The Tenth VIRTUE

Awakening

The Tenth VIRTUE

Awakening

M. C. MEINEMA

iUniverse®

THE TENTH VIRTUE
AWAKENING

iUniverse books may be ordered through booksellers or by contacting:

iUniverse
1663 Liberty Drive
Bloomington, IN 47403
www.iuniverse.com
1-800-Authors (1-800-288-4677)

ISBN: 978-1-4917-9257-5 (sc)
ISBN: 978-1-4917-9258-2 (e)

Library of Congress Control Number: 2016907234

Print information available on the last page.

iUniverse rev. date: 5/2/2016

To my Ben, Meegan, and lil Ben.
Never say *can't*; say *how*.

Thank you ...

This book was quite a journey. I have had the best support group helping me and, at times, nudging me along the way. Thank you all for believing in me and my story that yearned to be told.

To my husband, Wayne, thank you for all those TV shows that I made you pause so I could run away and jot down the story that was playing loudly in my head. You helped me talk out my thoughts and the twists and turns of the plot, and helped me come up with new and exciting avenues to take my characters on.

To our son, Ben, thank you for keeping it real and keeping me from using too many clichés. You helped me learn that ellipses have a limit, and it's because of you that my story has the beginning and the ending that it does.

To my best friend, Pam, thank you for getting me to think my storyline through and for our brainstorming sessions that lit my imagination on fire. You helped push me to keep writing it and believed that there was this amazing story deep within my brain.

To Meegan and Ben H., thank you for helping me come up with new characters and names. Your enthusiasm as we talked about the crazy characters and their abilities helped me develop a list of characters that I'll be able to use in the books to come.

To my beta readers, Wayne, Ben M., Pam, Derek, Meegan, and Jeramy, your insight was invaluable, and I treasure every jot and tittle you noted in my book. All of you made it what it is, and without you, I dare say, it would only be a dream.

To Gina, thank you for doing my graphic design work and listening to all my crazy ramblings. Your work with the photo was amazing, and I love the effects that you put into it.

To the group at iUniverse, thank you for all of your help and advice in publishing this book. Everyone was so helpful and kind. I couldn't have asked for a better experience.

And lastly, but most of all, thank you to my parents, Dale and Candy. You let me be who I am even if it didn't line up with society, and you encouraged me to just jump in and take a leap of faith at the beginning of this adventure. Without you two, there wouldn't be a Patrina.

Prologue

They had been traveling in an old green Caddy from the early fifties to see his brother. Izabella was overwrought with the impending birth of her first child, as she was due in nearly three weeks, but they continued on, desperate to mend the relationship between the two brothers, Vlad and Konrad.

Vlad wanted to be the most powerful, richest, and most desired man in the land. He would've been all of those too, had he not let his jealousy of his brother take over in his heart. As he learned the trade of importing goods from other lands, he became filthy rich. He then perfected his importing system, which made him the most powerful man in all of Poland. If a person ever wanted a nugget of treasure from another land, Vlad was the one to get it … for a price. He just couldn't seem to attain his one yearning—to be the most desired.

Konrad, his brother, was a man of integrity, honesty, and loyalty, and he was handsome too. He didn't have much money, but it didn't bother him. The ladies all swooned over him as he passed by in the streets. He didn't dress as showy as Vlad, but the way his stature exuded such confidence, well, money just couldn't buy that trait. It was this confidence and his integrity that won him the heart of Izabella. She was the one woman Vlad wanted but could never win.

When Konrad and Izabella got engaged, Vlad smiled and acted as though he was happy for them, but at night, in the darkest parts of town, Vlad started traveling down the path of destruction. He had money to burn, and he spent it on the hardest liquor in town. When that ran out, he imported more liquor from lands that were not known for their standards. So while Konrad and Izabella were beginning a new adventure into a life everlasting, Vlad was becoming more and more unlikable with every drop.

Years passed, and word came to Konrad and Izabella that Vlad had married. There was one picture of him and his new bride in the local newspaper, and neither of them was smiling. It turned out that the woman Vlad had married was not only very rich but was also the heiress to an export tycoon. This had been a business venture, not a marriage, and Vlad had now become both the import and the export source for all of Poland.

Vlad had been married for two years when his wife disappeared. No one ever saw her again. Vlad didn't seem to miss her and simply kept going on with his life. Right around the time of his wife's disappearance, Konrad and Izabella found out they were to have a child. They decided that since they hadn't talked to Vlad in a very long time and they wanted to make things right with him, they needed to visit him. They saved up for months so that they would have the money needed for the trip. Once they had enough, Konrad and Izabella set out for the long journey, even though it was very close to the expected arrival of their new little one.

The night they finally arrived at Vlad's castle-like mansion, the temperature had plummeted, and dark clouds rolled across the horizon. They decided they had better bunker down for the night because it looked like a massive storm was coming their way. Izabella made her way into the house as Vlad and Konrad brought in the necessities from the car. Vlad showed his two guests to their room upstairs, and after dinner, Konrad and Izabella resigned for the night. They slept through most of the storm until the lightning started to light up the sky. With each boom and flash of light, a new contraction seared across Izabella's belly. In all the years, never had there been such a storm as this in the little town. The storm continued throughout the night, but when the thunder and lightning died down, the wind picked up, whipping violently around every tree and structure. It invaded the estate through every tiny crack and crevice, and as the day broke over the horizon, the new baby girl made her entrance into this world. There was the kiss of a bitter breeze on her wet cheek, the bright shock of light trying to pierce through her eyelids, and then the soft warmth of a blanket encasing her in a protective shell. She was given the name Patrina Nadine Palinski.

Konrad and Izabella stayed with Vlad until Izabella was able to travel again. Once she was up to it, the new little family started the trek back to a shack on the outskirts of a small town that they fondly called home. While their two-bedroom shack had quite a few windows, they had blankets over them to keep the heat inside. This made the house rather dark, but the glow from the fireplace made it feel cozy. The leaves had all fallen from the trees, and the tiny snowflakes were beginning to build up around their little house.

Konrad was working at a small desk in the corner of the living room that day. He was using an old stool that he had found alongside the road to sit on so he could work on clocks and wristwatches for people in the town. He could fix just about anything.

Izabella had just placed her little girl in the makeshift crib in the bedroom near the rear of the house and set out to the kitchen to work on dinner. While her husband was doing his work, Izabella was in the kitchen whipping together a feast— well, a feast in their eyes. She could make something out of nothing in the kitchen. Nobody ever knew how she did it, but she could go into a nearly empty kitchen and come out with a feast fit for a king. They were content in their lives even though they seemed to have relatively little.

No one smelled the smoke.

At first, little wafts of smoke slid under the doors, behind the blankets on the windows, and under the desk where Konrad was working. Then it crept into the kitchen, behind the stove, and under Izabella's feet as she stepped. The flames started to lick their way up the wooden planks, down the floorboards, and soon, before they knew it, the fire had taken over the walls of their little house.

No one heard the panicked screams of Izabella or the voice of Konrad trying to calm her down. He kept telling her to get the diary, but all she wanted to get was her little girl.

The fire had slithered up between them and their daughter, blocking their way to the little room where Patrina was lying. The wispy smoke danced along the walls of the little girl's tiny bedroom as the fire dove in and out of the corners.

Nobody heard the crash or the screaming come to an end.

As little Patrina lay there in her crib, the fire tried to creep closer to her. The orange flames reached in vain across her ceiling, but its fingers were shoved back by something greater, leaving not even a gray trace of its presence.

Soon, the fire stopped growling, the smoke stopped dancing, and all that was left was silence and the pit-pat of the snow falling outside. There was no creaking of wood being eaten, no fire cracking its teeth, and no smoke slithering around corners anymore. And while the rest of the house was incinerated, Patrina's room was untouched.

Suddenly there was a rustling and scraping of someone trying to make their way to Patrina's bedroom door. Burnt chunks and piles of ash were pushed aside as Old Miss Latterly made her way through Patrina's shell of a door and up to her crib. As she looked down onto this newborn babe, a single tear slid down her cheek. This little girl was all alone now.

Old Miss Latterly grabbed the blanket Patrina was lying in and wrapped her tightly to protect her from the wintry breath of the season. She gently scooped the little girl up and held her tight to her face as she whispered over and over, "May the Monarch protect you."

She tucked Patrina tightly under her long, gray woolen coat as she turned to carry the little girl back to her own old farmhouse down the road. The snow was beginning to cover the roads, and it was getting harder for her to walk through the drifts formed by the blasting icy shards of air. Old Miss Latterly finally reached the sagging porch of her farmhouse, and the frigid gusts stopped blowing long enough for her and Patrina to sneak inside through the misaligned farm door.

The living room was dark except for the dance of the firelight on the walls. She had a small flame flickering in the fireplace on the far wall that barely took the chill out of the room. She gently laid Patrina on the green, velveteen sofa next to the fire so that the little girl could warm up while she went into the next room.

Suddenly there was a man's low, grumbling voice vibrating the walls of the old, drafty house. Only the thunderous tones of him talking to Old Miss Latterly and the low murmur of her responding could be heard. Soon, the voices fell silent, and when Patrina looked up, she saw the face of the man the voice came from … she would come to know him as Uncle Vlad.

As he bent down to grasp her from the sofa's warm embrace, she looked into his eyes. They were like dark, foreboding pools where all hope was drowned out. She was helpless as he wrapped her blanket tightly around her and over her head, blocking her view of where he was taking her. His walk out to his car had jostled her just enough that a tip of the blanket slid down from her face. Even the outside of his car looked as dark and uninviting as his eyes, and for the first time in her little life, Patrina knew fear.

He recklessly placed her in the backseat and slammed the door. The sound reverberated through her tiny head and made her ears throb. She rustled a little and was able to peek out of her blanket a little more, only to witness this giant of a man climb into the driver's seat and start the roaring engine. He drove for a long time, never saying a word to her as they wound their way through the snow to his grand estate.

Eventually he slowed to a stop and silenced the engine. He turned to glare at the little girl in his backseat, his brow furrowed as he pursed his lips. There was no love from this man … not like her parents. He got out of the car, slammed his door, and quickly opened hers. His hands were so large that he carried Patrina's little body in the palm of his hand. He threw her up to his shoulder, slammed the door, and carried her into his estate—the place she would be forced to call home.

Once inside, Vlad handed her off to a quaint old lady who was half his size. Patrina would come to know her as Miriam, and she would be the little girl's nanny. Miriam spoke quietly, and her touch reminded Patrina of her mother's. As Miriam cradled Patrina against the cream-colored woolen shawl that covered her chest, Patrina quickly fell asleep. When Patrina awoke, she saw ceilings that were so far away they were covered in shadows. The room felt ominous in the dark and drafty corners, and as she whimpered, Miriam lifted her once again and cradled her.

In time, Patrina would realize that every amenity for a little girl was encased in this room. She had a large closet, lined with hangers full of clothing from faraway lands in all sizes a growing girl could need. There was even a spacious bathroom, fully equipped with all of the necessities a little girl could need, and some that a growing girl would eventually desire. All around the surrounding walls, there were long, rectangular windows high up that showed only the sky and the tops of the trees. The sunlight would trickle through these panes of glass and dance through the dust to illuminate a brass, heart-shaped lock that threatened to forever imprison her in this grand estate.

One

Uncle Vlad made sure that nobody but he and my nanny ever entered my room. Miriam has been my nanny ever since that day my uncle brought me here. She has tried her best to give me a relatively normal childhood, even though I've never seen another child in person. The only interaction I've had with my uncle, until recently, was when he brought new books in for me to read. Those books were my education and my way to escape these bedroom walls.

Miriam taught me many things about the world and life in general. In fact, she taught me to read when I was only two years old. It was easy for me. I just understood it. A lot of things have come easily to me. There are some things I just know. I've always thought this was normal, but now, as I near the age of twelve, I'm noticing that there are more and more changes happening in my surroundings that only I seem to be able to see.

It's early in the morning, and the sun is just about to break the horizon. I'm not allowed a clock in my room, and Miriam has told me that there are no clocks in the house at all. Uncle Vlad's jealousy of his brother and the way he could fix clocks has intruded into the lifestyle of everyone who lives here. I've been raised to wake when the sun is rising and go to bed when the sun is setting. This is the schedule Uncle Vlad insists that Miriam keeps me on.

Today, Uncle Vlad left to go on a business trip. Miriam has promised me that, once he's gone, she will come to my room and allow me the chance to finally explore his estate. She tried to give me the chance to explore when I was around the age of four. However, just as I was out of my room and barely twenty feet down the luxurious walnut hallway, she came running up to me and snatched me into her arms. My uncle had come back home because he wasn't feeling well. She had to rush me back into my room as quickly as possible so that he wouldn't find out that I had been let out of my prison.

This time, though, she's making sure he's been gone a few hours.

Suddenly I hear Miriam's key entering my door lock. I turn in my bed to watch the lock change color as it is manipulated from the outside. No two objects ever seem to be the same color. Metals gradually shimmer to a bluish teal color when they are being changed, and that's what happens to my shiny, brass lock. It really is quite beautiful. Just as the lock reaches its full color, Miriam comes through the door.

"Good morning, sunshine! Are you ready to go on an expedition today?"

Miriam is so good at making my life in this prison a new adventure every day. The wrinkles on Miriam's face give away that she is older, well past the age of having her own children, but she has said that the Monarch blessed her the day I came here. She said that because He protected me from the fire, He allowed her the chance to raise one of His little ones—one of His special ones. That's what she has always told me.

I bound out of bed, having already gotten dressed in my long jean skirt and flowery T-shirt, and clumsily skip across the room. I must've grown since I last wore this because my bony ankles are poking out from under the hem, and the top is tight across my widening shoulders. My red hair is still a sleepy mess, but I don't care as I run to hug her.

I love Miriam as I would've loved my mother. She's short, barely two inches taller than me, and she's soft in all the right places. Her gray hair is held back on the sides with little gold clips, and she always wears a tattered, red plaid apron. She folds me in her arms and tells me that today is the day. My uncle has boarded the flight to the States, and we have nearly eight hours to explore this grand palatial estate.

"I'm very ready, Miriam! I've been waiting hours for you to change the lock to blue!"

"Blue?" she asks. "Why would it change to blue?"

"Because you were unlocking it, silly! Let's go, let's go, let's go!" I ignore the puzzled look on her face as I grab her warm hand and pull her toward the open door to my freedom and to the secrets waiting for me to find them.

The hallway is dark, as dark as I remember it being back when I was four. As we walk down the hallway, I notice that it curves around my room. There is one other door and a window to my left that looks out onto the sky and the tops of old oak trees.

"Where are we, Miriam?"

"This is the tower, sweet child. Your uncle was quite determined to keep you safely away from anyone who might find you and sway you to do their bidding. He wanted to keep you pure."

"Pure? What do you mean? And how would I do anyone's bidding?"

"There are things you know now, and there are things to come, but the things to come haven't made themselves known to you yet because you're not ready. There is more to who you are than you realize." Miriam leans over toward me and squeezes my shoulders. I'm puzzled as to what she is talking about. What kinds of things? When am I going to be ready?

I'm ready to know now! I decide to just let it go and continue on with my exploration. I can tell from the look in Miriam's eyes that she isn't going to go any further with the discussion anyway.

The curved hallway seems to have a downhill slope, and soon I see a staircase going down. I look to Miriam, my eyes pleading to proceed, and she nods. This is so scary and exciting!

There must be at least twenty steps, and they wrap around in a spiral all the way down to the floor below. As I slowly wind my way around, I can sense something calling to me, something drawing me onward. I step off the last step into a long, dark walnut wood hallway. I walk through the hallway and see door after door on the left side of the hall. I can tell by the color of most of the doorknobs that they're locked. There is one door in the bend of the hallway that's not locked, and it is bigger and more ornate than the others. I'm surprised when it starts to glow as I go closer.

"Look, Miriam! It's glowing!"

"What's glowing? All I see is a lot of dust that I will probably get yelled at for not cleaning."

"That door!" I exclaim as I point down the hall. "It's glowing. Don't you see that?"

Miriam looks at me with a puzzled look that melts into understanding. It seems as though Miriam knows a lot more about me than she lets on. For now though, I just want to get through that door.

The closer I get to the huge, adorned door, the more it glows. The door is engraved with a beautiful picture of a forest. There is a tree winding up the left side by the hinges, and its leaves blend into clouds at the top. The rays of sun shine down onto a river that has an assortment of rocks in it that turn into gems the closer I get to it. As I get up next to it, the scene engraved into the door becomes alive. The tree looks so real that when I touch it, I can feel the sap running between the scales of bark. The clouds appear fluffy like cotton balls but are only moist air to my touch. The sun warms not only the door but my hand as I follow the rays down to the river that is gurgling over diamonds, emeralds, and rubies.

Miriam stopped about three steps behind me. I look back at her, and she has her hands folded in front of her over the old, tattered apron. She smiles and asks, "What do you see?"

"I see paradise."

Two

"Don't you see it? Can't you see the tree moving in the breeze or hear the river lapping over the gems?"

Miriam gazes at me with a twinkle in her eye. "You have to let me see it, Patrina."

"How can I let you see something that's in front of both of us? Am I standing in the way?" I move to the side to make sure she can see past me, but she just looks at me and grins.

"In a manner of speaking," she replies. Miriam comes closer and takes my hand, and when she does, the door casts a light across her face. Now when she looks at the door, her eyes light up like she's able to see it for the first time, and she gasps. "That's beautiful, Patrina! Simply stunning …"

As she lets go of my hand, the glow from the door fades from her face. I'm not sure I understand what's happening.

"Miriam, how could you see it when you touched me but couldn't see it when you weren't touching me?"

"Sweetie, there's a lifetime of mysteries wrapped inside your DNA. You are special, much more special than you realize. Some of the things you see, only you can see unless you let others around you see them too. I don't know how to tell you how to do that, but I do know that others like you are able to open the eyes of those around them. When I touched you, I was able to momentarily glance into what you're seeing. I can only do it for a short time because it's too powerful for me now."

"What happens if you hang on to me for too long?"

"When you choose to open the eyes of those around you, it's like you're a buffer. It would be easier to compare it to sunglasses. Without sunglasses, the sun on a very bright summer day is too much to handle and can end up causing a headache. That's why we wear sunglasses. You are the sunglasses, my dear. When you open the eyes of the people you want to be able to see with your mind, you shield them from the intensity of the power that is before them. But when they just touch you, they are getting the full force of the vision. It's like throwing open the curtains in a dark room and letting in the full afternoon sun. Only the special ones can handle that. That's how your mother explained it long ago when we were helping someone."

I knew that Miriam knew my mother, but I didn't know the extent of the relationship. I only knew that Miriam was able to tell me stories about my parents.

"How close were you and my mother?"

"We were friends a long time ago … a very long time ago," she says as her gaze drifts off. She quickly refocuses and says with a grin, "Well, are you going to open the door or what?"

I grin and turn to find the handle. The doorknob is masquerading as a ruby in the river. I stick my hand in the icy cold river and grasp the perfectly round ruby. It's a little slippery, but I'm able to turn it. Slowly the door returns to wood again as it glides open to reveal wall upon wall of books as high as I can see. This must be Uncle Vlad's library.

The room is huge. The ceilings are at least twenty feet tall. It has a ladder that can roll around against the shelves so someone can reach the books that are up high. There is a big dome-shaped window in the wall at the far end of the library, letting in the morning light that illuminates swirling tornadoes of dust particles in the air. A dark mahogany desk sits in the middle of the room, with a high-armed desk chair neatly tucked behind it. Piles of dusty papers decorate the corners of the desk and flow over the edges to form heaping mounds of papers on the floor. There are folders strewn across the top of the desk as though someone has been searching for something.

I walk toward the nearest wall of books, but my mind is so focused on the myriad books displayed before me, it is as though I float to the wall. There are big books and old books, new books and hardcover books, books of maps, books promising secret treasures, books about myths and angels, and even books about animals.

Miriam stays back at the doorway to the hall and watches me explore. She smiles at me, and I smile back as I turn to a new wall of books and find that I am within inches of the ladder. I grab the sides and climb about four feet. I can see through the dome-shaped window out into the backyard behind the estate. It's glorious! There are little white picket fences around gardens of different flowers and huge ornate topiaries guarding the entrance into something that seems to be a maze carved out of hedges. I recognize some of the flowers from a book that Uncle Vlad brought me recently.

I'm so entranced that I nearly forget I'm standing on a ladder four feet in the air. Suddenly the ladder jolts me back into the library. I could swear it jiggled beneath me!

Climb higher, a small, still voice whispers. I look behind me, and no one is there. Miriam is still at the door, now leaning against the doorframe, looking at a fraying hole in her apron. I look below me, and no one is there either.

Climb higher, it whispers again.

"Miriam," I call out, "did you say something? I thought I heard a voice."

She looks up at me, shrugs, and shakes her head. "What did it say?"

"He told me to climb higher," I say, clinging to the sides so I don't fall off.

"If he whispers to your heart, then you are to do what he tells you to do. That is The Guide leading you in the way you are supposed to go next. It's okay. Let him lead you."

I start to ascend the rungs, higher and higher. I don't know how far I'm supposed to climb. The whisper wasn't clear. Just as I am about to give up, now nearly fifteen feet in the air, with only five shelves before I reach the ceiling, I hear it again but I realize that it's not from outside of my head that I hear it. It's in my head, like it's whispering right to my heart.

This is good. Now, let it glow.

I don't understand. Let what glow? How can I *let* something glow? Shouldn't it just glow by itself?

Calm yourself, dear one. Breathe. And then let it glow. The whisper is kind and gentle. It calms me. I quiet myself, slow my breathing, close my eyes, and release the tension I was holding within as I was climbing to this great unknown.

I slowly open my eyes as I feel myself at ease. I start to see a glow on the next shelf up than the one I'm facing; it's dim. I wouldn't even say it was a glow—maybe a glimmer. I breathe in deeply and let it out, feeling the air leaving my lungs. My chest lowers, my shoulders relax, and then it glows as bright as a star in the darkest part of the night.

This is yours, Patrina.

The whisper tells me something I somehow already know in the deepest caverns of my being. I stretch my hand out and grasp the glow that is above me. I slide it off the shelf and see that it's a book but not just any book. This book is leather and old. It's tied shut with a leather strap. I untie the strap, letting it drop and billow in the breeze that is circling me. I carefully crack open the binding, and on the very first brownish-yellow page, there is something written in black ink. As the glow fades, the words become clear, and I'm able to read what it says: "Diary of Izabella Palinski."

This was my mother's diary.

Three

I am so stunned at finding my mother's old diary in my uncle's library that my feet teeter on the ladder rung, and I nearly fall off. I quickly grab the side of the ladder, steady myself, and then wrap the smooth leather strap back around the diary. I gently tuck it in the pocket of my skirt and start the long climb down the ladder.

When I look down, I see that Miriam is no longer waiting for me at the door; she is hanging on to the ladder at the bottom. She is watching me as I climb down, and the look on her face tells me she is about to burst with anticipation.

"What did The Guide tell you? What do you have? Is that a book? Where did you put it?" She's asking so many questions that she can barely breathe in between them. By the time I reach the bottom rung, I'm pretty sure she has asked me at least twenty questions.

I hug her when I reach the bottom, and the smile on my face feels like it's about to break through to my ears. "Did you see the book glowing? It started glowing on the shelf! The Guide told me to let it glow, and I did!"

"Patrina, only you can see the glow, but I did see the expression on your face and knew something great must be happening. What happened?"

"The Guide told me to go higher and higher, and then it finally told me to stop. I didn't know what to do, and I sure didn't think I went that high! Then he said I had to be calm and let it glow. So I did what he told me to do, and when I opened my eyes, there it was! It's my mother's diary!" I exclaim as I take it out of my skirt pocket.

Miriam's face shows how stunned she is, and we both come to the same conclusion at the same time. Why is it in my uncle's library? Uncle Vlad is a collector of things, mostly rare antiquities, but there are some items that he likes to collect, and nobody but him knows why.

"Why would he have this, Miriam? This seems too personal for him to have," I say, holding onto the worn leather book.

"I don't know. Your mother and Vlad were always at odds with one another. Vlad loved your mother, more than any other girl around, but she didn't feel the same. Instead, your mother loved Vlad's younger brother—your father, Konrad. Konrad made her so happy. She told me years ago, when she and Konrad were just dating, that whenever Vlad was around, all of the hair on her neck would stand up. She could always feel his presence."

Uncle Vlad has never really been around me. He just pops into my room to drop off some books or an odd trinket and pops back out. Rarely does he even say hello. So my knowledge of my uncle is very little. I wonder what went on back then to make my mother feel the way she did.

Before I could have another thought, Miriam motions to me that we should keep going if we're going to explore as much as we can while my uncle is gone. We are careful to make sure everything is back in its place. The ladder is on the same bookcase, the papers are still in mounds, and we quietly walk out of the library and close the paradise door behind us. Miriam is only a few steps ahead of me when she stops and turns to grab my hands in hers. "Whatever you find here is

14

what you are meant to find, and whatever you learn is what you are meant to understand. This is your path, Patrina. Your mother's diary is a key to understanding. Whatever you do, do not let your uncle know that you have it. It was hidden high up on the shelf for a reason. Vlad does not want anyone to know he has it. I don't know why, and only The Guide can explain the knowledge it contains, but hide it and hide it well."

I promise her that I will hide it as soon as we are done, and I give her warm hands a quick squeeze. I turn and start heading down the hall. We don't walk very far before the hall opens up on the right to a large room. There are no windows in this room. I think we are in the center of the mansion. Everything is so maze-like that I've lost my sense of direction.

This room has a huge burgundy leather sofa with little, ornate, gold balls that wind up and around the ends of the arms and the back of the sofa. In front of the sofa is an old coffee table with claws for feet. The top of it is glass, but I can't see what's under the glass from where I'm standing. I walk across the room to take a look, and what I see through the glass tabletop surprises me so much that I stagger back a few steps. A stuffed lion's head sits inside the table and is looking up at me through the glass. It's so creepy!

I stand frozen; staring at this king of the jungle trapped behind a pane of glass, before I shake it off and return to exploring. The sofa faces a stone fireplace in the corner of the room that is so large I could easily walk inside it. At the back of the room is a long wooden bar with barstools tucked under the ledge. The wood on the bar is so sparkly it's like the wood has flecks of real gold in it.

Off to the far side of the room is a half-circle sofa that has the same burgundy leather fabric as the sofa by the fireplace. There is a circular table in front of this sofa, with claw-like feet and a glass top like the other table. I'm afraid to look inside at first, but my curiosity gets the better of me. I cautiously walk over to the table and peer into the glass. There isn't any animal. There are different trinkets in this one. I sit down on the sofa and look at the treasures Uncle Vlad has confined inside this table. There is an old leather-bound book, similar to my mother's diary, next to a folded piece of paper that is long and rectangular in shape, like a map. There are five stones, all similar in size but different colors, and then there is a big brass ring with three old keys on it. They remind me of those old-time keys that I read pirates used for dungeons deep within the bowels of their ships.

This table sparks my imagination so much that Miriam has to come over and remind me that we are limited on time and better keep going.

As I get up to leave, out of the corner of my eye I see something that looks out of place. An old painting on the wall is a little crooked, but that isn't the only thing that seems odd to me. There is a line running down the wall just behind the painting. If the painting had been in its place, I never would've seen it, but before I can go and inspect it, Miriam calls to me. I reluctantly decide that the line in the wall will have to be another day's adventure.

"C'mon, Patrina, there's lots to see, and your uncle will be home soon."

Walking out of that room, I feel as though something is trying to pull me back in, but the opportunity to see the house like this is a one-in-a-million chance. Uncle Vlad rarely leaves for a whole day. He works in town normally, so he pops in throughout the day. Miriam has wanted to show me the house for years. She thinks it is awful how he keeps me locked away. Is he really protecting me from something?

Four

We walk out of that massive party room and start following the maze-like hallway through the rest of the house. As I am looking at the random paintings of people from another time, I notice that there is a new scent in the air. Something smells like my favorite beef dish, and it's making my stomach growl!

"Are you ready for a little lunch?" Miriam asks.

"I guess I am. Something smells delicious!"

We come to another opening in the hallway, except this one opens up to the source of the wonderful beefy smell. I am so overcome by the scent dancing in my nostrils that I forget to watch where I am going.

"Oh!" I exclaim as I come face to chest with a beastly man in a dirty white apron.

"Bao, this is Patrina. You know, Vlad's niece." Miriam gives him a stern look.

Bao quickly adjusts his gaze, goofily bows to me, and reaches out his huge hand. I place my hand in his, and he says, "I am very pleased to finally meet you, Miss Patrina. I hope that you're hungry. Lunch is almost ready."

"Bao is your uncle's chef. He's been here longer than you have, my dear. He and your uncle go way back. Maybe Bao will tell you the story," Miriam says with a wink to the giant chef. She seems to have a way with getting people to talk. She gets me to talk all the time.

"Oh, Miriam, do you really think this poor girl would want to be bored with my story?"

"Bao, we all have a story of how we became a part of Uncle Vlad's possess—I mean life, and it would be wonderful if you would tickle our ears with yours over lunch."

"Very well." Bao pulls out some stools and sets them at the island in the middle of the kitchen. Everything is spotless—everything except Bao's apron, which seems to be crusted with the fixings of our lunch. I hop up onto the stool and hook my feet behind the rungs as Miriam climbs onto the stool next to me. Bao dishes out two heaping bowls of goulash, sets them in front of us with spoons so large they could be ladles, and pulls up a stool for himself.

"Aren't you going to eat any of this, Bao?" I ask.

"How can I weave a story fit for a princess in a tower if my mouth is full, Miss Patrina?" His eyes give a little twinkle as he grins at me from across the island. I have never felt so protected and loved before. This is turning out to be an amazing day!

"Where shall I start, Miriam? The beginning or the *very* beginning?"

Miriam looks at him, contemplates for a moment, and then says, "I think she would love to hear the *very* beginning."

"I was thinking the same thing," says Bao as he leans on one of his massive elbows and starts to paint a story for us.

"When I was a very little boy, my parents, who were quite wealthy, decided that they didn't have time to raise a good little Polish boy, so they sent me away to a boarding school in Warsaw. I had a room with five other little boys from all over Poland. There were many nights when we all cried ourselves to sleep. It was hard being away from my parents and my home. I missed them dearly. One day after school, I was walking through the hallway to my room, and I ran into your father, Konrad."

The shock must show in my face because Bao laughs and says, "Yes, even I knew your father back then."

I smile timidly and go back to eating, trying hard not to interrupt him with a bunch of questions. There is so much I long to know of my parents, and I didn't realize that the people I've had around me my whole life hold the keys to my past.

"Your father was a wonderful boy who grew into an outstanding man. We were great friends. Konrad and I would always meet after our classes. Many days, we would run to the huge field out back behind the main building to kick around a ball. When it was rainy or too cold, we would head down to the common room and play cards. Your father was very good at cards but very bad at bluffing. He couldn't tell a lie if his life depended on it!" Bao belts out a hearty, belly-jiggling laugh. He stops, breathes in deeply to catch his breath, and when he exhales, his face turns serious.

"One cold and dreary day, as your father and I were playing cards, in walks this boy who looked very much like your father. He walked with more arrogance than your father though. I looked at your father sitting across the table from me, and he sighed as he told me that was his brother, Vlad. And then he apologized to me! I didn't understand then why he would apologize because nothing had happened yet. He told me that he was apologizing for whatever his brother was going to do. I didn't think anyone could be that awful that someone would have to apologize for them ahead of time, but that was before I spent any time at all with your uncle.

"Vlad came over, pulled out a chair at our table, and told us to deal him in. I didn't really care if he played. We were playing poker, and poker is a lot more fun when there are more people. What I didn't know was your uncle was the king of deception. We only played for pennies because that's all we had, but in just a couple of hands of poker, your uncle won all our money. Once he had won everything, he gathered up his winnings, scooted his chair noisily across the cold concrete floor, and walked away laughing. I looked at your father, in shock at what had happened, and he apologized again. He shrugged as he said, 'Vlad always gets what he wants.'

"Day after day, I watched your uncle swindle other boys our age out of their favorite books, favorite jackets, and even their favorite shoes. He didn't just do it by winning a game either. Sometimes he managed to convince people that they needed to give whatever it was to him. I tried to stay clear of your uncle, but your father was my best friend, and Vlad just had a sense of where Konrad was, even when we were trying to be sneaky and leave Vlad in the dust.

"One day, Konrad and I went out to the back edge of the field where this dense wall of trees was parted by a small path. We had followed it in a little ways before, but that day we were bound for a grand adventure. We decided to see where the path led and hurried so Vlad couldn't follow us.

"The path swerved and looped around giant trees that must've been there longer than either one of us had been alive. The path rose over hills and dipped down into steep valleys. Eventually it came out to this clearing that ended with a drop-off that was a lot farther down than I cared to examine.

"Your father and I were joking around when out from behind the giant oak tree next to the path steps your uncle. He was upset that we knew of a secret place and hadn't told him about it. I think he was more upset that we didn't invite him along, but then again, we rarely invited him anywhere.

"He started yelling at us, but it wasn't a normal yell. The louder he yelled, the deeper his voice got, and the blacker his eyes went. It was not the nicest thing I've ever seen—that's for sure. He kept yelling at us, backing us up to the very edge of the cliff. I could feel the rumble of the earth shifting out from beneath my heels. Konrad was right next to me and started to slip. I reached out and grabbed his arm just as he started to fall backwards toward the canyon below. Seeing his brother nearly fall to his death snapped Vlad back into reality, and he lunged forward and pulled us both off the edge. Even then, Vlad never apologized.

"Years went by, and we got used to having Vlad around. Sometimes it worked in our favor because he rarely had to pay for anything. Quite often we were able to get an extra cookie from the lunch lady if we were with Vlad. He had a tongue that could spread words like honey and convince people to give him whatever he wanted. That was nice for us because we usually got in on the goods that Vlad was getting. It stayed like that throughout the rest of our time at that boarding school, and when we graduated, we all parted ways.

"I didn't see your father or your uncle for probably five years, and in that time, I made a rather huge mess of my life. I lost most everything I owned in card game after card game. I hadn't realized just how much influence your uncle had on the events around us until he was gone. I thought I could win on my own, but that was not the case. I ended up sleeping in the alleyway between two of the dirtiest bars in town. I begged on the street during the day and drank my earnings at night until I fell into a stupor in the alleyway. And then I would start the whole cycle again the next day.

"It continued on like this for a few months, and I lost so much weight that I was barely half the man that stands before you today. One evening, as I sat at a table in the corner drinking my last one for the night, in walks your uncle. He was dressed from head to toe in clothes that cost more money than I had ever made in my life. I tried to slouch into the corner so that he wouldn't see me, because I was ashamed of what I had let myself amount to, but he saw me nonetheless.

"He sauntered over to my table, pulled out the chair across

from me and sat down. He looked at me like he had just found a gem among the stones. 'Bao,' he says to me, 'you're looking rough. Squandered everything away, did ya? Well, I came for my payment.'

"I told him that I didn't know what he was talking about, and even if I did, I had nothing to pay him with. I didn't even have a pillow to lay my head on, but that just made him smile. As the black crept into his eyes like it did back on the cliff, he leaned across the table and said to me in a voice that shook the liquid in my glass, 'You owe me your life.'

"He went on to say that he was coming to collect on the day back at the cliff when his yell forced me and your father to the edge and he pulled us back. I remembered that day, but I never thought I would have to pay for it.

"Your uncle leaned back in his chair, folded his hands on the table, and calmly said to me, 'A life for a life. It's all equal, my friend. I saved your life on that cliff, and you owe me your life in servitude. I will give you a roof over your head and food in your belly, but you will serve me in my estate. If you choose not to, well … let's just say you'd be better off choosing to be my chef.'

"He could be a very ruthless man if he didn't get what he wanted. I had seen what he had done to others who didn't do as he wished, and because I didn't have any other better options, I came to work here and have been here ever since.

"Some days I wonder if I would've been better off choosing not to be the chef," he mumbles.

Bao inhales deeply and then seems to notice that my bowl is empty. I didn't even realize I finished it because I've been so intrigued with his story. The only reason I know I did eat the bowlful of goulash is the wonderful peppery flavor lingering on my tongue. Bao reaches for my bowl and starts to ask if we want more when Miriam gets off her stool. She smiles and says to Bao, "Thank you, dear friend. We must keep going. We have a lot to see, and we rarely know if the time we think we have is the time we actually have."

He nods and smiles as he places our bowls in the sink. I don't understand what Miriam meant. What did she mean about time?

Five

At the back of the kitchen are two doors that look like shutters. I look at Miriam as if to ask if that's the way we should go, and she nods. I push on the doors, and they swing out into this huge, light blue room. There is a cherry wood grand piano with real ivory keys off to the right of the room. Someone left the lid open, and I can see the piano wires strung beautifully inside, waiting for someone to come and tap on its ivory keys, bringing it to life.

This piano looks exactly like the toy one Miriam brought me years ago. She said it was from one of my uncle's trips. He had gone to Bombay, India, and found this tiny grand piano. The person who was selling it showed him that it was a real working piano and it could be played with a toothpick. It had taken a team of men six months to craft it, and from what I've learned, anything that rare is something my uncle has to have. I don't know exactly how much he paid for it, or if he paid anything at all. After listening to Bao's story about my uncle, I am beginning to think there is a lot about my uncle I don't know.

I walk to the middle of the room and feel the sunlight warming my shoulders from above. I look up and see a large rectangular window above me, but it doesn't look out to the sky. There's something there, like liquid, because I can see the ripples glistening in the sunlight.

"What does that go to?" I ask.

"That is a reflection pool on the roof that your uncle had put in years ago. Actually this whole estate was built according to his liking. If we have time, I can show you the gardens up on the roof. They used to be quite spectacular."

I like the idea that there is a garden so close to my room. I bet it would be easy enough to sneak in and out of.

On the walls are paintings of people that are dressed like they are from another time.

"Who are these people?" I ask Miriam.

"Those are your ancestors. They come from your father's side. There's your grandfather at the end. He's the one with the grumpy look on his face. The funny part is that was how everyone sat for paintings. They didn't smile like we do now. It was thought that if they smiled in a picture, that meant they were crazy.

"The lady next to him with all of her hair piled on top of her head is your grandmother. I only knew her in her older years, and she was very kind. She was probably too kind because she gave Vlad and your father whatever they wanted … except Vlad took advantage of her. She died completely broke and living in a shack down by the lake out back."

"Wait, there's a lake? Where?"

"That's for another time, dear Patrina. Yes, there is a lake on the property, but it's a long walk, and it's surrounded by a wall of trees. It is quite lovely though."

She gives me a wink and then points to the last painting on the end. It's of a beautiful woman with long, golden curls the color of sunshine. Her eyes are blue like the sky on a clear summer's day. Unlike my grandparents, she's smiling and radiating a sense of peace and joy.

"That's your mother, Izabella. Your uncle was so smitten with her that he convinced her and your father to sit for a portrait when they were here almost twelve years ago."

"That was when I was born, wasn't it?"

"Yes, it was an extremely hard winter that year, and I guess you were eager to see your new world. Those paintings were done in this very room."

"Where's my father's portrait?" I ask as I scan the walls looking for more faces. I don't see any more paintings.

"Your uncle and your father weren't exactly the best of friends. I'm not sure of this, but I'm guessing that the only reason he had both your father and mother sit for the portraits was just so he could get your mother to sit. I've never seen the painting of your father. This was the only one of the two that was hung."

I stare at my mother's painting and can't help but be in awe of her beauty. As I look at her longer, my world seems to dissolve around me. I can hear her soft voice singing to me. I feel the warmth of her arms as they hold me. I can see something on her neck glittering in the sunlight …

It is as if my real world comes snapping back around me. There really is something glittering in the painting! It's a necklace in the shape of a heart, but it looks like it's made of glass and glitters like a diamond. Whoever painted this picture captured the realness of the necklace amazingly. I look a little closer; there is something white inside the glass heart.

I turn to Miriam, who is now sitting on one of the chairs alongside the piano. "Miriam, did you ever see the necklace my mother is wearing in this picture?"

"I saw it a lot! She never took it off."

"What's in the middle of it?"

Miriam looks as though she's contemplating how to tell me something important. She sighs, unfolds her hands that were patiently laid in her lap, and gets out of the overstuffed chair.

She walks across the room to me, places her arm snuggly around my shoulder, and says, "That is a feather ... a small, white feather."

"Why is it in the middle of her heart?"

Miriam pauses. "There are things I can tell you, and there are things I'm not allowed to tell you. The Guide will tell you when the time is right. I know some of this seems very puzzling, but all in good time."

I look into her blue eyes and see that they might've been the same color as my mother's when she was younger. I don't understand why there are so many secrets, not only in this house but in my life that has been hidden from me.

In frustration, I shrug her arm from my shoulder and move across the room. Off to the left of the grand piano, there is a door, and the tension in Miriam rises as I make my way over to it. It's wider than most of the doors in the house that I've seen so far. And it looks heavy and solid, more so than the other doors. The door handle reminds me of something that came from a long time ago. It's ornate and made out of gold. I reach for the handle, and just as my fingers graze the shiny finish, my ears are pelted with a loud boom.

"Don't go in there!"

Six

The floorboards under my feet vibrate. Until now, I had never heard her raise her voice, and now I know why. The floor shakes, the walls shake—even the air shakes. It was almost as if there was a sonic boom flying across the room at me. My hand is trembling.

I am in such shock that I start crying. I can't help myself as the tears well up and stream down my cheeks. Miriam rushes over to me and draws me into a hug.

"I'm so sorry, Patrina! I didn't mean to raise my voice that far."

I brush my hair off of my wet cheeks as I draw back out of her arms. "Why did you yell? That was awful! And why did everything shake when you yelled?"

"I'm sorry. Truly I am. You just can't go in there. That room is your uncle's room and office. He knows when even the smallest detail is out of place in there, and if he found out you had been in there, he would be even more irritated than if he just knew you were out of your room."

There are many secrets, my special one, I hear The Guide whisper to my heart as Miriam continues to apologize. This is odd, to be able to hear with my ears and with my heart at the same time.

I whisper back in my heart to him, *Why are there so many secrets?*

There is good and evil all around you, and some things are hidden for a time. This is one of those times.

Miriam has continued talking to me about how Uncle Vlad's office is just off of his room and how his room holds many intimate details of his import and export business. Some of those things are so secret that even Miriam, who cleans and manages the household, isn't allowed to see.

I must have a strange look on my face. Miriam stops talking and holds me out at arm's length to look at my face.

"What is it? Did he say something?"

You may tell her I talked to you, but there will come a time when you mustn't tell her all the things I tell you. The Guide is still here. I don't think he ever truly leaves.

"The Guide told me that there are many secrets and this is one that needs to be hidden for a little while longer."

Miriam looks at me with a look of relief. She lowers her arms and stuffs her hands back into her apron pockets. She's very quiet now and looks off to the side. She takes in a deep breath and lets it out as she says, "The Guide is wiser than any of us. If he says that it needs to be hidden for a little while longer, so be it, but we can keep exploring. You haven't seen my section of the house yet."

I reach into my pocket and feel my mother's diary. It's soothing to my touch. Even though it's only a piece of her, I feel as though I have her heart with me now. I am really enjoying seeing this house that I've been trapped in, but at the same time, I'm curious to see what's in her diary.

Miriam leads me further into the grand piano room to a magnificent archway that leads out into a hallway. The hallway is dark and paneled in the same wood that's on the floors. I walk into the hallway and see two other doors, one on each side of the hall, and then a third door at the very end. The door at the end is different from the two on the sides. It looks stronger and bigger, and it has a window at the top of it. I strain my eyes to see out of the window, and I can tell that it's darker near the window and gets lighter as I look farther out. It's like there's shade right outside the window. Miriam stops at the door on the right side of the hall, but I keep walking towards the windowed door.

As I get closer, I discover that if I'm on my tiptoes I can peek over the bottom of the window. I stand onto my tippy tiptoes and crane my neck as long as it will go as the tips of my fingers grasp at the edge of the window. I struggle to pull myself up against the pain in my fingertips so I can glimpse outside. My eyes crest the edge, and I can see a long, covered porch just outside the door. The roof over the porch stretches out to the edge of the top stair that leads down and out into a yard.

The yard is beautiful and almost as immaculate as the back garden that I could see through the large window in the library. This one isn't as flowery as the back garden, but it has the most glorious stone fountain that must be the size of a pool. The bottom of the fountain has layer upon layer of stones, stacked in a circle, that hold the clearest blue water that shimmers and sparkles in the sunlight. In the middle of the fountain is a statue of a lady. She seems familiar to me. She's standing on the top of a round ball with bare feet. She has two wings, one behind each shoulder, and they must span at least six feet. One of the wings looks as though someone took a sledgehammer to it and smashed part of it off. She's cradling an open book with both of her hands, and the middle of the book is from where the fountain spills its water. It gives me a sense that the words she has in that book are meant for more than just her.

"Shall we continue, Patrina?"

I turn and see Miriam standing at a door to her right. She

turns the round brass knob and swings the door open. She motions for me to walk through the doorway with a grin and a twinkle in her eye.

As my feet creep past the entrance, I can see that this is Miriam's suite, and it's a whole world unto itself. It even smells different in here! It smells like my room when I can open the windows in the springtime, though all of her windows are closed. Her room has a rosy glow to it because of the sunlight dancing through the rose-colored sheers on the windows. She has plants in pots at various places along a makeshift windowsill she must've placed there years ago.

Along the far wall is a door that is cracked open enough that I can see a light on and her clothes hanging up. That must be her closet. To the right of that door is another door, but that one is open all the way, and it's dark in that room.

"What's in there?"

"That's just the bathroom. Other than a kitchen, I have most of what I need in here. Your uncle sees to it that no one ever needs to use the facilities in his section of the house by making sure his workers have their own. Even Bao has his own suite on the other side of the house. We passed his area on our way to the library."

I remember seeing a couple of doors in the first hallway we explored, and then I start to think about how long I have been here and how Miriam has always been in my life.

"How long have you been here, Miriam?"

"Since before you lost your parents. I was here when Vlad was having this estate built. He made this suite for me next to his so that he could keep me … well … close. We'll just put it that way." Miriam had put her hands in the pockets of her apron when we came in here, and now she has scrunched her apron in her fists.

"When will you tell me your story, Miriam?"

"Not right now."

I guess I knew in my heart that would be the answer. I love Miriam, and sometimes when she doesn't know I'm looking, I catch a sad look move across her face like a dark cloud. She has that look now, and I don't like to make Miriam sad, so I start asking about different things in her room.

"I love your blanket on your bed. Did you make that?"

Instead of the dark cloud leaving, it seems to park on her face as she says, "No, your mother did, years ago."

"Oh …" While I am very curious about her friendship with my mother, I can tell that there is a lot of history that brings back memories of a life that seems to make Miriam sad.

I decide to look in silence at the different trinkets decorating her room. Some are displayed on shelves, and some are scattered on the tops of tables or dressers. She has a tiny tree on one of her tables that catches my eye. It looks like a real tree, though it's only about ten inches tall. It doesn't have any leaves, just branches that stretch out at different angles and lengths. Miriam has been using it to hang her jewelry on. She doesn't have very many pieces on it—just a golden bangle bracelet on a lower limb, a silver chain made of tiny links on a limb off to the left, and a golden chain that seems to shimmer of its own volition with a pendant dangling at the bottom on the right side of the tree. It's placed a little farther toward the back of the tree. I turn the tree so that I can see the pendant a little closer. It looks familiar. I look at it a little harder; it's the same pendant that my mother wore in her portrait. It's the glass heart with the small white feather in the middle. Except this one has a crack right down the center.

Seven

Miriam comes closer to me. Her hands haven't relaxed yet in her pockets, and I can't tell how she's feeling. It's like she's hiding her feelings from her face.

"This looks like the one my mother was wearing in that portrait," I say, trying not to sound like I'm prying, but I really want to know if this is my mother's.

"Yes." Miriam keeps her answer short like she's afraid of saying too much.

Finally, I ask, "Is it my mother's?"

Miriam sits on the edge of her bed. The blanket, which was made by my mother, scrunches underneath her.

"No," she says quietly.

Miriam takes her hands out of her apron pockets and relaxes a little. She lays her hands on top of her lap, and the dark cloud over her face has changed. It looks more like defeat. Her shoulders slump as she seems to collapse inward. She motions for me to sit next to her and stretches her hand out so that I can place the pendant in it. I slip it off the branch from the tree and place it gently in her palm as I sit next to her.

"There are some things I can tell you now, but some things still have to wait. You will need to be accepting of the information I can give you, and you can't ask for more, okay?"

"Okay," I reply.

Miriam takes out a pocket watch that she must have hidden inside her apron, glances at it, and places it back inside.

"We only have a short while, and then we need to get you back upstairs. Your mother and I go back a long time. She and I were … in the same line of work, you could say. She had a different job than I did, but my job was to help her do part of hers. I was a sort of messenger, and I helped her with some of the people she dealt with."

"I know you said not to ask, but I don't understand why you both had these pendants." I am really trying hard not to pry too much. This is the most Miriam has opened up to me about her past.

Miriam looks as though she doesn't know how much she can tell me. Doesn't The Guide talk to her too? I thought he talked to everyone.

"Patrina, this is part of a life I lost. I made such a terrible mistake so long ago. Maybe it's time you knew who I am." She scoots so that she can face me. She takes my hands in hers and looks into my eyes with the saddest expression I think I could ever bare to look upon.

"Your mother and I … we were … angels."

Before she can go on any further, I snatch my hands out of hers in shock. How can she be an angel and live here? And why would an angel allow my uncle to lock me up in that tower my whole life? I am near tears at the very thought of this as I hear that small whisper in my heart again. *Listen to her, little one. Do not let your assumptions shut the door between you.*

"Patrina, please, let me finish." Miriam's eyes plead with mine as she takes my hands again. I don't fully understand, but I'm trying to calm down so that maybe I can.

"We were angels a long time ago. The feathers in the pendants are our first feathers. The very first ones that are like baby bird feathers that molt and make way for our grown-up feathers. The first feather that falls is collected by other angels that are watching over us and placed inside a pendant to symbolize our life's work that we have been made for. If you look closer at my pendant, on the back is the symbol of winged feet. This is the symbol for a messenger. My work was to bring messages to people and to other angels."

"Like when something important is going to happen?" I ask.

"Yes, or when an angel needs help to direct the one that they are assigned to watch over. I brought the messages to the angel. Your mother was one of those angels that I brought messages to, but your mother was a different type of angel than most. She was special because—"

Something slams somewhere in the house and startles both of us. Miriam stands up so fast that the pendant in her lap falls to the floor. She grabs my hands and starts to pull me toward her closet.

"What was that? Where are we going? What's going on?" My heart races inside my chest as she hushes me and tells me to be very quiet.

"Your uncle is back!" she whispers to me as she leads me into the closet and to the back corner behind her dresses. There is a seam in the wall, like the one I saw in one of the first rooms we explored today. She touches something, but it's too dark, and I can't see what she's doing. Then the wall pops out a little, and she slips her fingers under the edge. As she pulls it open, I can see that there's another room behind this one. Except it's not a room. It looks like a corridor.

"This house holds many secrets and passageways," she whispers to me as she grabs my hand and pulls me inside the hidden corridor. It's like a hallway in the main house but much tighter and there are only a few lights on the walls.

She pulls me along a little too fast, and I stumble over my own foot. Just as I am about to fall into the wall, she turns around so quickly that she's a blur and catches me. I stare at her in astonishment. I've never seen her move like that.

"Be careful. We don't want him to know you're out. He will be making his way up to your tower soon. He always buys you books on his trips."

We start off again down the dimly lit passageway. It turns to the left and then curves to the right. Small wooden steps lie ahead of us. They must be a back way to my tower. The steps are made of old planks, not the nice wood that's in the rest of the house. And they're very small, only about the width of two of my feet side by side. We have to turn sideways to squeak our way up the curve of this dark and drafty back staircase. At the top, Miriam runs her fingers along the wall until she finds another seam. She presses something on the left side of the wall, and part of the wall pops out, just like in her closet. Only this time it opens to the hallway right outside my bedroom door.

Miriam peeks down the hall, and once she sees that it's clear, she rushes me out of the back staircase and quietly closes the secret door. She reaches into her apron pocket and pulls a key out. It's old and looks like a key that would be used for a treasure chest in one of my books. She pokes it into the heart-shaped lock on my door and tries to unlock it, but it won't turn. Just as she takes the key out and tries again, I can hear footsteps starting up the staircase. They are heavy steps. These are the footsteps of my uncle.

Miriam hears it too, and I think she stops breathing for a moment because all I can hear are my uncle's footsteps pulsing in my ear. The panic in the air is so thick it's nauseating. She pokes the key in again, and this time it finally turns. With a loud thunk, the door unlocks and swings open. The sound of my uncle's steps stop for a second. Did he hear the lock open? Before I can even look at Miriam, she pushes me into my room and turns to look back down the hallway.

Eight

"Good day, sir. You're back early," Miriam says, opening my door.

"My trip wrapped up quite nicely, and I was able to get back on an earlier flight. What are you doing?" Vlad asks. He sounds suspicious, but I can't see him. I quietly tiptoe to my reading corner where I have shelf on top of shelf of the books he has brought me.

"Just going in for a little afternoon work, sir. Do you have any new additions for her today?"

"Yes, but I thought I would give it to her. Her birthday is soon, and she and I will need to get to know each other better. I have big plans for her."

Miriam steps aside and opens the door a little farther. Uncle Vlad walks into the room with an air of distinguished arrogance. His clothing is impeccable, and every little detail is in place. I never would've guessed that he had been on an airplane or that he had even sat down in the clothes he's wearing. My clothes get wrinkled almost immediately after I put them on. His clothes look as though they have just been pressed. He has his black suit jacket unbuttoned, and the crisp white shirt underneath is opened at his neck. His jet-black hair is combed back, making the blue of his eyes look like the pictures of the ocean in the books I've read. I try not to look like I am staring, but I think I see a scar on the left side of his neck just beneath the collar of his shirt.

"Hello, Patrina."

"Hi … Uncle Vlad."

He doesn't normally talk to me. When he brings me new books, he just comes in my room, barely past the door, and sets them on a table nearby that was placed there for his drop-offs. I don't know whether to get up and shake his hand or stay seated in my little armchair in the corner, so I just stay where I am.

"Do you like the books I bring you?" Uncle Vlad steps a little closer, close enough that I can smell his musky cologne. I feel like his eyes are burning holes into me.

"Yes, very much."

"I have a new one for you." He hands it to me. Every part of him is well groomed, even his hands. He wears a ring on his left hand that looks very old. It's gold and has a ruby with some sort of symbol on it.

I take the book from his hands. It's about the Great Lakes around a state in the U.S.A. called Michigan. It looks funny to me. The state looks like a mitten that I would wear in the cold … if I were ever let outside. I set the book down by my side as Uncle Vlad sits on the gold velveteen armchair that Miriam usually sits in. Where is Miriam anyway? I sneak a glance around the room but don't see her anywhere.

"You have a birthday coming up soon. You'll be twelve, and that's a big milestone for you. I'll be visiting more often. I have some projects in mind to help you develop the skills that you will use for my business. It's time to start earning your keep, Patrina." And with that, he slaps his hands onto his knees, pushes himself up out of the chair, and walks in long strides across my room. What does he mean "earn my keep" anyway? He's the one that keeps me locked up here.

I stare at the book he just gave me, and he locks the door on his way out.

The sun is starting to set outside my windows, and I feel the edge of the diary digging into my leg. I almost forgot about it in all the hustle of trying to get back into my tower. I slip my hand into my pocket and feel the smooth texture of the well-worn leather. It makes me feel like my mother is right here with me. As I take it out of my pocket, my stomach is in knots. I was only able to glance at the beginning part of the book earlier today, as we were so intent on taking advantage of seeing the mansion. Even though I feel like I learned a lot, I think I have more questions than answers.

"Maybe the diary can shine some light on all of this," I whisper as I unwind the leather strap and open the front cover.

I see the page I saw earlier and run my fingers across the handwriting. This is a piece of my mother. The edges of the pages are worn and look as though she flipped through this book often. I turn the page, expecting to see more of my mother's penmanship, but it's blank. I turn another page, and that one is blank too. I start to flip through the book at a panicked pace. All the pages are blank! Where are the answers I was seeking? Why would The Guide tell me that this is for me when there is nothing inside? I feel so confused and irritated. I just don't understand!

I angrily toss the book up onto my bed and slump into the chair. Even though I'm mad and feel like I've lost any hope I had, the chair is soft and soothes me. I sink into the chair and watch the sunlight start to dim. I start to recount all that I learned today: I met Bao and heard his story, and I also learned a lot about my uncle and his love for my mother. From the story that Bao told, Uncle Vlad sounds kind of scary. And there was that pendant that both my mother and Miriam had. We got interrupted before she could tell me her story.

As I'm thinking about all the little things that wove together to make an interesting web, my eyelids get heavy. My body feels like its being held down by a huge weight, making it impossible to move. I feel my head loll to the side, and I give in to the sleep that dares to snatch me away.

I open my eyes, but everything looks fuzzy … almost like a fog has crept into the outer rim of my eyesight. I'm standing outside in my bare feet on a sandy edge by a river. I can feel the grittiness of the sand between my toes. There's a giant weeping willow tree whose leafy green tentacles are gently wiggling in the breeze. The sun is shining, and I can feel its warmth on my shoulders. There's something in my right hand. I look down, and it's the diary. I can feel something in my other hand too. My fist is clenched around it, and it's starting to dig into the flesh of my palm. I can barely open my fingers. After a moment, I'm able to force my fingers to creak open, and I see something shiny … like glass … and small. It's the pendant that my mother and Miriam have! Why do I have it?

"Izabella! Don't! Please don't do it!"

I hear someone shouting off to my left. There's a woman with dark, wavy hair running to me, but I can't make out who it is. The woman looks at me as she begs me, but her face is a blur. Why did she call me Izabella? I'm not Izabella.

I hear myself say in a voice that's not my own, "You betrayed me. How can you ever help me again if I can't trust you? You're lost to me and to the Monarch. You will forever serve under him whom you have chosen to listen to."

The woman is sobbing loudly as she falls to her knees in front of me.

"No, Izabella, no! Please give me another chance! It was only a mistake! Please …"

I feel my hand clench around the little glass heart pendant.

It hurts so badly, but I can't make it stop. I look down at my hand, and it's starting to glow orange. It gets brighter and brighter as the pain sears through my fingertips. Suddenly a loud crack comes from my hand. My fingers slowly open of their own will, and I drop the pendant to the ground in front of the woman. There is a feather inside it, just like my mother's and Miriam's, but now this one has a crack in the glass.

I watch as it falls and sinks into the sand in front of the woman who is still crying at my feet. Her shoulders fall in defeat as she whispers, "I'm sorry." She tilts her face up to me, and I'm finally able to see who she is. It's Miriam ...

I'm jolted awake by the loud clack of my door being unlocked. It's dark outside. I have no idea how long I have been asleep. That dream was so real, and yet it wasn't me. It was my mother. How could I be dreaming that I was my mother?

Miriam opens my door quietly and peers just past the frame. "Are you sleeping?" she asks in a whisper barely loud enough for me to hear.

"I was, but I'm not now," I reply. I reach up and touch my hair. If it looks as bad as it feels, that really must've been some dream. Can I tell Miriam about the dream? She was in it ...

Just as I wonder that in my heart, The Guide whispers, *Yes. You may tell her. It's time you knew.*

Nine

"You look like you were sleeping well." Miriam giggles as she flicks on the lamp on the nightstand next to my bed. The light casts a golden glow on the gray hairs on her head, making them sparkle in the light.

"I had a dream … about you." I don't know how to tell her about what I saw because I don't know if it was a dream or something else. It felt too real.

"About me? What was I doing in your dream?" Miriam sits in the armchair on the other side of my nightstand. This is where she sat every night and read me bedtime stories when I was younger. Even now she likes to sit there and tell me stories of my parents as I drift off to sleep.

"It was a really weird dream. I was my mother, and you and I were out by the edge of a stream or lake—I don't know which. You were crying and begging me not to do 'it,' but I'm not sure what 'it' was. I had my mother's diary in my one hand and your glass heart pendant in my other hand. When I talked, it was my mother's voice that came out. I said that you had made your choice or something like that. And then I squeezed the glass heart until my hand glowed orange and the pendant cracked."

Miriam lets her head fall, and her shoulders slump. A tear

slides down her cheek. I didn't mean to upset her. It was only a dream, right? Miriam wipes the tear with the back of her hand, lays both of her hands in her lap, and sits back in the chair. She lifts her head and sighs as she says, "That wasn't a dream, Patrina. You're almost of age now, and you're going to start having new things happen that you're not going to understand. These dreams are one of them. I don't know if you're ready to hear this yet. I wish The Guide would just talk to me again!" Miriam slams her fist into her thigh, and what she just said finally sinks in. She can't hear him?

"Just as I'm an angel, and your mother was an angel ... you are an angel too. We aren't full angels ... this is hard to explain." Miriam reaches her hands to her face and rubs her temples as though she is getting a headache.

She lays her hands back into her lap and sits back in the chair. I can tell she's thinking by the erratic movement of her eyes darting around the room. "You've read that book that I snuck in here right? *The Book of Ancient Letters?*

Uncle Vlad brought me many books, but Miriam brought me a book that was comprised of ancient letters. She told me to hide it years ago so that he wouldn't know I had it. Just like any other book I've been given, I devoured every last word. What else is there to do when you're locked in a tower?

"I've read it a couple of times," I say, curious as to where this is going.

"Do you remember in the first letter where it speaks of giants and nephilim?"

Of course I remembered that! That was the part in the letters that talked about how angels came to earth and took up human wives and had children that were part-angel and part-human. They were called nephilim because they were the rejects. And from what I've read in other books, these would've been some very large rejects!

I nod my head in excitement and lean a little closer to her.

She starts to talk in a hushed tone, maybe so my uncle doesn't hear.

"*The Book of Ancient Letters* talks about the first nephilim, but about three hundred years ago, there was a revolt in Arcadia, the city of the Monarch. You know who the Monarch is, right?"

I nod. He is the creator of everything, the great ruler, the one and only. Not only have I read about him, but Miriam has told me about him. He is the almighty king of Arcadia, and he always has been. I lean forward in my chair and rest my elbow on the armrest as she continues.

"There were six angels who wanted to make their own army, an army stronger, smarter, and more powerful than any that was ever known to man … or to the city. They left Arcadia and came here. They learned from the past angels some of the things that went wrong with their first attempt to create an angel-human breed, and they have been tweaking it ever since. This is the age of the tenth genesis.

"Your mother and I are of the ninth genesis. That makes you the tenth." Miriam stops for a minute and looks at me. I feel dumbfounded. There is so much she just told me in such a short time. Is this what The Guide wanted me to know?

"I have so many questions. I don't know where to start." I sit in a glassy-eyed stupor as she patiently waits for me to come to my senses. "What's Arcadia? Let's start there. I've seen references to a place where the Monarch lives but never heard the name. Is it near here?"

Miriam smiles a little and clasps her hands together. "Arcadia is the most beautiful place you could ever see. Do you remember the paradise door?"

I nod, recalling the magnificence of it and how it came to life as I was near it. And it wasn't just a little life but abundant and overflowing life! It's the kind of magnificence that you don't want to ever leave.

"Uncle Vlad had that door made to resemble Arcadia because of his love for your mother. She talked about Arcadia to both your father and Vlad on a few occasions and described how beautiful it was and her love for it. Arcadia was the paradise that the Monarch made for him and his people, the ones who love him unabashedly and are wholly devoted. Some of the residents in Arcadia are the angels, the Monarch's servants. There are many different kinds of full angels there, and there are also the nephilim. That's what your mother and I are ... were. But only the nephilim that choose to be a part of Arcadia and serve under the Monarch are welcomed into the city. Those who choose to serve make a trip to the city when their first feather comes in so that they can receive their job. I was an archangel, or a messenger. I brought messages to people and to other angels. Sometimes they were messages from the Monarch, and sometimes it was from angels to angels.

"Your mother was a virtue. Virtues are a Monarch masterpiece. Since your mother was a ninth-genesis virtue, this means that you are the tenth-genesis virtue. You are one of the most gifted angels. One of the things a virtue does to keep their legacy alive is the mother passes down her knowledge, wisdom, and experiences to her daughter. Sometimes these come out as what seem to be dreams. These are not actually dreams but experiences that happened in your mother's life. I'm just sad that your first one was that one."

The happy glow from Miriam's face starts to fade as she continues, "The time I had with your mother was a blessing all by itself. The dream that you saw was the end of my job as a messenger. I made a poor decision, but that's for another time. To answer your question about Arcadia, it's not near here ... not in the sense that you're thinking. It's somewhere you have to be called to. Once you're called to it, you can go, but once you choose to abandon your job, you can never go back. I can't go back anymore."

Another tear slides down Miriam's cheek, and as she briskly wipes it away, she gets up from the chair, straightens out her apron, and smiles. "My dear Patrina, this has been a lot of information, and I still have some work I need to finish before I can finally go to sleep. Shall we pick this back up another day?"

I realize that I am still feeling quite tired myself. Today has been a long day with a lot to process. I nod my head, and she gives me a hug and tucks me under the blankets. She flicks off the light on my nightstand and quietly closes and locks the door behind her.

As I lay there with the moonlight shining in my windows, I start to feel myself sinking into a deep slumber, except I can feel the warmest, softest grass nestling up between my toes …

Ten

I look down and see my bare feet in the lushest, greenest grass I could've ever imagined. I've only seen grass in pictures in the books I've read. I never thought it would feel like this!

As I look closer, I can tell these aren't my feet. There are callouses where I don't have any, and my toes are smaller. They are very close to what mine look like, and I realize that these must be my mother's feet, except I can feel everything as if they were my own.

I glance at the ground ahead of my toes and see tiny droplets of water on each little blade of grass. This must be dew! The dew is so soothing to my skin. It's almost as though my feet are drinking it in after being parched from neglect. I can see my skin starting to soften and pink up as the gray, dry cracks in my heels begin dissolving before my very eyes.

I have no idea where I am, but this place is wonderful!

I look around me and see that I'm at the bottom of a hill. The hill is covered with grass and tiny white flowers that look like the snowdrops from my horticulture book. They're so delicate and beautifully placed across the hill. It's as though I'm standing in a piece of art.

I look off to my side and see what I think is the sky … except it's not the right color. It's a brilliant reddish orange.

It's a sharp contrast with the green grass but is stunning nonetheless. I recall from one of the ancient letters that a red sky is a warning of something … what was that again?

I start to walk up the hill, and the grass tickles the bottom of my feet. It's such a comforting feeling. The whole place is soothing to my innermost being. It's effortless to walk up this hill, and when I finally reach the top, I see the prettiest city imaginable.

There are buildings of every color of metal, even the rose gold that I see once in a while on a trinket Uncle Vlad brings me. The city itself seems to twinkle like a star in the night sky, except it twinkles in a light that doesn't come from a sun like what I've always known. The light is emanating from somewhere else. There are other people here. A lot of other people! They don't look like anyone I've ever seen … and they're glowing.

Someone is calling my name, but I don't see who it is, and slowly I feel myself being pulled back. "I want to stay!" I try to tell the force that is pulling me back, but the voice keeps calling to me. Quickly the city fades away, and I'm back on the grass I stood on in the beginning. With each mention of my name, this beautiful place dissipates. Where's it going? Why can't I stay?

Someone is shaking me … No, really! Someone is shaking me! I cringe against the light in my room and the rays of sun shining down on my face. As I struggle to pry my eyelids open, I finally look up into the face of Miriam.

"My goodness! You were out like a light, my dear! I've been calling your name for about ten minutes now. I was getting worried. Are you okay?" Miriam must've been worried because her hair, which is normally nicely held back with fancy little pearl clips, is all disheveled, and one of the clips looks as though it's about to fall out.

I rub the sleep from eyes and prop myself up onto my elbows. "I'm okay. I was just dreaming, I guess."

"Dreaming of what?" I can tell that now that Miriam has told me what my dreams really are, and the first dream I had was of her, she's a little worried.

I sit the rest of the way up in bed as the excitement of what I saw comes back in full color to my mind. "I dreamt of this hill with the most glorious grass and little white flowers all over it and there were all of these people that were glowing. And the sky—it was red! The sky is supposed to be blue, not red, isn't it? And my feet! They weren't my feet. I have never felt so secure and safe … and loved! I felt loved beyond measure! I wanted to stay! I wanted to stay so badly, but a voice kept calling my name, and every time it called, it pulled me farther and farther away. I couldn't make it stop!" I feel more and more anxious at the thought of losing some place like that, some place that my heart longs to be … forever.

Miriam pushes the covers over and sits on my bed next to me. She looks both happy and sad. She takes my hand in hers as she says, "Patrina, that was Arcadia. Your mother and I used to go there frequently because of the very thing you've discovered. It's home, and it feels so good to be there! It's refreshing and refueling. Your mother and I used to walk up that very hill you described, but the sky wasn't always red."

"Why would it be red? There's a part in the *Ancient Letters* that talks about a red sky in the morning being a warning and a red sky at night being a delight or something like that. I don't know what time of day I was there though." I lay my head back down and let it sink into my pillow. I used to think my pillows were the best thing on earth, but now I know differently.

"The sky in Arcadia has been red only two times that I know of—the first time the angels left to try to make their own breed of army radicals, and again about three hundred years ago. Given that you were there, I would say that it was the second time, but then I don't think it was your mother you were seeing through. That's odd ..."

My mind is swirling with thoughts and questions. What exactly does it say in the letters about the sky? I flip back the blankets to go get the book, and I look down at my feet.

They are covered in grass.

Miriam looks down where I am looking and gasps. "Dreams aren't supposed to come back with you!"

My sheets and blankets are drenched like I climbed into bed with soaking wet feet. I reach down and pull a blade of grass off my foot. It's as soft as it was in my dream, and it's still glistening. I gently lay it on top of my nightstand as Miriam watches. She stretches out her hand to touch it, and just as her fingertip touches the dewy edge, it disappears into dust and floats away like a dream when you first wake up. I look to my sheets, and they are now dry. All the grass on my feet has disappeared as though it was never there in the first place.

We stare at each other with questioning eyes, trying to make sure we both saw what we think we saw. "Maybe your mother's diary has something in it about dreams," Miriam says finally.

"There's nothing in my mother's diary. Just blank pages," I say dejectedly.

"What did The Guide say about it?"

"Nothing. I was angry, and I threw the book onto my bed." I look down, too ashamed to look Miriam in the eyes.

"Patrina, The Guide can only talk to you if you let him. When you're angry, your emotions shut him out. It's like slamming a door on him. There's probably a reason why you haven't been shown what the diary holds yet."

I look up at her, searching her face for hope. When I didn't find the answers I thought were going to be in the diary, it felt like my little bubble of hope had popped. She smiles at me and points to the diary that's on the edge of my nightstand. "Why don't you try again?" she says.

"Okay." I turn to sit on the edge of my bed and pull my nightgown over to cover my legs. My feet are completely dry but not the kind of dry where it makes my skin feel tight. They actually feel nourished and refreshed. I reach toward the diary, and it starts to glimmer. It makes me feel hopeful, like maybe there's something in it.

The diary is warm to my touch when I pick it up. Books aren't supposed to generate their own heat. I set it in my lap and unwind the leather tie. The glimmer has reduced to an iridescent shimmer as I open the front cover. I flip over the page that my mother's name is on, and the first page is blank, just like before. Wait … it's turning gray … is that a letter?

Eleven

The words start to form as though someone is actually writing them. The author of this page writes:

> I was awakened by a lot of shouting this morning, and as I looked out my window of this glorious mansion the Monarch has made for me, I see Coyle in the courtyard. I don't understand why Coyle always has to make everyone do things his way. And then when someone doesn't want to, he starts yelling, until the Monarch comes and makes him calm down.
>
> I can just barely make out what he's yelling. Something about taking over and making nephilims that are perfect. Strong.
>
> I just looked out the window again, and Coyle has gathered quite a crowd. Why is Engelbert there? He's like me. He shouldn't be there. And Mariangela is there too. She's probably fueling Coyle on.
>
> I hear someone coming. They're loud! I think they're coming in …

It just stops there. I turn the page to see if there's more, but that's it. That's all for now, I guess.

I look to Miriam, and she's just patiently watching my face. I look down at the diary.

"Can you see the writing?" I ask her.

She smiles, looks at the book, and shakes her head.

"No. That diary is for you and you alone. That may be why your uncle hid it from you. He wouldn't have been able to read anything either—well, other than the inscription in the front. I bet he knew that you'd be able to read it though. What did you see?"

"It was from another person that I don't think was my mother. She lived in a mansion in Arcadia and mentioned someone named Coyle and Mariangela."

Miriam's face has wrinkles between her eyebrows. "Hmm … the only one of your specific line that lived in Arcadia was Adena. She would've been the first of the ten, if she happened to be a part of it. Who were the other names again?"

"Coyle and Mariangela. Do you know them?"

"Coyle was the one who started the revolt. And Mariangela was like his right-hand guy, except she was a girl. Those two together would've set the world on fire if they could. Coyle didn't like being less than the Monarch. He wanted to rule over others like the Monarch, and Mariangela wanted to be a part of his uprising. What else does it say?"

I look back at the page again. "It talks about Coyle gathering quite a crowd in the courtyard, and then she heard someone coming. It just stops, like whoever was coming actually came in there. Do you know what happened?"

"I only know what has been told to me through the years. Coyle was a vicious and jealous angel, and he had a few followers. Coyle wanted to make nephilim who would be stronger than all the rest and not be so obvious like the giants from the stories in the *Ancient Letters*. Coyle wanted certain angels who were made for particular jobs in his army. One of those kinds was virtues, like you and like Adena. Adena could control elements, and that's probably the gift you're tapping into when you see objects glow or change colors. Adena could manipulate objects that were made from various elements, like metals. Coyle was one of six angels who revolted and took angels with them. Some of them went willingly, and some didn't. Adena was one of them from the sounds of her entry in the diary."

"But Coyle was in the courtyard, so it couldn't have been him that was coming for Adena." I can feel the fear in the pages of the diary as though it is me that is there.

Miriam takes my hand. It's warm and soothing. I know she's been placed in my life for a reason. I don't know why yet, but I appreciate how she can calm me.

There are so many questions swirling about in my mind, but one stands out more than the rest. I look up at Miriam as I ask, "How can this be Adena's entry in my mother's diary? It just says that it's Izabella's diary in the front."

There's a twinkle in Miriam's eye as she says, "Izabella was the last one who had it. The diary holds all of the entries from your entire lineage. It's been passed down from mother to daughter since the revolt. I guess The Guide and the Monarch wanted you to learn from the beginning what had happened."

She pats me on the leg and starts to get up. "Well, my dear little angel, you need to get up and get dressed. You have a very full day ahead of you. Your uncle is home, and he has asked that you come down and have breakfast with him."

I don't want to go have breakfast with him—even though I am excited that I get to leave my room. I climb out of bed and find a lime-green T-shirt crumpled on the floor next to a dark blue pair of pants. I start to put them on when Miriam pulls out of my closet a dress Uncle Vlad brought back from Indonesia when he went there a couple of months ago.

I stop midpull with my pants at the base of my thighs and look at her. Miriam shakes her head and says, "Oh, you need to dress accordingly, dear. When you're up here, you can dress however you wish. But when you are down there, you have to dress for the occasion. Breakfast is a little less formal than dinner, but you still need to wear a dress. And shoes! Good thing your uncle bought you this!" She has a dress draped over her arm, white shoes dangling from her index finger, and some white see-through stockings that seem to be slipping off the top of the dress.

When he brought me these clothes a few months back, I thought it was rather odd. I don't go anywhere and don't need anything like that. Now I can see that he has been planning this for a while.

The dress isn't very pretty. It's a navy blue with strange pink flowers all over it that remind me of a watercolor painting in one of my books. Miriam hands me the white stockings that I have to wiggle my way into before I can put the dress on. She calls these horrible things "nylons." It's like wedging myself into a pair of pants that are three sizes too small, and it pinches my waist.

Once I get the nylons on, Miriam slips the dress over my head. The dress has little pearl buttons at the neckline, but they don't do anything. They're just for decoration, I guess. The sleeves aren't short, and they aren't long either. They fall just below my elbow, and when I bend my arm, it cinches tight and squeezes my forearm. The dress is just long enough to cover my knees, but it poofs out at the bottom. I bet if I twirl around, it will float up and make a perfect circle. Just as I'm about to test my theory, Miriam grabs my arm.

"We don't have time for twirling!" Miriam says. Sometimes I swear she can read my mind.

I slip my feet into the shiny, white patent-leather shoes that have a buckle that goes across the front of my ankle. They are the least annoying part of this whole outfit. Why people wear this stuff to a meal is beyond me!

Miriam stands back and looks at me with a goofy grin on her face. "You look beautiful, Patrina! And you'd look even prettier if you'd smile." She winks and turns me so that she can clip my hair off of my forehead. It pulls a little, but it feels good when I feel the air hit my face.

"There! You are ready for breakfast with your uncle!"

I'm itchy and feel pinched and awkward. How can this be beautiful? I guess my emotions are written all over my face because Miriam gives me a look and says, "Straighten up and behave like a lady."

I guess the sooner I behave like a lady, the sooner I can get this over with and get out of these clothes!

Miriam takes my hand, and we walk to the door of my room. She opens the door, and I see the familiar curved hallway. That door to the left must lead to the rooftop garden. Maybe she'll let me see that after breakfast. We make our way down the stairs and through the halls. We pass the paradise door and round to the kitchen.

"Your uncle thought you would like to have breakfast in the glass room."

I don't remember seeing a glass room. Just as I am about to utter a hushed word to Miriam, she leans and whispers in my ear, "There were a few rooms you didn't see. This is one of them, and it's just off of the arboretum that houses some of your uncle's plants. The dining room is another, but I'm sure you will see that later."

My stomach does flip-flops as I get nearer. We walk into the indoor greenhouse that she referred to as an arboretum. There are different plants all over this room. There is no door into this room, just a doorway. We follow a path that weaves through this leafy green space. It's like a place that is meant to be walked through, not to sit in and enjoy. A door off to the left is made of etched glass, and there's a picture of a beautiful garden with a lady sitting on a bench. She looks familiar to me, like the statue in the front garden.

Miriam opens the door and ushers me through. The sun is shining outside and as the rays of sun glisten through the glass ceiling, their warmth is trapped behind the panes with us. There are huge palms in here that hang over a white stone path. I almost feel as though I'm walking through a jungle. This glass room feels more like a greenhouse than the one designated to be one!

Something flits past my left cheek. I turn and see that it's a butterfly! There are butterflies in here! I look at the plant I'm standing next to and see three more. I'm so mesmerized by their little fluttering wings that I don't realize that Miriam has left me.

Or that my uncle is standing right next to me.

Twelve

"I acquired these butterflies on one of my trips a few months ago," Uncle Vlad says as he stands towering over me. The scent of his musky cologne invades my space and makes me feel like he's too close. When I turn to face him, I see that he's dressed in navy slacks and a cream-colored shirt that is unbuttoned at the neck. I can't help but realize that we kind of match.

I really don't know what to say to him, so I turn and look at a nearby hibiscus. It's a brilliant red with a yellow stamen. I remember reading about this flower in one of my books. This is a tropical plant.

I keep looking around and see more and more flowers that don't normally grow around our area. Our temperatures are too cool for most of these. They are flowers that a person would see in a warmer, more southern climate. There's even a bamboo tree growing in the corner next to a quaint little table set for breakfast.

He motions for me to go over and sit down. Without a word, we both go to the small, round, cast-iron table. As I'm about to reach for my chair, he quickly grabs the back of it and pulls it out for me. I cautiously sit down and scoot forward so that I'm closer to the table. He sits across from me and snaps his napkin in the air so that it unfolds, and then he places it across his lap. I quietly unfold my napkin and place it in my lap, trying to do as he does so that I don't upset him. I remember Bao's story about how he can have a temper.

The plate in front of me holds a pile of golden scrambled eggs, a few glistening chunks of cantaloupe, a couple deep red strawberries, and two crispy strips of bacon. My mouth starts watering. I pick up my fork and start digging in as Uncle Vlad laughs. "I guess you were hungry, weren't you, Patrina?"

Maybe I should've waited for him, but I just couldn't help myself! The scrambled eggs are so delicious that they melt in my mouth, and the bacon is the right amount of salty crispness to balance out the sweet nectar of the fruits.

"Do you remember when we talked yesterday?" he asks as he takes a bite of bacon.

I finish off my last bite and nod. I try to remember the etiquette that I learned in one of my books and lightly dab the crumbs from my mouth with my napkin and then place it back into my lap.

"I am in the business of imports and exports," he continues. "Do you know what that is?"

"You order stuff to be brought into our country and fill orders that need to be brought to other countries?" I ask.

"Basically. There are products that we make in our country that other countries can't make and vice versa. Therefore, we work together to make sure that everyone gets what they want."

I have no idea where he's going with this. I remember him mentioning that I was getting old enough and that I could start helping him with his business, but how am I supposed to help him with this? My mind drifts a little, and he shifts in his chair. I guess he can tell that he lost my attention. He leans forward and places his right arm on the table, and as he does that, I see the scar on his neck below his collar. That's the scar I thought I saw yesterday!

"Patrina, pay attention!" he says as he slams his hand on the table. The sharpness of his voice snaps me back and makes me feel uncomfortable. He leans back in his chair and readjusts his collar, hiding the scar.

"I'm sure by now that Miriam has explained to you who you are?" I can tell he's fishing for me to volunteer information. *Be quiet, dear child.* The Guide has become a part of me as though it is ingrained in every neuron in my brain. I don't understand why I should be quiet, but I trust The Guide and just look at my uncle. I try to hide from him any knowledge that I have and just raise my eyebrows in a silent question.

He looks like he's starting to get angry. Maybe I should've just said that she told me everything. *Be still, child. Hold on.*

His face is reddening as he starts to rant, "I told her that she needed to tell you everything! That way we would be able to start work today! Now she's put me behind schedule! Again!" He rips the napkin from his lap and whips it onto the table. My knees are starting to tremble, as I'm only about two feet away from him. I realize that I am definitely within his reach should he choose to take his anger out on me.

Almost, dear one. Just a little longer …

I am trying not to stare at his face, but the veins in his head are throbbing. I look into his blue eyes as he's ranting at me, and the blue that once reminded me of the ocean pictures in my books has gotten murky, and the very edge of his iris has turned a jet black. Bao mentioned something about his eyes in his story.

Breathe, little one. Keep breathing.

I feel The Guide as though he's right here with me. I calm my breathing, my knees stop knocking, and I smooth the napkin on my lap. Suddenly, Uncle Vlad stops yelling, takes in a deep breath, holds it for a few seconds, and then slowly lets it out. I look up at him and see that the black around the blue in his eyes has started to recede, and the veins have gone back into his head. He seems to be calming himself down.

With another deep breath, he says, "Patrina, sometimes you just cannot depend on other people to do the job that you should've done yourself. Let that be a lesson to you … and to me."

He picks up the napkin, folds it into a smaller square, and lays it gently on the side of his plate. He looks at me from across this small table, and I have to look away. His gaze almost hurts because it's so intense.

"Looks like I'm going to be the one to tell you who you are. You are Patrina Nadine Palinski, daughter of Konrad and Izabella Palinski. Konrad is my brother, as you know. Izabella … Izabella was your mother, but she was much, much more than that. She was quite powerful. I discovered her gifts shortly after your mother and my brother started dating. I had started my own business of importing goods when my brother brought her around me. I don't think he actually wanted to introduce us, but, nonetheless, I ran into them when they were out at a pub in our town.

"She was beautiful. I invited myself to sit with them at the corner booth that evening, and as we talked, I could tell something was unique about her. She got up and excused herself to go to the ladies' room, and when she did, she accidentally knocked her glass off the table. Fortunately it was mostly empty, but the glass got a crack in the side when it hit the floor. She sat it back onto the table, and when she thought we weren't watching, she took her finger and touched the very end of the crack. I tried not to let on that I was watching, so I looked out of the corner of my eye as her finger started to glow. It was as if she were melting the glass with her touch. I couldn't believe what I was seeing, so I quickly turned my head to watch as she dissolved the crack right before my eyes!

"Your father wasn't very happy that I had witnessed this

and quickly gathered up their belongings and whisked her out of the pub with some foolish excuse. I sat there dumbfounded for hours as I ran my fingers across the smooth glass where there once was a large crack.

"Shortly after that, I decided to do a little digging into her background. She wasn't who she said she was exactly. And you're not who you think you are either. Izabella has a lineage that holds many secrets and powers. It didn't take me long to see that her lineage only goes back about three hundred years, unlike mine and your father's. Her family tree, so to speak, just popped up out of nowhere, and all of the women in the line are special.

"I wasn't able to find much information on all of them at first, mainly just the last five, but I did find countless stories about these abilities they had that seemed to be passed on to the next generation. And that's when I found Miriam, but I'll let her tell you her lovely little story some other time.

"Miriam did, however, fill in quite a few gaps for me, and I was able to figure out a lot about your lineage. It turns out that there were nine generations of you young ladies, all of which were given special gifts and abilities … talents that accumulate with each generation. Izabella was the ninth in the line, making her have nine of the gifts, but she didn't have them all—unlike you. You are the tenth, the golden child. The one who is going to make me a lot of gold!"

He starts to laugh, not just a giggle or even a snicker, but this booming, loud, engulfing laugh that makes every bone in my body shudder. All at once, I don't feel like a niece to him. I don't feel like any kind of family at all to him. I feel like a possession.

I am a possession.

Thirteen

I don't know what to say to him, and I feel as though I am frozen in silence in my little bistro chair. He seems to finally get a hold of himself and stops laughing. He greedily grabs his crystal glass and gulps every last drop. As he wipes his mouth with his napkin, he has not stopped looking at me. I look down at my lap and rustle my napkin with my hands.

"Now that you're up to speed on who you are, you should know what you can do. Or rather, what you should be able to do. Do you even know the talents each of your ancestors were able to do?"

"No," I mumble. Miriam hadn't told me much of this. And it was only yesterday that anything showed up in the diary. I barely know about the first of my lineage. I really didn't want this information to come from my uncle. I don't really know him, and from the stories I've heard, I don't know if I even want to know him.

"Well I shall give you a crash course, my dear." And with that, Uncle Vlad pulls out a black, leather folder that holds a giant pile of papers of what I can only imagine is the details of my lineage.

"Miriam didn't divulge the information of how your line came to be. She only told me that you're from a line of nephilim, and the first of your line was named Adena, which meant 'fire.' Oh, and you should know that every one of you has a name that has something to do with your talent. That's what Miriam told me. Adena was very good with elements, manipulating them, combining them, making them do what she wanted. She was able to melt metals with just a touch of her hand. Or melt glass back together. This is the talent your mother was using that night in the pub.

"Adena was married to a blacksmith named Tyson. I found that the spouses and their jobs were very fitting to your nephilim ancestors as well. Quite intriguing, actually. Adena and Tyson had only one child, a little girl, and they named her Geena, which means 'earth.'

"Geena was a nature nephilim and was able to grow whatever she wanted. She could make trees and flowers grow while at the same time making weeds die. She married a man named Demeter, and he was a farmer. So Geena's talent was very profitable for their little family. Along with her talent of controlling nature, she found that she could also manipulate elements the way her mother could. This was the first of the nephilim kind to have more than one talent.

"Geena and Demeter also had only one child. In fact, all of your ancestors only ever had one child, always a girl. Anyway, this little girl was named Diona, which means 'from the sacred spring.' Diona, from very early on, could control the seasons, which also helped her parents with their farm. Geena and Demeter became very wealthy with the help of their little Diona, and they were able to run their farm from the comforts of their plantation home by using the help of the slaves they bought."

"Slaves? My ancestors had slaves?" I boldly interrupt him because I am shocked that my family has had anything to do with the awful slavery that I've read about in books.

"Yes, my dear, slaves. It was very common back in those days. Shall I continue?" he says with an impatient sigh.

I look down at my hands in my lap and remember that I'm supposed to be a lady, and a lady doesn't interrupt. "Yes, Uncle Vlad."

"Diona grew up and went out on her own, which her parents were not happy with at all. Without Diona's talent of manipulating the seasons, it made farming harder, and they eventually lost their wealth and their slaves.

"Diona, however, left their plantation and never looked back. Diona moved to the quaint little town of Kazimierz Dolny, here in Poland. It was there that she met Caldwell. I was told it was fate that they met because one day she went down to the bank of the Vistula river and saw him sitting underneath a great oak tree, whittling a piece of driftwood that had floated down the river. They saw each other and were wed the next day. Diona and Caldwell had a little baby girl under the stars nine months later and named her Kerra, which means 'dark.'

"I was told that Kerra was able to manipulate the night skies, tampering with how the readers of the night would interpret signs. Kerra's talent and her teenage hormones are what instigated Napoleon's defeat at Waterloo in 1815. Kerra had been a scholar of battle and, through her inquiries, was able to attain the position of assistant to none other than Napoleon himself! Kerra, however, did not agree with Napoleon's tactics and was able to tell the enemy's night readers when and where Napoleon would be and just how many he was sending, all with the stars that were under her control.

"After Napoleon's defeat, Kerra ran and hid in the Mountains of the Crosses for fear that those in charge would find out about her tampering. The story I found says that it was at the base of the mountain, a crossroads, where Kerra met her husband, Travis. Travis had built a church on the top of the mountain, and it was there that Kerra and Travis lived and had a baby girl. They named her Mika because she was born on a new moon.

"Mika was a force to be reckoned with, from what I was able to find. Mika was the first to really have some information about her, and not just from the stories that Miriam told me. I found snippets about her all over the place, from the farmer's almanac to even the history books that are in the schools. Except they don't call her by name; they just talk of her works."

Just then there's a knock on the glass door. We both look, and it's Miriam with a tray of something. I can't tell what it is from where I'm sitting. Uncle Vlad holds up his hand and wiggles two of his fingers to signal for her to come in. She balances the tray on one hand and pulls the door open with her other one.

As she nears our table, Uncle Vlad says, "Miriam knows of Mika's works, don't you?"

I can tell that Miriam doesn't want to say anything. She looks uncomfortable.

She sets the tray down on a nearby stand, and now I can see that she has some sort of a breakfast crumble cake. It smells wonderful. I didn't know breakfast was followed by dessert!

"Yes, I know all too well the works of Mika, sir," Miriam says as she sets the little plates of deliciousness in front of us. My plate has a beautiful triangle of a cream-colored coffee cake drizzled with caramel. Next to it lays a tiny silver fork. I've never seen one this small.

"Why don't you tell Patrina about Mika's temper, Miriam?"

Miriam sighs as Uncle Vlad leans back in his chair with a grin.

"Very well. Mika was someone my grandmother would deliver messages to. She was quite powerful, as she could control elements, nature, the seasons, and the stars along with the moon. She really enjoyed her power, and it fed an unnatural temper she had developed. Mika was a beautiful nephilim and had many a man trying to woo her. Even from her early years,

Mika had men of every age proposing to her, saying that they would whisk her away and give her everything she desired.

"But there was a young man by the name of Iko who was in her town on business. He was from Japan, and he wasn't like the other men. Mika would've been about twenty years old at the time, and most twenty-somethings were already married. Not Mika though. She was a romantic and was looking for the perfect man. She thought she had found him in Iko … until my grandmother had to deliver a message to her.

"All of our messages come from the Monarch and are of utmost importance—and they are also nonnegotiable. What He says, we do. I was told this was the first message the Monarch had brought to a nephilim, but He was trying to keep her from heartache. Even though the nephilim were born and bred out of evil, the Monarch still loved them and wanted them to come back to Him.

"The Monarch didn't want Mika to be defiled and had grandmother tell her that Iko had a wife and three little kids back in Japan. When she told Mika, it devastated her. She had longed for a man that would be her one and only, but Iko would not be him. The next day, as she was bidding him farewell, Mika's heart broke in two, and any sense she may have had in her head left her. Iko boarded the train that would take him across the continent to the boat that would take him to his final destination. Mika cried for days. Nobody really knows how she knew where he was, but she must've known when he boarded the boat because it was then that Mika cried out. As tears streamed down her face, the biggest tsunami in the history of Japan rolled through. It took out Iko's boat, and everyone on board died in the depths of the ocean. Her pain was so intense that the tsunami also took out 15,000 homes. One of those was Iko's wife and children. They also perished in Mika's aftermath."

I look at Uncle Vlad, and he seems to be overjoyed at this

tale. He starts clapping his hands and says, "Good story! Such power!" He sets his hands in his lap again, looks at me with an evil twinkle in his eyes, and says, "We are going to have such fun!"

Fourteen

Miriam motions toward the sun and says, "Sir, I believe it's getting late."

"Oh! Yes, I will have to pick this up another time. I have a meeting to get to." He stands up, straightens his shirt, and turns to me. "Patrina, shall we continue later?"

I don't know why he's even bothering to ask, as I really don't have any other options. I just say, "Yes," thankful to have this awkward breakfast over.

He smiles at me and saunters out of the room, leaving Miriam and me to clean up the dishes. Once I see that he is out of sight, I quickly kick off the shoes that have been pinching my feet since this whole extravaganza began. I can't wait to get out of this costume.

I start stacking up our breakfast dishes to take them into the kitchen when I notice that Miriam is crying.

"What's wrong?" I ask her. I set down the stack of dishes and wave my hand at her, trying to get her attention, but she won't look at me.

"I'm sorry, Patrina. I meant to tell you all of that stuff about your ancestors. I thought The Guide would tell me when I could, and I kept waiting, but he never said anything to me. He hasn't said anything in a very long time." She sniffles and tries to regain her composure by smoothing down her apron and throwing her shoulders back.

"I thought The Guide talked to everyone. He doesn't?"

"The Guide doesn't talk to the angels, or nephilim, who have fallen and chosen a separate path. We aren't like full-blooded humans. We don't get a ton of chances to correct our ways and get back onto the path of the Monarch. Angels, and nephilim like you, once they've chosen to revolt, their hard hearts cut all ties they have with The Guide. It's actually painful ... as if someone is ripping out part of your heart. Your first dream ... that was what was happening to me."

"Miriam, I'm sorry. Can you please tell me your story?" I ask as I sit in one of the bistro chairs and wait for her. She stops wiping the table and sits down across from me, where Uncle Vlad sat just a few moments before.

"It isn't a pretty story ... and I'm not proud of it." She sets her hands in her lap, and the pride falls out of her shoulders as they slump inward.

"It was quite a few years back ... around 1970, I suppose. Your mother and I were working with a couple who was in need of some direction. I had met your uncle three or four weeks before. He was very persuasive and convinced me that what he wanted of this couple was very important.

"He and I met for coffee one day to talk. He knew of Izabella's and my upcoming meeting later that afternoon. I didn't realize that he had been following what we were doing. Vlad had also been meeting with the husband of the couple on the side. The man was involved in importing food and setting the prices in the marketplace. The Monarch had sent The Guide to me to have me tell this man not to raise the prices of the food and that he needed to just trust the Monarch. The Monarch would make everything all right in the long run. Vlad had other intentions and wanted the power that this man had in the country. Vlad convinced me that if I told this man not to raise the prices, the whole country's import market would fall, and no one would have enough food to eat. 'Millions will die from starvation.' That's what Vlad said.

"I didn't talk to your mother about this because I believed Vlad. I didn't want millions to die from this one man's supposed mistake. So later that day, your mother and I went to the meeting we had set up. We were talking with him, and your mother was telling him that the Monarch had sent him word. I interrupted her and told him that he had said to raise the price of food because otherwise millions would die of starvation. Your mother was stunned long enough for the man to gratefully accept this information, and he quickly left us to sit in awkward silence.

"I knew what I had done was against our code. We aren't supposed to tell someone our own word and say it is the Monarch's word. But I thought that what I had done was necessary … that the Monarch didn't know what was right in this situation.

"Your mother started walking away from me, toward the banks of the river you saw in your dream. I could feel in my deepest parts that I had done something terribly wrong. Izabella, being a virtue, ranked higher than me, and she could dole out the punishments given down to her by The Guide.

"I chased her to the weeping willow, crying after her. I knew what was coming; I had seen this before with other angels and nephilim. She ripped my glass heart off from around my neck, and I begged for her not to crack it. That heart is our key to Arcadia. Without it, we can't return to Arcadia after our first feather has fallen.

"She told me that what was done was done and that I had chosen who I was going to follow … Vlad. I didn't realize that when I decided to believe him and do as he asked it would tie me to him forever. She used her gifts to crack the glass of my heart pendant, forever severing my link to Arcadia. And then she walked away. I never saw her again.

"I found your uncle downtown and told him what had happened. He wasn't sad for me. He was actually really happy that I had done what he had asked. All that I had lost didn't seem to cross his mind as he told me that I was his now and would serve him. Then he put me in charge of the construction of this estate."

Miriam looks as though she is completely spent. All of her vigor and light has left, and all that sits before me is a shell of the woman I have grown to love. I dare to ask, "What happened to the man that you gave Uncle Vlad's advice to?"

"Oh, he raised the food prices, and there was such a commotion about it that the country revolted, he was stripped of his power, and he and his wife had to leave the country for fear of their lives. Your uncle now has the power of importing food and setting the prices. That's what he wanted the whole time, and no one but he and the Monarch knew this. That was why the Monarch had The Guide tell me to give the message to the man not to raise the prices. But we don't always see the bigger picture like the Monarch does."

I didn't realize just how powerful my uncle really is, I guess.

I can see that Miriam is thinking of the days when she was still linked to Arcadia. She's looking sadder now than she did before when she was telling me the story.

"Here, I'll help you take these things into the kitchen," I say, trying to change the subject. "And after we do that, we can go out to that roof garden!" I say, smiling at her with a twinkle in my eye.

She looks at me and starts to grin. My enthusiasm must be catchy because her grin gets bigger, and she starts to giggle. "Yes! I do think that's a wonderful idea. And I'll tell you about the rest of your ancestors, seeing that I was supposed to do that anyway. I'll pick up your uncle's folder of the articles he's collected on our way up."

We grab the dishes and silverware we stacked, and I toss the napkins on top of my stack as she opens the door. I start to walk toward her when my foot kicks something and I hear it skitter across the floor in front of me. I look down and see that I almost forgot to get the dreadful shoes I kicked off earlier. I reach down, twist the straps around one of my fingers, and carry the remains of my awkward morning back into the mansion.

We swing by the kitchen to drop off the breakfast dishes on our way up to my tower room. I want to say good morning to Bao, but I don't see him, so we continue on through the hallways. I'm not sure where Miriam found the folder, but when I turn around to see if she's behind me, she already has it in her arms. I'm nearly skipping through the halls, giddy with the thought of going outside.

We finally get all the way upstairs, and I start undressing as I walk in. These clothes are awful and uncomfortable. When I take off the nylons, I can feel the dent they've left in my skin all the way around my waist. Finally I feel like I can breathe!

Miriam is picking up the clothes as I'm taking them off and hands me the jeans and T-shirt I originally picked out before I knew about the etiquette rules of eating downstairs. I quickly put them on and find a pair of socks. I slip those over my feet, and when I look up, Miriam has a pair of slip-on tennis shoes. I put them on and am surprised that they're comfortable. They almost feel like my slippers. I've never had the need for outdoor shoes before now.

Miriam disappears into my closet to put away my breakfast clothes. She left the folder on my bed, and one of the papers has slipped out. It looks like a newspaper clipping. It says, "Great Fire in Poland."

Fifteen

When Miriam comes back in, I glance away from the newspaper article that's on my bed. "I'm ready when you are," I say to her as she walks toward me.

"I haven't been teaching you all that you should have been learning … according to Vlad." She mumbles the last part about my uncle under her breath. "So we are going to have a little crash course in elements."

I freeze where I am standing, fearful of what's to come. I thought we were just going to go outside to the rooftop garden. I muster up the courage to ask, "What do you mean a crash course in elements?"

"You are a tenth-genesis nephilim, which means you have all of the powers of your ancestors before you. You need to learn how to harness them before you accidentally do something. Some of the worst catastrophes in this world's history happened because the ones before you didn't know how to use their gifts, and their emotions took over. You'll learn about those as soon as you open this lock … without your hands." She has locked the door to my bedroom and stands next to it now. She motions to the lock and smiles at me.

"I don't know how to do that!" I exclaim. I'm so frustrated

because now I have to magically unlock this dreadful lock before I can go outside to a garden I've been so excited to see.

Calm yourself, my child. The Guide is here with me again. I'm slightly irritated that even he's in on this whole extravaganza.

"Patrina, you remember how you can see the lock change colors when I'm unlocking it?" Miriam asks. I'm so overwhelmed that the lock on the door is turning black, not the blue color that it turns when Miriam unlocks it. It's not even the brass color that it normally is when no one is touching it. This is not going in the right direction at all.

Breathe, dear one. Just breathe. Take a deep breath, release your fists, and relax your shoulders. Breathe …

With an agitated sigh, I do as The Guide says, and I can start to feel the tension leave my body. I look up and say to Miriam, "Yes, but *you're* unlocking the door. *You're* the one doing it, not me. I only watch it happen."

"You have to picture it in your mind. May I touch your arm while you're doing it? Then I can help you because I can see it change colors," Miriam asks as though her touch would be a violation of my gifts. I agree and close my eyes. I picture the key going into the lock and sliding under the pins within, moving them up and into place.

"You're doing it, Patrina! It's changing colors!" Miriam exclaims. She grabs my arm a little hard out of excitement, and it hurts. I open my eyes and glare at her. "Oh! I'm sorry!" she says as she lets go of my arm a bit.

I go back to concentrating, and I can see in my head the key turning and the locking mechanism release when I hear the familiar clunk coming from the door. I open my eyes and see that the brass is a brilliant blue and the lock that has encased me in this tower has now been unlocked.

"I did it! I actually did it!" I exclaim to Miriam, jumping around and holding her hands as she grins back at me. I stop jumping as a thought occurs to me. "Does this mean that I can do this to other locks too, or do they all have to be made out of brass like this one?"

Miriam is still grinning at me as she says, "You really have no idea the extent of your gifts. You can manipulate elements, so that means any metal, any element that is on that periodic table in your science book, you can manipulate. It'll take some practice, and you'll need to understand the elements and how they function on their own and together, but you'll get it. Shall we go out to the roof garden?"

In all my excitement, I momentarily forgot about the roof garden. And now I'll be able to go out there whenever I want … as long as my uncle doesn't find out. Maybe I can ask him if he will grant me a little freedom. And maybe if Miriam says it's to help me develop my gifts, then he might let me.

We open the door to my bedroom and walk down the curved hall. We don't have to walk long before we come to the door off to the left. I saw this door when we were exploring the house. It has a tiny silver lock on it.

Miriam gestures to the lock and says, "Why don't you see for yourself? It's a different lock completely, but it's still a lock. Try to unlock this one. Just close your eyes and see it unlocking in your mind."

I close my eyes and try to visualize it. I can see the lock, but it won't budge. The tumblers inside won't move. I open my eyes and look at it. It's not glowing at all. It's still the same color it was when I started. I don't understand what's going on. I close my eyes again and just try to relax. Maybe all of my excitement has interfered in the process. I take a deep breath in and relax my shoulders. I can see the lock in my mind like before, and it's starting to move. One tumbler moves, then another tumbler, and soon I have all of them out of the way except one last one. Just as it's starting to slide upward, I smell musky cologne and hear heavy footsteps fall behind me.

"What do you think you're doing?"

I whirl around to face Uncle Vlad, who is looming over me. I start to tremble, but Miriam isn't even flinching.

"You wanted me to train the girl, and I am. How else is she supposed to fully understand her gifts unless she can use them?" Miriam snaps back. Uncle Vlad clenches both of his hands into fists, and I wonder how Miriam can be so calm in the face of such fury.

"That's not what I meant! You showed her the very first day how to escape from her room and manipulate locks in other doors. She almost had that one to the garden!" he yells as he points at the tiny silver lock.

How does he know how far I got the lock? Miriam can't even see the colors, and she's like me. What is Uncle Vlad? I didn't think anyone could see this stuff unless I let them, and I wasn't even focusing on that. I was just trying to get the lock to release.

I am so lost in my thoughts that I didn't hear what Miriam and my uncle were talking about, but whatever it was, he seems calmer now as he tells me to continue with the lock. He makes me nervous though. I'm comfortable with Miriam, yet it's hard to do the locks with her watching. How am I supposed to concentrate with him here? Where's The Guide?

I try to stop my hands from trembling and my knees from shaking. Uncle Vlad seems to have this effect on me. Miriam says that he had an effect on my mother, but it was just the hair rising on the back of her neck. I feel like every nerve is convulsing in my body.

"C'mon, girl! You know how to do this, so do it! We don't have all day!" Uncle Vlad is so testy with me. I'm just learning how to do this. I close my eyes and release the tension in my shoulders. I take in a deep breath and block out the sound of him breathing down my neck by focusing on the lock in front of me.

One tumbler, two tumblers, three, and then four. I'm finally seeing the fifth one lift and my surroundings disappear. It's just me and the lock. Everything is quiet and peaceful. The fifth tumbler lifts into place, and the door clunks open as the lock releases. I hear Miriam shriek with delight as Uncle Vlad says, "Finally!" and my surroundings come crashing back around me.

I timidly touch the edge of the door, beckoning it open with my fingertips as a warm breeze dances up my arm to my shoulder and across the right side of my face. It feels like the gentle touch of my mother when I was a baby. I peek through the opening and see the most amazing rooftop garden I could have ever imagined.

I step through the doorway and down a tiny step onto the first level of this forgotten garden. There are multiple levels surrounded by raised gardens by the edges of the roof. It would be easy to get lost in thought out here. It feels like anything could happen up here.

Uncle Vlad is right behind me and snatches the folder out of Miriam's hand. He angrily says, "I'm back now, thanks to a meeting that went all wrong. I'll do the rest of her lineage since you can't seem to handle it." His words come sliding out of his mouth and slice through any happiness Miriam might've been clinging to.

She glances to me when he looks away and mouths, "I'm sorry."

"If you're quiet, you may stay and watch how someone should teach," he says to her over his shoulder as he walks down the steps that take him to the lower level of the garden. He flicks his hand toward a nearby bench, motioning for her to sit there. Miriam walks to the bench with her head held low, and as she sits down, I can tell she's trying to keep her composure.

"Patrina!" Uncle Vlad impatiently snaps his fingers, trying to get my attention back on him. I'm guessing he thinks everyone's attention should be on him. I look at him and fold my hands behind my back like I'm standing at attention waiting for orders.

"Just because you now know how to unlock doors at will does not mean that you can come and go as you please. There are still rules in my house, and if I have Miriam put you in your room, you are to stay there. Understood?"

The more I'm with him, the less I like him.

"Yes, I understand," I say, trying hard to stay focused on him. There's so much to look at and touch that it's hard to pay attention to this demanding uncle in front of me. Not to mention, the more insistent he is, the less I want to follow his rules.

"I suppose you want to know about the garden before we get back to business?"

I eagerly nod. The garden is quite a wonder, especially since it's on the roof. Who takes care of it? Does anyone? The closer I look, the more I see that parts of it have become overgrown.

"This garden was your mother's. They lived here for a short time. She loathed the dark and cold season that we were in at the time. So in hopes of getting them to stay a while longer, I started the construction on the rooftop garden. She never saw it though. They left with you before it was completed.

"Every flower up here was one of your mother's favorites. Some were her favorite because of how they smelled, some because of their shapes, and some because of what they could do. She was into the homeopathic stuff, though I'll never understand why she wouldn't just trust the pharmaceutical companies. They are trained to make medicines to help people, after all.

"Nonetheless, this garden was for her. I tried numerous times to get her to come and see it once it was finished, but my brother had a fit and ended up not letting her speak to me. So here it sits."

It is hard to tell what flowers are supposed to be here and what flowers are here because weeds have taken over. I've come to the conclusion that a weed is only a weed because someone deemed it wasn't good enough to be a flower in their garden. I'm sure the homeopathic plants are weeds to my uncle. One of the businesses that he owns is a pharmaceutical company. He is probably just biased ... or greedy. At this point, I am starting to think it is more greed than anything that drives my uncle.

As I am looking at one of the echinacea plants that has begun to bloom, he calls me over to an old cast-iron table that sits next to a raised pond in the middle of the roof. This must be the reflection pond that I could see from the piano room.

Excited to see this pond from the top now, instead of the bottom, I quickly skip over to it, and to him. He is impatiently sitting at the table with the black folder full of my lineage. Just as I get close to it, he points to the chair on the other side of the little table, and I know that I have to sit down and listen instead of going and looking into the pond. He seems to know how to suck the fun out of everything.

He opens the folder on the table and readjusts himself in the chair. He doesn't look too happy that we are doing this up here, but I can't tell why ... until I look past him at the water in the pond. I can see his profile reflecting in it ... except it doesn't look right. I can see the top of his scar on the side of his neck poking out of his collar when I look right at him, but when I look at his reflection, that scar is glowing red.

Sixteen

I gasp and look away in terror. How could an old scar glow red? Why does it make me want to run for my life?

He stops shuffling papers and looks at me. It makes my skin crawl. "What's wrong with you?" he asks.

He's getting angrier by the second, so I pretend to cough and say, "A bug flew into my mouth."

My uncle seems to accept my answer because he goes back to his collection of papers.

"Here we are! This is where we left off. Mika had just killed off the man she wanted to wed, oh, and all of his family and thousands of others. She was quite powerful!"

He's so nonchalant as he recounts the horrors that my ancestor caused, as though he's proud of her. It's unsettling, but I try not to look like it bothers me so that he will go on.

"Mika eventually found another to wed named Kyran. Kyran worked on the railroad that Iko travelled on. How's that for irony?" he says with a chuckle. "Mika gives birth to a baby girl whom they named Eleana. To Mika, Eleana was the beginning of a new day as she continued to try to control her anger and raise her child up in patience.

"Eleana grew into quite a wondrous young lady who had all the abilities before her and could control the sun. When she was about your age, she discovered that she could align the moon in front of the sun, blocking the sun's light out, all while moving stars around and making comets dance across the sky. They called these 'eclipse comets' because only when she blocked out the sun could other people see the comets she moved across the sky.

"One night, while she was putting on a show for her parents, a young boy her age, by the name of Sam, saw her directing the objects in the sky from his hiding place behind a tree. He was so enamored by her that he continued to follow her to see if he could watch her do this again. He was the first known 'eclipse chaser,' and when she saw that she had an admirer, she wanted to know him more. They eventually wed during the longest-known eclipse to man, and later that year she gave birth to their little miracle, whom they named Jacey.

"Jacey was similar to Kerra in that she was very much involved in the politics of Poland. When Poland came under attack by the Russians, Jacey was serving alongside Jozef Pilsudski, Poland's commander in chief. Jacey was able to work miracles, astounding turns in events that no one was able to fully comprehend, and the Battle of Warsaw was one of them. Pilsudski was at his wit's end and figured the only thing his army could do against Russia was a counterattack from the south. Against all odds, somehow Jacey caused such mental confusion in the Russian armies that they were taken off guard and retreated. It's still called the Warsaw Miracle to this day, but few know of Jacey's participation.

"Jacey met a man named Galen shortly after this miracle at one of the army hospitals. He was serving in the war that she had just helped them to win, but he had been winged by a stray bullet. His upper arm was starting to turn black, as gangrene was setting in and taking over his system. Jacey was immediately drawn to him because of how calm and comforting he was even in his state of distress, and with one touch of her finger, she was able to heal his arm and bring him back to health. They were wed shortly after that and gave birth to the woman you're middle name is from … Nadine."

Uncle Vlad stops all of a sudden and looks to Miriam, who has been sitting silently on the bench he shooed her to at the beginning. "Miriam, get us something to drink. I'm feeling parched. All of this talking and the outside air is drying me out."

Miriam doesn't say a word as she gets up quickly and disappears inside the house. Uncle Vlad pauses for a bit, cracks each knuckle on his left hand, and then proceeds to crack every knuckle on his right hand. He seems to be waiting to get a drink before continuing. Or maybe he's waiting so that he can continue showing Miriam how to teach. He's weird.

We sit in awkward silence for a few more minutes, and then Miriam comes back out with a glass pitcher of iced lemonade and three small drinking glasses on a tray. She sets the tray on the wall of the reflection pond nearest to my uncle and places our glasses on the table in front of us. I realize how thirsty I am when I see her pouring the cold lemonade into the glass in front of me. The last drop barely makes it in before I am guzzling it down. When I set my glass back down, I look up to see Miriam and Uncle Vlad staring at me. Miriam looks amused; my uncle definitely does not.

"Have you taught this child nothing?" he booms at her. Miriam pours more lemonade in my glass and then a first round into his and finally the last few drops into hers as he continues yelling at her. I'm too busy downing my second glass to pay him much attention. It's just more commotion about her teaching me to be a lady, waiting until she's done pouring, something about my pinky sticking out … I really don't know. Some of this etiquette stuff seems a little too pretentious to me.

Now that he is done yelling, and Miriam has gone back to sitting on her bench, I finish my second glass of lemonade.

I guess he isn't parched anymore because he starts back up again with my ancestors' stories. I still don't fully understand why he wants me to work with him, but I definitely know I don't want to have him as a boss.

"Nadine had the courage of a bear. From early on, she was busy making sure people weren't being bullied and that things were fair. She was raised in the time when Adolph Hitler had decided he was going to annihilate all of the Jews. She instigated the Warsaw Uprising against the Nazi's back in 1943, but Nadine had something that plagued her more than any of her other ancestors before her: doubt. Doubt is more powerful than any gift, talent, or ability and needs to be squashed before it ruins you or the ones you are trying to help. Just as the uprising was starting to turn the tide, Nadine lost her courage because someone doubted her actions and she listened to them. It was because she listened to them that the Nazis gained a foothold and, in turn, destroyed the little city Nadine was trying to protect. She ran away up into the hills, ashamed, but one of the men in her resistance followed her. His name was Randolph. He came at a time when she needed protection from herself and the doubt she had allowed to seep into her heart. She fell head over heels for him, and they were wed under the stars. Nadine and Randolph are your mother's parents.

"Izabella was born at a time when Nadine had given up hope that she wasn't doing anything worthy of the Monarch. The Monarch has kept all of your ancestors prisoners to serve him the rest of their lives. When I met your mother, I saw it in her eyes that she wanted to be free. Nadine had told Izabella all her life that she was the Monarch's promise to her mother and that her lineage would live on, and one day there would be one from her line to save them all. One who is noble and strong, one who has valor and courage, and one who will control all the abilities. Your mother was a dreamer, dear

Patrina. She didn't do anything like your other ancestors. She met my brother, fell in love, and lived a peasant's life. She could've been rich beyond her years and been with me! Look at all I could've given her, but she didn't want any of it.

"You are stronger than all of them, and with me teaching you, together we can conquer everything! You don't have to be like the rest. You don't have to go to the Monarch. You can be your own person! You can control your own destiny and do what you want to do!"

The more he talks, the more confused I get. I thought I wanted to go to the Monarch. If I don't, then I won't be able to have The Guide help me, and I will never be able to go to Arcadia. What does he mean I could be my own person? Isn't my purpose to go to the Monarch and receive my job?

I glance over my shoulder at Miriam, and she has the look of fear on her face. Is he telling me the truth? Why didn't Miriam tell me about this? Was she keeping this from me?

Just as I'm about to ask him these questions, he closes the folder, gulps down his drink, and says, "Well that's about it for today, Patrina. I have some work I need to do in the library, so I will let you work on your newly found abilities up here with Miriam." He stands up and pats me on the shoulder as he walks past me. I feel so lost, and I don't know who I can trust anymore.

When he saunters up the steps and back into the house, Miriam stands and starts to walk toward me. I'm so irritated that I don't even want to be around her right now. I just want to be by myself so I can figure this entire thing out. Where is The Guide anyway? Why isn't he explaining this to me!

Dear one, I never left. Some things are better learned on your own.

I really don't want to learn this on my own, and right now, I don't want Miriam explaining anything to me. I don't know what to believe.

Seventeen

I turn to look at the reflection pond so I can't see Miriam's face. I feel so torn up inside. I don't know what to believe anymore, and the last day and a half has been filled with so much more than I ever thought possible. I didn't realize how much there was to my little life outside of my locked room. I didn't know I had such a big decision ahead of me either.

"Patrina ..."

I can feel Miriam standing behind me. Maybe like how my mother could sense my uncle's presence. Her presence feels warm and soothing to me. I'm still very upset with her, no matter how soothing she may feel.

"Patrina, I know you're confused, but you need to understand that we all have free will. Your uncle wants you to work for him, and if you work for him, you can never work for the Monarch. My life is a testament to that."

I turn around to face her, and a tear betrays me as it slides down my cheek. "How could you not tell me all of it? I didn't know I had a choice! I thought I was just supposed to go to the Monarch when it was time, and that was it. What if I don't want to be ruled over like Uncle Vlad says my ancestors were?"

"Sweetie, that's not exactly true. Everyone picks a side

basically. You either pick to work for the Monarch and all that goes with it, or you pick to serve the other side."

"What's the other side? Uncle Vlad?" My patience has grown so thin trying to figure out everything that's going on. I wish she would just be straight with me. I let my anger seep out as I yell, "Just tell me everything!"

Patrina, calm down. You will know all of it in time. Be patient, dear one. I know it's hard, but let her explain it to you, The Guide says as I'm about to lose control.

Miriam takes my hand and leads me to the edge of the reflection pond. I am so over this game. When we get to the pond, I snatch my hand from hers and sit on the edge. There aren't even fish in this pond. Nothing makes any sense.

She sits beside me. As I look down into the pond toward her reflection, it looks strange. Her reflection isn't what I see when I look at her. I try to my find my reflection, but all I see is a hazy, rippled mess. This pond isn't normal.

"Let me explain it, okay? I know you're upset and confused. There are two sides, and only two sides, to this world. There's the Monarch's side, and there's the Fallen side. The Fallen side was started when the first angel decided that he wanted to rule the world and thought he could do a better job than the Monarch.

"The angel that started the Fallen was from a very long time ago. The Monarch won that battle, and the original Fallen have been imprisoned ever since. However, about three hundred years ago, another group of angels defected and reestablished the Fallen's work and creed to conquer the world.

"They are known as The Six, and each one has a power different from the other. They were the ones who started the new genesis line that you and I are a part of. Coyle is their leader, and he's the one you read about in your mother's diary. There are five more, and my guess is The Guide will show you more about them in her diary too.

"Since you are a virtue, you came from Engelbert's lineage, though I don't know how he got all messed up in this. He was known as 'the bright angel.' He was one of the Monarch's favorites. The Monarch has a special place in his heart for the virtues. Maybe that will be explained in the diary as well.

"Anyway, when your first feather is starting to come in, which is going to be right around your twelfth birthday, you have a choice to make: the Monarch's side or the Fallen's side. Once you choose and your feather has fallen, the one who catches your feather is the one you serve. Your first feather is your contract for life.

"How do you have your feather then? I saw it in your heart pendant. My mother had one in her pendant too." I'm still confused.

"There is a lot involved with your first feather, and it all depends on which side you choose. If you choose the Monarch's side, you will need to make a trip to Arcadia. Your first feather is your calling to Arcadia. It's like an open invitation for your entry there, but you will need to start your journey just as your first feather is about to poke through. There are many trials you will encounter along the way—trials that will make you feel as though you won't make it in time. This is the work of the Fallen.

"If they can cause you to get lost along the way, long enough for your feather to fall before you can get to Arcadia, someone from the Fallen will appear and snatch your feather away from you, sealing your fate of serving the other side. Then you cannot work for the Monarch. You will automatically be serving the other side.

"Not only do they own your life's work, they steal your free will as well when they keep your feather. You will mindlessly serve the Fallen. If you make it to Arcadia and one of the enlightened angels catches your feather, it will be blessed, encased within the heart pendant, which is a symbol of the

Monarch's love for you, and given back to you with your job engraved on the back. This is a symbol of not only your choice to serve the Monarch but also that he is protecting your free will and will guide you throughout your adventures."

I readjust myself on the concrete edge of the pond, wishing I had chosen to at least sit in the chairs. This is more complicated than I had realized, and yet it sounds like I have to serve one side or the other no matter what, and that choice is only a few weeks away. I look down at my hands that I have been mindlessly wringing.

"Why does Uncle Vlad want me to choose to be my own person, as he says? It doesn't sound like I can be my own person … ever."

"Oh, dear Patrina, it's not like that … well, unless you choose the Fallen side. The Monarch isn't a dictator who makes you do everything his way. He allows you to find your own unique way of doing the job he has chosen for you. Your mother was a wonderfully creative virtue. I really wish she was around longer for you. She could bless a multitude of people with something as simple as a rainbow, or a warm southern breeze, or even a still lake to mirror the mountains. She was courageous to be her own unique kind of virtue, no matter what anyone, including your uncle, thought of her. What your uncle didn't tell you was your mother's gift. Along with the eight gifts that came before her, her gift was grace. And grace isn't an easy thing to do. It's also not an easy gift to understand for some. She chose to work alongside me, a messenger, not only to give me courage but also to show grace to the one who was receiving the message, because some of those directives can be a little rough to hear.

"Your uncle …" Miriam stops midsentence as though she senses something, and she looks around the rooftop garden. She then leans toward me so that her mouth is within inches of my ear, and I can feel her warm breath on my neck. Just as

I think she is about to say something, she glances once more to the door, and when she does, I look at the water in the pond and can see her reflection now, clearer than before. She has a white glow all around her. I'm about to point it out to her when she shatters my world as she says, "Your uncle wants to catch your feather because if he has your feather, not only are you Fallen but then you will mindlessly do his will."

Eighteen

What? I don't want to mindlessly do anyone's will! I must not have said anything out loud for quite a while because Miriam says, "Patrina! Are you okay?"

I look at her and see my fear reflecting in her eyes. "How can this be? How could he do this to me? I thought he loved my mother. Why would he do this to her daughter? And how could you let him?"

I'm angry at everything and everyone right now. How could the old lady who rescued me just hand me over? How could Miriam just let him lock me away to keep me hidden so that he can catch my feather and rule me for the rest of my life? Where are my parents? They never found the bodies, so nobody really knows what happened to them, and they just left me to become my uncle's slave!

Miriam stammers, "Patrina, I'm sorry, so sorry, but I couldn't do anything. He owns me now that I broke my contract with the Monarch. I still have free will only because I kept my feather, but he owns my life. I had to keep you hidden. I had to keep you a secret. And I had to keep your gifts hidden from you until now because otherwise he would've made me do much worse jobs than watch over you and tend to the house. You're only just now starting to see who he really is, and I'm afraid it might be too late."

"What do you mean too late? I don't have my feather yet! Let's run away!" I say in a panic. "We can escape, and he won't find out until it's too late and I'm far away!" I'm already planning our escape route in my head as she drops my hand and looks at me with defeated eyes.

"I can't escape, dear. He owns me. I have to serve him. Something happened to him a long time ago. He has power, Patrina. I don't know where he got it or who he got it from, but he has an evil power within him, and he keeps me close so that I can't run away."

Things are starting to make sense to me. Why wouldn't she leave, or Bao, unless they couldn't? And that scar on his neck that I saw glowing red … there's something to that. Maybe that's how he got his power.

"Miriam, how much do you really know about my uncle?" I ask as I'm starting to ponder who my uncle is and how he's been able to accomplish so much.

"I met him a long time ago, but he was already like this. I heard from your mother that he wasn't always this way. She said that Konrad told her that when they were boys, he used to be nicer but that something happened one night, and he has never been the same. That was before their parents shipped them off to the boarding school. She said that Konrad and your uncle didn't start out at boarding school. They started out at a different school. I don't know what happened … she never did say, and I'm not sure she even knew. But Konrad did, and he didn't want to mess around with making his brother upset."

"When we were sitting here this morning," I say, "I saw something in the water."

Miriam doesn't seem surprised. "Water is an element too, remember? And water can be a pretty powerful tool for you. From what your mother said, water can be used to show a person's true self." She leans over so that she can see herself in the pond. "I only see me and you. What do you see when you look in?"

I look over at her reflection and say, "I can see you. You're glowing white. It's very pretty."

"What do you see when you look at yourself?"

I look down and then off to one of the gardens across the roof.

"I don't understand what I see. I see a smeary, rippled mess. I can't even see my face."

Even the water doesn't know my true self. This is pretty pathetic.

Miriam taps me on the knee and giggles. I don't know why she thinks this is amusing. It's kind of depressing to me.

"You can't see yourself because your path hasn't been set yet. You haven't chosen. That's a common issue with virtues. Their true self isn't determined until they choose their path, and then they can see themselves. Don't worry, dear. Once you've chosen with your heart, you'll see who you are."

I shuffle on the cement edge, kind of relieved at what she just told me but concerned at what I saw earlier. "I saw my uncle in the water."

"You did? What did you see?" Miriam is back to whispering again and leaning in close. I don't think she wants me to say what I saw very loudly. So I lean in close to her too.

I whisper into her ear, "I saw his scar glowing red."

Miriam leans back as she gasps. She has the look of terror on her face, much worse than before. She wrings her hands in her lap and then stands up and starts pacing.

"Oh ... this is bad ... this is very bad," she starts murmuring as she paces.

"What's bad? Is the red glow bad?"

Miriam stops pacing and comes back to sit on the edge of the pond with me. She takes my hand, leans in, and whispers, "Red is the color of the Fallen."

"The Fallen?" I nearly shout as I stand up.

"Sssshhh!" Miriam tries to hush me as she stands up next to me. Her face is within inches of mine now. "Not so loud! We can't let on that you saw the red. Your uncle would be totally relentless at making sure that you are never let out again if he knew that you know about him."

Her last words make my head spin. "Isn't this what he wanted? He wanted you to train me so I could learn to use my gifts."

"He only understands *some* of your gifts. He only knows you can manipulate elements. He doesn't know that some of the elements show you things, especially not what water can do. If he knew that the water in the reflection pond would show you his true nature, I can assure you that he would've had it drained. You must keep this to yourself."

I feel like I'm drowning in a giant black pool of secrets that are coming out of nowhere.

I don't know what to do or how to handle any of this. I walk out to the farthest garden by the back of the house and look out across the backyard. I need a moment to breathe, but as I'm looking out on the yard behind the house, I am stunned by what I see. What I thought was the entrance to a maze really is a maze! And it covers a lot more space than I realized. Just beyond the end of the maze, I see a forest of trees.

I don't want to be stuck here the rest of my life, mindlessly serving my uncle. In the deepest part of my heart, I realize that I've made my decision and that decision is to go to Arcadia. It would be better serving the Monarch than my uncle. If I'm going to make that journey to Arcadia, I'm going to have to escape. And if I'm going to escape, I'm going to have to get through that maze.

"Miriam, what's past the maze?" I ask as I'm staring out across the great expanse that is my uncle's land.

"The forest with the lake that I told you of earlier. What

are you thinking about?" I can feel her looking at me, but I keep staring out to the trees.

"If I were to make the journey to Arcadia, I'm going to need to escape, and that's the only way I'll be able to disappear, isn't it?"

She touches my shoulder and turns me to face her. "If you really want to make that journey, you can disappear that way. But you have a lot to learn before you can do that. Are you ready?"

"I don't see any other way," I say softly.

"Well then! We better get started! You're training for something far greater now, dear. It's not going to be easy, and you will need to have a lot more patience than you've shown up until now, but you can do it. All the other virtues before you didn't have one thing that you have," she says with a glimmer in her eye.

Her enthusiasm must be contagious because I'm starting to feel like I can conquer the world. I smile at her as I ask, "What is that one thing?"

She giggles and wraps me in a hug as she says, "Me, silly! You have someone who can train you!"

She holds my shoulders at arm's length and says, "We really should go back inside for now. There are some things we can practice later, but it's getting late, and I have a couple of errands I need to run before dinner tonight."

We begin walking across the rooftop garden to go back inside, and as we walk past the reflection pond, I glance inside. I can see my face now ... and I'm glowing white!

Nineteen

Once inside, Miriam walks me to my room and tells me she will be back a little later after she runs into town but that my uncle is still home. She tells me that she thinks if I'm quiet that he will forget about me and get wrapped up in his work, so that she will be back before he insists on meeting with me again. It's hard adjusting to him wanting to be around me so much now compared to the years I've lived in his house without him being interested in me.

As she leaves and locks the door behind her, I see the calendar off to the left of my door. I walk over to it and realize that I need to flip the page to show the new month. It's already a week into this month. I count out the weeks until my birthday, which is on the autumnal equinox in September. There's only six weeks left until my birthday. My feather will be coming in then, so I need to learn everything I can and escape soon.

I figure that while I have a few moments of quiet time, I should go look in my mother's diary. I can just barely reach behind my headboard to the hiding place. I'm hoping there will be something in it, not just blank pages. I need to learn more about my past and these gifts I have inherited.

I feel the familiar leather book and pull it out. I lean up

against my bed and lay my mother's diary in my lap, tracing the worn edges with my fingers. I unwind the leather straps that are used to keep it shut and take a deep breath in hopes of something being shown to me. I open the book and see my mother's name, but it's starting to fade. It looks as though someone is erasing it and writing my name in its place before my very eyes. Soon my mother's name is just a memory, and mine is there instead. I wonder if my decision to go to the Monarch is the reason this diary is now mine.

I flip the page and see the entry made by Adena again. It's haunting how her entry just ends, but I'm glad that it's still there. I was worried that it would disappear as quickly as it appeared and I would never be able to see it again.

I turn the page and find the next one blank, but it's starting to write itself, just as Adena's first entry did. The author of this page writes:

> Brox came here yesterday. He's such a brute! He nearly knocked the hinges off the wall when he busted in through my door. It seems as though he's working with Coyle now. So is Engelbert. I really liked Engelbert, but now I'm not so sure about him, not if he's siding with Coyle. Coyle is trying to get a group of us to revolt and reestablish the Fallen, but I don't want to do that. Brox said that I could either come willingly or he would make me. I'd like to see him try! I made my doorway super strong now so that even Brox can't break through!
>
> I'm supposed to hang out with Gyan today. I love her. She's so smart and talented. Everything just makes sense in her head. She can take a piece of wood and build something amazing out of it. I wonder what we're going to …

As I am reading the latest entry, the letters start to fade and erase themselves in the order that they were written.

Put it away, little one. The Guide just pops in out of nowhere.

"Why must I put this away? It was just starting to get good. Did you make it erase?" I ask out of irritation.

Put it away, Patrina!

"Fine!" Just as I put it back behind my nightstand, in walks my uncle. I didn't hear him coming! If he caught me with the diary, there's no telling what could've happened.

He glances around the room and then finally spots me on the floor leaning against my bed. I must look really awkward because I don't have anything that I'm doing. I look like I'm just sitting there being weird, but he doesn't seem to think anything of it.

"There you are! Who were you talking to?" he asks as he glares at me with condemning eyes.

"Just myself. When you're alone a lot, you tend to talk to yourself." I say as I stand up and sit on the edge of my bed.

"Well whatever. I thought since Miriam is running errands that you and I could try working on your gifts." He comes near me with a glass in his hand. I have no clue what gift he plans for me to work on with a glass.

"I found this glass the other day at one of the nearby taverns. It's almost identical to the one your mother fixed back when I first met her." He has a crazed look in his eyes as he takes the glass and taps it hard against the corner of my dresser. It doesn't just crack; it breaks a huge V-shaped piece off, and he stands there holding it like I'm supposed to do something.

"Well, c'mon, girl! Fix the glass!" he insists as he sticks the broken glass in my face. I take it, and then he bends over and picks up the chunk that broke out of it and hands that to me as well. I sit on my bed holding the glass and the chunk and just look at him.

"Miriam hasn't taught me how to do this yet."

"Girl, these are natural abilities and gifts! You should be able to figure them out on your own. You shouldn't have to have someone walk you through it. Put it back together!"

I scoot farther onto my bed and place the glass and the chunk on top of my bedspread. I don't know how to do this, but if I don't do it, he's going to be mad, and I don't want to see what would happen if he gets truly angry. I take the chunk and place it back in its spot in the glass, and it fits perfectly. Now what?

Stay calm, dear one. The more upset you get, the less you can control your gifts.

I'm thankful that The Guide is here, and I'm also thankful that my uncle doesn't know that I can talk to him or that he talks to me. It seems like Uncle Vlad wouldn't like to know that The Guide has been coaching me since he doesn't want me working for that side.

I close my eyes and steady my breathing like I did with the locks. I can feel my uncle staring at me, and I try to block him out. His presence makes concentrating difficult. I focus on the glass and the chunk, and I can feel my hands heating up. They almost feel like they're on fire! I wrap my hands around the glass and can feel the glass melting and shifting beneath my fingers. I find the crack between the glass and the chunk and run my finger along it, and as I do, I open my eyes.

Steady now, Patrina, The Guide says.

I watch the glass that was once two pieces start to melt back together as my finger runs along the crack. It's as if I'm painting it together with my fingertip. As I reach the rim after fixing the left side of the V-shaped crack, my finger leaves the glass, and I see my uncle staring at me. The look in his eyes stuns me out of focus, and I'm left shaking. His eyes are not only edged in black, but there are flecks of red in his irises that I have never seen before. Red like his scar!

"I can't do it!" I say as I push the glass toward him and get off my bed on the opposite side as my uncle.

"What do you mean you can't do it? You've been doing it! Now finish what you've started!" His yelling at me is definitely not helping my nerves.

I glance toward my door that he left open. Maybe I can just make a run for it. As I'm contemplating a narrow escape, I see someone's face looking in around the corner of my doorway. I didn't hear anyone come up.

I try to see who it is without letting on to my uncle that someone else is here. I don't think my uncle is even aware of anything other than making me finish fixing this glass as he's picking up the cracked glass and bringing it to me. My uncle's distraction gives me enough time to figure out that it's Bao at the door.

As I look at Bao once more, he raises his finger to his lips as if to make sure I keep his presence a secret. His presence soothes me, and I'm not afraid anymore.

Uncle Vlad roughly hands me the glass. "Finish it!"

"Okay," I say as I take it from his hand. I sit on the chair in my reading nook and place the cracked glass in my left hand as I trace up the other side of the V with my right finger. It's not working. It's not melting like it was before.

"Finish it!" He's becoming impatient, and it's not helping my nerves.

Find your peace, little one, The Guide says. *Calm yourself and find your peace. Only then can you finish your task.*

I take a deep breath and block out my insistent uncle. *Focus,* I tell myself. *Focus and breathe.* I take my finger once more and start at the bottom of the V. I can feel the heat in it like before and see the glass melting beneath it. It's working! I slowly trace my finger up the side and remold the glass back together. Just as I reach the rim, Miriam walks into my room.

"Oh, excuse me, sir. I didn't realize you would be training her today."

He snatches the glass from my grasp and whirls around with insanity in his eyes as he exclaims, "Look what she can do! She can fix glass! This is amazing!"

Miriam steps to the side of the door as Uncle Vlad walks out, holding the glass and rambling on and on about what I just accomplished. Bao must've returned downstairs because he didn't see him on his way out the door. As his footsteps disappear within the house, Miriam closes the door and looks at me with questioning eyes.

"It's okay. The Guide was with me. And Bao too," I say to her, relieved that the whole ordeal is over.

"Bao? He's not even here today. He's out getting groceries for this week's menu."

Twenty

"What do you mean he's not here? I saw him! I saw him standing at the very edge of my door," I say as I point to the now closed door to my prison tower.

"I don't know who you think you saw," she says, "but that couldn't have been Bao. His vehicle was still gone when I pulled in."

"But I saw his face, and he looked just like Bao!" I start to recount seeing this mysterious person standing in my doorway, and the face was Bao's ... but the height ... the height was different.

"How tall is Bao?" I ask, now curious as to who was peering in at me.

"Around six feet. Why? How tall was the person you saw?"

"He was much taller than that. His face was near the top of the corner of the door. And he looked like he was bending over to look inside the door. How tall is my door?" I ask as I try to find a tape measure that I have for some of my math lessons.

"I'm not sure, but I believe your tape measure is in your top dresser drawer, if that's what you're looking for." She never ceases to surprise me with how she knows what I'm thinking.

I go to the dresser, and sure enough, there's the measuring tape right on top of my math books. I take it, stretch it out, and let it fling itself back inside. I stand next to my door and look to Miriam. "Can you hold this please?" I ask as I point to the bottom of the tape. She comes over and holds it as I get a chair to stand on. My door was custom made to be taller and look like one of the old Victorian doors I've seen in some of my books. I stand on the chair and stretch the tape measure up as Miriam holds the bottom. When I near the top edge of the door, I read that it's ninety-six inches.

"It's eight feet tall!" I say as I hop down off the chair. "That means that whoever was looking into my room would've been closer to nine feet tall since he was crouching to look inside."

"And you're sure he was a he? And that he looked like Bao?" Miriam slides my chair back across the room to my desk as I head to my reading nook. There has to be a book about giants in here somewhere.

"I'm sure! Like positive sure! Where would I look to find something about giants?"

"I'm not so sure it's a giant you're looking for."

I stop and look at her with a puzzled look. "What about *Jack and the Beanstalk*? Nobody could've just made that up, right?"

"*Jack and the Beanstalk* is a fairy tale, but you're right, there's usually some truth in it somewhere, but giants aren't just … giants. Maybe you should get out the *Book of Ancient Letters*. I think we're dealing with something much older than fairy tales."

"You mean like the nephilim from the first time the Fallen came to be? Wouldn't that make whoever was looking in my room really super old?" I ask, pulling the *Book of Ancient Letters* from the shelf. There's no way that could be who it was! That would mean that the Bao lookalike is over 2,000 years old. That's nuts!

"Yes, I mean like the nephilim. They don't die off like humans. They're more like the angels in that they live more lifetimes than you can fathom. Even I am older than you'd think. Most nephilim disappear, not die, including your ancestors. It's said that they go back to Arcadia, but I don't know if that's true."

"But why would he be here? Looking at me? And how can he look like Bao?"

"Some nephilim, especially the older ones, can shift their appearance. They can look like anyone they wish, except they haven't figured out the height issue. They may have the face of someone you know, but they will still be nine feet tall. Some of the younger nephilims, through careful gene selection, are able to control their height now so they can totally look like someone else regardless of height. I'm thinking the one at your door was one of the older ones … one of the first ones."

"What would he want? And how could he be here? I thought the older nephilim were imprisoned and that was why the Fallen made new ones." I'm getting really freaked out. How can someone that big get into the house without my uncle or anyone else knowing about him?

"There's no telling what he wanted. And while many of them were imprisoned, there's no way to know if all of them were. What did he do?" she asks as she sits in her favorite chair near my bed.

I set the *Book of Ancient Letters* down onto my bed and climb on top. My skin is crawling from fear that someone, or something, just waltzed in here and knew how to find my room.

"He looked at me, and when I noticed him, he raised a finger to his lips to make sure I stayed quiet because Uncle Vlad was in here. He didn't seem threatening. But he had Bao's face, so that helped me feel relaxed."

Miriam just sits there and tucks her hands into her apron. She pulls out her little watch that she keeps hidden inside and looks at it. I can tell it's getting close to dinnertime because my stomach is starting to growl.

"We'll have to think on this for a while. How about we head down to the kitchen and grab a bite to eat? I can hear your stomach from all the way over here," she says with a giggle. She doesn't seem too worried about my afternoon visitor.

"That sounds good to me … but what if that nephilim is still in here? And do I have to wear some dumb getup or can I just go down there in these clothes?" I really do not want to wear nylons again! Ever!

"I have a sneaking suspicion that whoever that nephilim was, we aren't going to learn anything by sitting up here, and we'll just eat in the kitchen, so what you're wearing is fine. C'mon, let's go. If your stomach gets any louder, the next town might hear it!" We both laugh as I slide off the bed. I'm starting to feel better now.

As I near my bedroom door, I know that it's locked. I can feel it in my heart. I look to Miriam, and she's looking at me with eyes that are silently asking if I'm going to unlock it. I'm starting to get the hang of this. It seems to have a lot to do with having peace and being able to focus. When I'm around her, it's easy to focus, so I just close my eyes for a second, and there's a loud thunk as the lock unlocks and the door swings open a bit.

"You've come a long way in such a short time!" Miriam comes next to me and gives my shoulders a quick squeeze. I wish I could just stay with her and train the whole time. Uncle Vlad makes me nervous, and now something is lurking in the house that can shift to look like someone else. I wonder if I can learn how the writer in my diary made her door super strong against … who was that again? Brox? What an odd name!

Twenty-One

We walk down the hallway outside my room and make our way down the spiral stairs to the long hallway below. I think Miriam said the doors on the left were part of Bao's wing in this giant house.

"Are these Bao's rooms?" I ask, pointing to the doors as we near them.

"Yes, both of these doors go to Bao's rooms. He has a room with a bathroom, like mine, and a separate room he uses as a giant pantry when he finds grocery items on sale and there's no room for them in the kitchen pantry."

As we are walking past the second door, I can see that it's not latched all the way and is slightly ajar. I peek through the crack and see Bao tinkering in his room. It looks like he's putting something away in a drawer, but he's normal size. That's scary that someone can look just like someone else.

We continue on in silence as we make our way down to the kitchen. I'm famished at this point, and it doesn't look like Bao has been home long enough to make anything for dinner. I'm sure he will at some point, but I'm hungry now.

Once inside the kitchen, Miriam opens the fridge and pulls out bread, ham, and lettuce to make some sandwiches. She sets out a plate for each of us and starts to make the sandwiches.

"There will come a day when you are no longer here, and you will come across many who are unexpectedly not like you. Be wary of those with whom you cross paths. Some will be great and trustworthy friends, and others will be your worst enemy, seeking only your gifts for their will. You're only safe place to go is Arcadia."

Just as she finishes saying this, Bao walks into the kitchen.

"Why hello! I did not expect anyone to be in here this time of day. I'm guessing you and the tower princess are hungry?" he says with a chuckle as he reaches for his apron that is hanging on a hook near the sink.

"Bao," I say, "have you seen anyone unusual around here? Someone who's never been here before? Somebody really tall?"

He thinks for a moment as he ties the apron strings around his waist and says, "No, I don't think so. I don't go to too many places in this house because I'm usually cooking, but I haven't seen anyone different. Why really tall? Did you see someone?"

I look to Miriam and raise my eyebrows as if to silently question whether I can tell him or not, and she nods in approval. "Someone was here earlier, outside my room, looking through my door. But he looked ..." I pause because even I doubt what I saw. This whole thing just sounds silly. Miriam looks at me and nods one time as if to nudge me to keep going. "He looked like you."

"Like me? How can someone look like me?"

"He had your face, but he was really tall. I thought it was you up there trying to calm me as my uncle was pushing me to fix a glass he broke."

Bao stops putting away the dishes from the dishwasher and looks at me. "How can you fix a glass?"

I look to Miriam. She just finished making our sandwiches and places mine on a plate in front of me. She looks at me wide-eyed and slowly shakes her head no. Why can't he know about me?

There are a lot of people in this world who cannot know what you can do, The Guide says.

I really wish they would've told me this before I started talking to Bao. "Uh …" I stammer, "I had some glue leftover from one of our science experiments, so he was making me glue it back together."

"Oh, that must be some great glue! I haven't seen any broken glasses that look like they were glued back together." Bao just accepts what I've said and continues on with the dishes in the dishwasher. Miriam sits on the stool across from me and gives me a wink as a token of her approval.

We sit in silence as we eat, and I ask in my heart, *Why can't Bao know about me? He seems like a trustworthy kind of person.*

All humans have a thread of greed running through them. No matter how trustworthy they may seem to be, they all have a part of themselves that will take advantage of your gifts, sweet one. Having The Guide with me is like being able to hold a conversation with someone inside your head, and nobody outside of your head knows what's going on. It's nice.

But I don't think Bao would do that. He's nice to me, I continue on silently.

Bao is trapped here, just like you and Miriam, The Guide says. *Never underestimate what a trapped person will do to escape. If he knew of your gifts, he would be doing the same thing that your uncle is doing. Be still, little one. Learn, listen, and grow, and when the time is right, I will tell you when to go.*

I am about to protest and question about where to go, how, when, and with whom, but I can tell that now isn't the time. I finish my sandwich and watch as Miriam places the last of hers in her mouth and takes our plates to the sink. I'm tired. These days have been overfilled with learning and drama. I yawn and close my eyes for a moment when Miriam says, "Looks as though someone could use an early night."

I nod without opening my eyes. I look up and see Miriam

smiling at me from across the room, and I slide off the stool. She reaches around my shoulder and bids good night to Bao.

I realize how tired I am as we climb back up the stairs. Every step feels two feet tall, and there are so many of them. Once we reach the top and open my door, I head to the closet and change into some warm, squishy, soft pajamas that have the little footies attached to the bottom. I come back out, and Miriam has turned on my nightstand lamp and flipped back the covers to my bed. As I climb in and slip my feet beneath the blankets, Miriam covers me up and tucks me in. I'm barely in bed before I'm fast asleep …

I'm suddenly walking through a forest, but it's a strange forest. It's different than most, and I don't understand why. I look up to the treetops, and they feel a mile away. I think I just saw something flit into one of the trees up ahead.

I follow the dirt path that is riddled with rocks and twigs and find a branch that has fallen, making the path impassable. I reach down and touch the branch, but it's not a normal branch. It sparkles when I touch it. This must be some kind of a magical forest!

I'm able to lift the branch with just a single touch of my finger, and as it's floating off the path and into the woods next to me, I see up ahead a tree trunk that's the size of a house. How peculiar!

I walk to the massive tree and look up, but it's so tall that I can't see the top. As I reach out and touch the bark around it, something pops, and a door opens just enough for me to see that there's an entrance. I wiggle my fingertips around the edge and pry the door open. It's so very dark in there. I reach my arm in to feel around, but I feel nothing. I'm afraid to go inside, but something in the very depths of my being knows that this is the way I have to go. This is my way to freedom.

Just as I'm about to walk through the doorway, into the darkness that is before me …

It's morning, and I'm standing at the doorway to my closet, stretching my arm inside. That dream was so real! What was that all about? I feel like I need to find that tree and that door.

That's where your real journey will begin, The Guide says.

Twenty-Two

My real journey? Just as I'm about to ask The Guide what he's talking about, Miriam walks in. I'm still standing outside my closet.

"What are you doing?" she asks as she sets down a tray that carries a small glass of orange juice and a blueberry bagel.

This is one of those things you mustn't tell her, The Guide whispers. *Continue on into the closet and get ready for today.*

"Oh ... I ... uh, was just getting dressed." I step inside the closet and pick out some jeans and a T-shirt.

As I'm changing, Miriam talks to me from the room. "So your uncle visited me last night. He has decided to give you permission to use the rooftop garden whenever you wish! How very exciting for you! I thought we could use it to train this morning."

I step outside the closet in disbelief and see her standing near the tray with a huge grin stretched across her face. I'm ecstatic that I've been given permission to use the garden. And I'm excited that we can start training so I can figure my way out of here.

"What are we going to learn today?" I ask as I reach for the bagel. Miriam already smeared it with cream cheese just the way I like it.

"Well, I was thinking you're going to need to learn how to tap into your nature talent. That is the second talent, which started with Diona. If you're going to make your way through those woods, you're going to need to know how to disappear."

"I'm going to have to get through that maze too. When I was looking off of the roof yesterday, I could see that the maze is pretty big."

"Yes, your uncle is a bit paranoid. He's very rich, and others have tried to break in, so he had multiple gardeners put that maze in place over the years. Different gardeners meant that no one really knew the extent of the maze." She hands me a pair of socks and my new tennis shoes. I put them on after I shove the last creamy bite of bagel into my mouth.

"There's something you need to know about that maze though." She pauses for a second and checks to make sure that the door is closed and there's nobody lurking around. "The maze is enchanted. It's not as simple as walking through it. I don't know how he had it enchanted or who did it, but it's a shifting maze. I tried to escape myself a while back. It was shortly after the maze was put in. I thought that if I did it while it was still new and not fully rooted that I could make my way through, but it didn't seem to matter. With every twist and turn, there's a new turn that opens up, and eventually you take a turn and you're right back where you started. It works the other way too so that whoever is in stays in, and whoever is out stays out."

As she was saying this to me, I start to feel my hope of leaving dissipate into nothingness. "How am I going to leave?" I ask, sitting on my bed with my shoulders slumped. All of my excitement has fluttered away from me like a butterfly eluding being caught.

"There has to be a way because Vlad has gone through it before. That's the only way to the woods out back, and he's done it. I just don't know how," Miriam says as she hands me my juice. "Finish your breakfast. Don't lose hope."

"I'm trying not to, but it sure feels like everything is going against me," I say and then guzzle down the last bit of juice.

"I know that feeling, but there's always a light somewhere leading the way out." She takes my glass from me and sets it on the tray, and then we walk toward my door. "When your mother would unlock a door, she would just snap her fingers, and it would unlock, or lock, depending on what she wanted it to do. Why don't you try that? You seem to have the hang of it by now."

"Sure, yeah, okay … I'll try it," I say as I snap my fingers, and the lights in my room dim.

"Uh, that's not right." I snap them again, and the lights go off altogether.

"You might've just destroyed the filaments in the lightbulbs. I think you need to focus more on the lock and less on snapping your fingers." As I turn away, I can hear her mumble, "I'll have to replace those bulbs now."

I walk closer to the door and focus on the lock. As I'm staring at the lock, I snap my fingers, and the door unlocks and opens a little. "I did it!"

"Yes you did! Now do it to the garden door."

We walk down the hall, and as I near that door, I look at the lock and snap my fingers. That lock unlocks too! This is very exciting!

I open the door and am greeted with a warm breeze and the scent of flowers blooming. "It's beautiful up here, Miriam! Why couldn't I ever be up here before? Why hide this?"

Miriam was right behind me as I walked through the door, but now she's off to the side looking at one of the flowers.

"Because this garden wasn't for you. It was for your mother. It was a gift of love, my dear, and that's hard to let anyone have once it's been dedicated to someone else. But now, since your mother has been gone for a while, your uncle has come to the conclusion that it might help you work on your gifts." She picks one of the long-stemmed purple flowers and continues talking as she walks to me. "He doesn't fully understand your gifts, but I explained to him last night that a growing girl needs fresh air when trying to work on something as hard as you are, and he agreed. So here," she says as she hands me the flower, "put this back on its stem."

"What?" I ask in puzzlement as I take the flower from her. "I can't put it back. You picked it."

"It's nature. You can put it back together since it's a fresh pick. If it had been picked a while ago and the ends were brown, then no, you wouldn't be able to because that part would have died. Go ahead. Try."

Part of me thinks she's lost her mind, but there's a small part of me that wonders if I can really do this. She knows a lot more than I do about these gifts. I walk over to the garden she was just at and find the stem where she picked this flower. I look at the stem that is in the ground and the bottom of the stem in my hand, and they aren't even. If she had cut it, then it would've been an even line that might've been easier to put back together. This has to be lined up just right.

I begin turning the stem, trying to find which way it'll line up, when Miriam comes over to me and touches my shoulder. "It doesn't have to be this difficult. You're overthinking it."

"How else can I put it together? It has to line up, doesn't it?" I'm getting frustrated. Why couldn't the diary have been more of an instruction manual so that I knew how to do this stuff?

"You just have to see it in your head being back together. Your mother could just touch the two cut ends together, and they would meld back into one."

The mention of my mother and my lack of being able to do this sends me into a whirlwind of despair. "I'm not my mother, and I have never had my mother!" I exclaim in frustration.

"Why did she have to leave me? Why couldn't she be here and help me out?" The tears are flowing down my cheeks, and even though Miriam is here, I feel so alone.

"Oh, Patrina! She didn't leave you because she wanted to. Nobody really knows what happened, but I knew your mother, and she loved you. She would've never left you unless something made her. Come here," she says as she pulls me into a hug. "Let's dry your eyes." She wipes my face with a corner of her tattered apron, and I'm starting to feel better.

"I just don't understand why I couldn't have my mother with me. Why would the Monarch allow something like this to happen? Why couldn't he make it so that she could stay with me, and then I wouldn't be in this situation?"

"Honey, the Monarch allows things to happen so that we can grow and be the best we can be. I don't know his plans for your life, but I'm sure the Monarch knows, and we have to trust that he knows what's best for you. What I do know is that we have to get you to Arcadia if you are going to find the answers to your questions. Shall we try again?"

I sniffle and wipe the back of my hand across my cheek. I still have the picked flower in my other hand. "Yeah, I guess. I'm not learning anything crying." I try to smile, but it doesn't fix the fact that I don't know what I'm doing.

I decide that I'm just going to try it my mother's way. I walk up to the broken stem in the garden. I take the flower in my hand and hold it so that the stem touches the stem in the garden. I take a deep breath and close my eyes and picture them back together in my mind.

"You did it!" Miriam grabs my shoulders and shakes me out of excitement. When I open my eyes, I can see that I really did do it! It's one piece again! This is great!

"There's something else your mother could do," Miriam says as she takes my hand. She pulls me toward the larger gardens near the edge of the roof. There are two gardens back here with steps that walk up in between them to a covered gazebo at the top. My uncle spared no expense for this garden.

These back gardens have a lot of foliage in them. There are different kinds of ornamental grasses and the prettiest golden, star-shaped flowers. These look like the sedum from one of my books. I can smell the sweet fragrance of the lavender before I see it billowing in the breeze next to brilliant red coreopsis flowers. There's ivy here too, but it looks as though the ivy has taken over a lot of the garden because it's flowing over the edges and drowning out the tiny white asters that are desperately trying to reach the sun.

"She could move the plants with just a wave of her hand. Why don't you try that?" Miriam grins as she urges me closer to the garden.

"What? I could barely get the stem back together!"

"Just relax and imagine your hand is a big sweeper that is pushing the plants out of your way. You can do it!" Miriam is surer of my abilities than I am.

"How about we just go up to the gazebo and look out on the maze? I need to know how big that maze is, don't I?" I take her hand and try to get her to go up to the gazebo with me, but she is not budging.

"How about you move the plants and then we will go up there? Like a little reward?"

She gives me a wink as she tugs on my hand. I don't think there's any way out of trying to do this.

"Okay. I'll try." I give in and find a patch of flowers that look like they will bend easier than something like the ivy. *Maybe the wind will help me out,* I think to myself.

The wind will be another day's lesson.

I sigh as The Guide reminds me that I have a lot to learn. I forget there's quite a bit my ancestors could do. I'm just glad The Guide and Miriam are here to help me figure it all out.

I calm myself, like I've been taught to do, but this time I

leave my eyes open so that I can see the plants move. I haven't seen any of this happen so far because I've had my eyes closed, but I'm not going to be able to just close my eyes if I'm caught in the middle of something. I take my hand and wave it over the plants that I want to move, and they just barely move. I really want to go up to the gazebo, so I take my hand, but this time, I imagine that my hand is a huge sweeper. As I push my hand toward the plants, they move as though they are magnets, repelling the leaves away from me.

"That's wonderful!" Miriam says. I forgot she was there for a moment.

"Now we can go up to the gazebo, right?"

"Yes, we can go up now." She gives a little chuckle as I start sprinting up the stairs.

There are only five steps up to the gazebo, but it feels like we're really high up, and the view is glorious. The maze is huge … much larger than I originally thought. Up here I can see that it wraps all the way around the mansion, with only the grounds closest to the house clear of the hedges for gardens and general open space. Out of the corner of my eye, I see something move at the far edge of the maze.

"What's that?" I ask, pointing toward the line of trees.

Miriam turns to look in the direction I'm looking but now, whatever was there is gone.

"I didn't see it. What was it?"

"I'm not sure, but I think … I think it was a guy."

Twenty-Three

"A man? You thought you saw someone out there?" Miriam asks as she cranes her neck, looking. "I don't see anyone, but the maze will keep whoever it is out," she says as she takes my hand and starts to go toward the stairs. "We probably should go back inside."

"What if that was the nine-foot-tall guy who was wearing Bao's face? Maybe he can get in and out of the maze like Uncle Vlad." I don't want to go down the stairs, so I pull my hand out of her grip. "Can't we just stay up here a while longer?"

"Patrina, we don't know who or what that was that you saw. There are many who would love to have you on their side, doing their dirty work. We can stay for a few more minutes, but let's work on one more thing, okay?"

She's at the top of the stairs, motioning with her hand for me to walk in front of her. I suppose I don't have much of a choice right now. But later, when no one is around, I'm going to come back out here and see if I can see anyone.

I do as she wishes and walk down the steps with her right behind me. "Okay, what's the last thing for today?" I ask, grinning at her over my shoulder.

"I didn't say the last thing for today but one more thing for now. I have some other work I need to do, but we will pick this up again later," she says with a wink. "Now let's go back to the garden where you learned how to push the plants. One of the most important things you will need to learn is how to disappear. Especially out there," she says as she points to the forest and beyond.

"This little trick means you have to get into the garden. So hop up there and have a seat next to the lavender."

The garden is at least three feet tall, and it's hard to get into, so she sticks out her hand for me to hold as she and I hoist myself up over the stone wall that holds in the garden. When I stand up in the garden, I can see over the tall edge of the roof that lines the edge of the gardens. I can just make out the very edge of the maze and the forest beyond. I don't see anyone though, so I turn around and sit down cross-legged in an open spot of dirt among the towering stalks of lavender.

The lavender smells sweet and soothing. It's relaxing. As I'm leaning in to smell a cluster of blooms, Miriam says, "Your mother used to love lavender. She said that it helped her sleep." Miriam runs her palm across the tops of the blooms and then smells her hand. "The fragrance will stay with you even after you climb out. Now, let's focus. The trick to disappearing is to use the foliage around you to cover you. Before, you learned how to bend it away from you. Now you need to draw it into you, to cover you."

"Um ... and how would you suppose I do that? The sweeper I have in my head from earlier probably wouldn't work."

Miriam stops and contemplates for a second as I sit and enjoy the smell of these tiny little purple flowers. "Maybe you can imagine that these flowers represent your mother and they're bending in to give you a hug?"

The thought of being able to get a hug from my mother is bittersweet. It would be wonderful, and yet the notion that I'll never get one makes me sad too. As I sit among these beautiful flowers, I imagine my mother being here, wrapping her arms around me. At first, I feel a tickle, and then I feel little tickles all over my arms and the back of my neck until I'm completely wrapped in lavender. When I look down, my body, from my neck down, is entirely encased in these long purple blooms, and I feel happy and at peace, as though my mother really is giving me a hug. I look up at Miriam and see that she is beaming with joy.

"You're finding your gifts, Patrina! You are truly becoming … amazing."

She stretches her hand out to me so that I can get out of the lavender, but it has totally surrounded me. It's as if it has made a cocoon to preserve me. I look to Miriam for some sort of suggestion and she just raises her eyebrows as if to ask, what are you going to do?

I can just barely reach up with one of my hands and wave it over the long tendrils. When I do, they move away from me as though they are now repelled by me. It's all starting to become easier now that I know that this is who I am … who I am going to be.

Now freed, I take her hand and climb out of the garden. She helps brush the dirt off of me, and we start back toward the house.

"I have some work to get done, and I do believe you have some schooling to attend to. Aren't math and history on your agenda for today?"

"Ugh! Can't I just skip it and practice my gifts instead?" I ask as I put my hands together under my chin, thinking that maybe if I give her my big puppy-dog eyes that I'll get my way.

"I don't think so," she says with a little pat on my back. "While working on your gifts is important, learning about the world in which you live is too. You get your work done, and I'll get my work done, and then we'll meet around lunchtime. How does that sound?"

"Like torture," I mumble. I figured I wasn't going to get out of working on my schoolwork, but it was worth a shot.

Once we get inside, she shuts the door to the roof and locks it, and then we head to my room. I walk over to the drawer that holds my textbooks and take out my math and history books. I don't feel like working on this stuff at my desk, so I put the books, pencils, and notebooks on my bed and climb on top. Once there and settled, Miriam says, "All set?"

I nod in response, and she says, "Very well. I shall see you in about two hours. Work hard so that we can go back outside, okay?"

I nod again as she walks out my door and locks it from the outside. I don't know why she locks it because I can unlock it whenever I please now. It's probably a rule made by my uncle. Maybe that rule will no longer exist soon, and I can have more freedom.

I open up my math book to the page that I'm on and start working through the examples. They seem pretty easy. I wonder what it would be like to go to a school with other kids my age and listen to a teacher go over this in class. It sounds like it would be a big waste of time. I can usually get my work done in an hour or two, and I've heard that kids go to school for seven to eight hours a day! That's like having a full-time job!

I work through the problems at the bottom of the page and check my answers with the answer key in the back of the book. Looks like I managed to get them all right, and it's pretty easy. I close that book and drag my history book across my bed to me. I open it up to where my bookmark is and see that today will be about the American Civil War.

Just as I start reading about the Confederate states, something lights up my room. I look around to see if one of my lights just magically came on by itself, but none of them are on. Plus, I'm pretty sure I broke all the bulbs earlier when

I was trying to unlock the door anyway. Where is that light coming from?

I look behind me and see that it's coming from behind my nightstand ... where I hid the diary.

Twenty-Four

I hop off my bed and kneel on the floor so that I can reach behind the nightstand and pull out the diary. As I clear it from the bed skirt on my bed, it's glowing so bright that it's a little hard to look at. I wonder why it's doing this. Did it want my attention?

I set it on top of my history book and climb back on top of the bed. The diary is warm to my touch, and I decide that now is as good a time as any to open it and see what it wants. The confederacy can wait until later.

When I open the cover, I see my name instead of my mother's. I miss seeing her name, but for now I need to figure out why it's glowing. It's never done this before, and the glow has centralized onto one of the pages within as I flip to find which one it is.

Suddenly it starts to dim. I flip to the front where there was writing, and it's all erasing itself, word by word. The last time this happened, Uncle Vlad was coming! I quickly shut the book as I look and see my lock turning blue like it does when it's being unlocked. I twist around and shove the diary under my pillow just as Uncle Vlad walks in. That was way too close.

"Good morning, Patrina!" he bellows as though he's addressing a room full of people.

"Uh, good morning? I didn't think we were scheduled to meet today."

"Oh, I had a meeting in town that was cancelled, and since Miriam is working around the house, I thought it would be a wonderful time for us to catch up and see how you've been progressing. Miriam says you're picking up on your gifts fairly quickly."

He saunters across the room and sits in one of the chairs in my reading nook. Did I cover the diary enough? I was just trying to cover it so he couldn't see it at the angle he was standing in, but now he's all the way on the other side of my room. And I can't exactly look because then he will wonder what I'm doing. I need to get him out of here.

"I'm doing pretty good … at least I think so. We could go out onto the roof garden, and I can show you what I learned this morning," I suggest, not only in hopes of getting him out of my room but also because then I can go back to the garden.

"That sounds like a great idea! Let's go! And then you can show me how easy this is coming to you. I heard you have a new trick with unlocking locks now?" He gets up out of the chair and starts to walk across the room and then stops. He's looking at my bed. Oh no! Is the diary sticking out? I need to distract him, and the only way I know how is to do something that will shock him.

"Uh, why don't you go and lock my door?" I stammer, trying to distract him.

He looks at me confused, but shrugs and with long strides, makes his way to my door, and then shuts and locks it in one fell swoop.

I quickly lean forward and snap my fingers at my door. Just as I do, the lock to my room gives a loud thunk as it unlocks.

He looks at me with a shocked expression. "You just snap your fingers, and it unlocks?"

"Yep! Miriam taught me how to do it," I say as I climb off

my bed and walk toward my door. I slip on my shoes and hope today isn't going to be one of those days where it's all close calls like this one. I may end up having a heart attack!

We walk down the hallway to the rooftop garden door. "Do it again," he says excitedly.

I lift my hand next to the lock and snap my fingers. It unlocks, and the door opens a little, just enough to slip my fingers around the edge to pry it open the rest of the way.

"Amazing!" he exclaims. "That is simply astounding! What else has become that easy?"

"Well nothing has really become *that* easy yet. I'm still learning a lot. The locks were the first things that I learned to work with, so I'm hoping that other stuff will become easier the more I work with them." It's actually kind of fun showing off a little.

The Guide whispers, *Be careful, little one. He mustn't know all that you can do … remember the lavender.*

Right! He can't know that I know how to disappear. I almost got so excited about showing him all the new stuff I can do that I gave away my escape plan.

We walk over to the first garden off to the right of the door. "Go ahead, pick a flower," I say as I motion to the different asters that are growing in this garden.

"Any flower?" he asks.

"Sure, any flower," I say as I watch him bend over and pick a black-eyed Susan from a corner. "Now what?"

"Hand it to me, please." I take it from him as he hands it to me, and I walk over to the corner he picked it from. As I touch the stem of the flower with the remaining stem that's in the garden, the two join ends and become one flower again. I let go of it and watch it sway in the wind and then turn to look at my uncle.

"Bravo!" he says, clapping. "That was magnificent! If you weren't already going to work for me, I would say that you would make a fine magician!"

I was excited until he reminded me why he wants me to learn all of this. I don't want to work for him, but for now, I don't want him to go back to my room and find the diary.

"Let's go over to the gardens by the gazebo," I suggest Maybe while we're back there, I can ask him about his maze.

"Yes, let's!" He motions with his hand for me to lead the way, and I walk on ahead of him to the back gardens. Too bad he doesn't walk in front of me because then I could try to look at his reflection in the pond as we pass it.

We walk up to the lavender in the garden that I climbed into this morning, and I'm surrounded by a warm feeling of security. I imagine this is how my mother would make me feel if she were here with me right now. Then again, if my mother were around, I dare say I wouldn't even be here.

"Miriam just showed me how to do this, so it's not as easy as the locks yet," I say. I want to warn him in case it doesn't work the first time. I can't focus when he yells, and that would just make it worse.

"Okay, fair enough." He's standing off to my left with his hands crossed in front of his waist over the suit jacket that he never seems to be without. He's always pristinely dressed as though he's meeting someone very important. I can't imagine those clothes would be even a little comfortable.

I regain my focus and find the foliage that I pushed earlier. I hear him sigh as he waits for me to find the right spot.

"Okay, I'm ready," I say as I reach my hand near the plants, and they barely move.

"Was something supposed to happen?" he asks. He's starting to grow restless.

"Yes, please be patient with me. I'll do it again." I place my hand by the plants once again and move my hand toward them, but they don't move away. They move toward me! Oh no! He isn't supposed to see me do that!

"Did you just draw those leaves toward you?" he asks,

standing right next to me as though he's trying to get a closer look.

I quickly reply, "No, that was the wind. It didn't do what I was trying to get it to do."

He looks at me, and his brows furrow. "I didn't feel any wind," he says. I can tell he doesn't fully believe me, but maybe if I can get the plants to bend away from me, I can calm his suspicions.

"Let me try one more time, okay?" I ask, hoping he's not going to blow up at me.

"Fine, one more, but my patience is wearing thin with you, girl."

I'm starting to freak out. What if I can't do it this time? Is he going to yell at me? There's no telling what kind of punishment he will deal to me if I can't perform the tricks he wants to see.

Calm yourself, little one, says The Guide. *Breathe. It's when you let your anxiety get the better of you that your gifts backfire and do what they shouldn't. Remember, this is why Miriam is training you. So you don't make the same mistakes as your ancestors.*

I do remember Miriam saying that, and I start to relax. I have to focus on just what is ahead of me and try to block my uncle out. I take in a deep breath and move my hand toward the plants, imagining that they are being pushed away with a giant sweeper like before, and as I do this, the whole front row in the ten-foot garden moves backwards, away from us!

"Wow! Now that was impressive!" he shouts. "I didn't know you had such power! You moved the whole front half of the garden!" He is stunned, and so am I. It didn't do this last time.

I'm trying to hide my shock and pretend that I knew this could happen. "Yes … it is amazing how some of these gifts work. Well, that's all I've learned so far." I decide to use this moment to see if I can get him to talk about the maze. "Miriam and I were up there earlier," I say as I point to the gazebo, "and

I noticed you have a gorgeous maze that winds around the house. Would you tell me about it?"

I've come to understand that Uncle Vlad is very proud of his power and his riches. I'm hoping that if I can get him to talk about the maze, I will learn a better way of escaping here.

"Why, of course! That maze cost a pretty penny and took years to build," he says as we're walking up the steps to the top. As we near the top and are standing at the railing of the gazebo, he continues telling me the story of how it came to be.

"This is my hedge of protection, so to speak. After your parents took you back to live in their shack, I was here one night working alone in my library. I heard a loud crash coming from down the hall and decided that I had better go check it out. I pulled one of my swords from off the wall that I had acquired from a pharaoh in Egypt and started down the hall."

I can tell he loves telling this story because he's holding an imaginary sword over his shoulder and tiptoeing in place in the gazebo. Just watching him makes me want to giggle, but he's being very serious.

"I passed by the great room and looked inside, but everything looked undisturbed in there. My next guess was that maybe Bao had dropped some pots and pans in the kitchen. I quietly made my way to the kitchen, and Bao was nowhere to be found, and the kitchen was immaculate. I looked on up ahead toward the arboretum, and I could see shattered glass spread out across the hallway. Someone had broken in!

"I tiptoed up to the entrance of the room, as quietly as my designer shoes can do on my finely imported floor, and I could hear someone talking in the room amongst my plants. He's mumbling something, and I couldn't quite make out what he was saying. I decided to slip inside the room just behind one of my giant ostrich ferns that was potted in a fifteenth-century high-shouldered jade vase from China.

"I peeked through the foliage to see a beast standing among

my precious plants! He had busted through the north window and was standing amidst a sea of glass. But that wasn't the weirdest thing about this whole burglary. This man wasn't just a man—he was a giant! He was at least nine feet tall!"

As he's describing the burglar, he's standing up as tall as he can, with his arms stretched up as far as they go to show the massiveness of his intruder.

"Nine feet?" I ask. "I've seen him!" I blurt out without thinking.

"What do you mean you've seen him?" Uncle Vlad stops acting out his story, letting his arms fall back down, and stares at me.

"When you came to my room to start training, you know, with the broken glass, he was standing in my doorway. At first I thought it was Bao because he had Bao's face, but he was too tall to be him. And then when Miriam and I were out here working, I looked out across your maze, and I saw someone," I say as I point to the place I saw the mysterious giant exit the maze.

"What? Nobody can get through that maze. You must've imagined it."

"No!" I exclaim. "He was right there!" I look to where I'm pointing, and just off into the very edge of the woods, I see him standing there … watching us.

Twenty-Five

I quickly duck down behind the railing that surrounds the sides of the gazebo in hopes that the man didn't see me.

"What are you doing?" Uncle Vlad says impatiently.

"Don't you see him? He's right out there," I whisper as I creep up to look over the edge and point to the woods where I saw him.

I watch my uncle's face as he squints to look at where I'm pointing. Suddenly he bends over to hide behind the railing next to me.

"Go inside and lock your door. I'm going to go get this guy and make sure he can never return!" Uncle Vlad grabs my arm and pushes me on ahead of him, ushering me back into the house. He points to my room and then locks the garden door behind him. I head to my room and close the door as he runs down the hall to the stairs. I stand and wait just inside my door as I listen to his footsteps disappear. The only way for him to catch the nine-foot guy is to go through the maze. Maybe I can sneak back out to the roof and watch how my uncle can get through the maze because no one else can do it. At least up there I will have a bird's eye view of the maze.

I wait another minute or so and then open my door and go to the garden door. I snap my fingers, trying to unlock it, but it's different this time. There's something blocking me. How can that be? Uncle Vlad just locked it, and he doesn't have any gifts like me ... or does he?

I try again but can't seem to get to the lock. Something is blocking my way, and I need to move it before I can even start to unlock it. Whatever is in my way feels dark ... and evil.

You're right, dear one, The Guide says. *Your uncle enchanted the lock out of fear, and there's only one way to undo a dark enchantment. You must tap into your courage gift. If you truly believe that you can undo the lock, then it will be undone.*

"I haven't even gotten to that one yet," I say aloud to The Guide, even though I could've just said it in my heart and he would've heard it just the same.

You have to believe you can do it. Do you believe?

"Uh ... not really. I'm barely getting the hang of this as it is, and that was without any other dark enchantment or random magic."

Do not forget that you were gifted for times like this ... and much more that lies ahead of you. If you believe you can do it, with my help, nothing is impossible. Have a little faith, dear one.

It's true; he's never left me, so I know he will always be with me no matter what I end up doing. And I know that I can unlock this door because I've done it before ... although it didn't have some magic barrier keeping me from it. Have a little faith, that's all I need ... just a little faith that I can do this, and The Guide will help me.

I try again, except this time I look past the barrier and imagine it doesn't even exist. It's taking a little more work, but I can finally see in my mind the tumblers lifting into place until I hear the all-too-familiar thunk that the lock makes once it lets go.

I did it! Now to see how my uncle is going to get through that maze!

I race to the gazebo and crouch below the railing. At some

point, I'm going to have to stand up and watch, but I haven't figured out how to do that without being seen. I look to the side of the gazebo and see one of the giant marble pillars that hold the roof up. That should be big enough to hide behind and still look over the edge.

I shimmy up next to the pillar and feel invincible as I peer out from my cover. I look down at the maze and see the hedge walls moving. They seem to shift on their own. My uncle just walks, and the hedge walls move out of his way. He zigzags back and forth through the maze, one wall at a time, and I realize that the maze is far more complicated than I imagined.

As if he can sense me, he stops and looks up at the gazebo. I quickly tuck myself back behind the pillar. And after a second of waiting, I barely peek out from behind the pillar just to see if he's still looking. I don't think he can see me because he turns back around and starts moving the walls again.

I scan the edge of the woods where I saw the nine-foot guy before and can't find him. I don't think he's there anymore … but then something catches my eye by the woods. The maze is moving down there too! That guy is coming at my uncle in the same way that my uncle is moving the hedge walls! I didn't think anyone else could move the maze like Uncle Vlad. Wasn't that the point of him enchanting it? Although, now that I think about it, he never said that he was the one who enchanted it.

Uncle Vlad is moving through the maze much faster than the strange man-giant, and soon I can only see the hedge walls moving. I can't see my uncle or that guy anymore, but the pieces that are moving are getting closer and closer to each other.

One more wall, and they will be face-to-face. My curiosity has gotten the better of me as I step out from behind the pillar to see if I can watch a little better. I figure that if I can't see them, then they can't see me, right?

The last wall slides out of the way, and at first it's just silence. I expected yelling, at least from my uncle. He has one of those voices that can shake the floor. And then I start to see it.

There's a glow.

At first there's only one color, a golden hue coming from the open space in the maze. And then I see the other color— red. It's the color of the scar that was glowing on my uncle's neck that day in the reflection pond. I don't know which color belongs to who, but if my uncle doesn't win, then that giant is going to have no problem getting into the house.

The red glow grows and forms a dome of color over the maze on the end my uncle came from and slowly takes over the gold. Soon the gold starts to move away, toward the woods, and the red is following it. I wish I knew who was what color!

The gold has almost made its way out of the maze with the red following close, and just as the last hedge wall opens and the gold starts to exit the strange, enchanted maze, the red gets huge and snuffs out the gold with a puff of smoke.

The red is starting to dim now, but it's moving in the wrong direction for it to be my uncle. It's going toward the woods. The color is almost gone now as I see a man exit the giant maze. I strain my eyes to make out who it might be. What is that he's wearing? Is it a … suit?

I lean out over the rail as far as I can go when suddenly the man turns around, looks up at me, and stops midstep. I realize it at about the same time that he does; that's my uncle, and he's mad.

He starts storming back to the maze toward me. He takes both of his arms and with a giant sweeping gesture forcefully motions his hands down toward the ground. The maze obeys his command and opens a straightaway going from the woods where he's standing right back to the entrance near the house. He's coming … and I know deep in my heart that I need to hide.

Twenty-Six

I scramble off the gazebo and sprint across the garden and through the door. I have no place to hide other than inside my room. If I made my way down the stairs, he would catch me in the hallway. Wouldn't he? But he would know to look for me in my room. I have to risk finding another hiding place.

I don't even bother locking the garden door behind me. I skitter down the curved tower hallway and around the spiral stairs as fast as my feet can take me. The moment my feet hit the floor of the hallway below my tower prison, I hear a loud boom coming from the other end of the house. I can only imagine that this must mean my uncle has made his way back to the house.

I try the first door, Bao's door, but it's locked, and I've never worked with this lock, so I don't know if I can unlock it fast enough. I pass it and go to the next door, which is still part of Bao's suite, but I think it's his storage room. It's locked too. By now I can hear my uncle tearing through the house, and it sounds like a thundering train moving in my direction.

Just as I'm about to scurry back up the stairs to my room, Bao peeks out his door and whispers, "What did you do? I heard a loud thunder and looked out my window to see Vlad storming up to the house. I've only seen him this angry one other time, and it was directed at me."

"I don't have time to talk. I need to hide!" I whisper insistently.

He steps aside and motions for me to come inside his room. I don't know Bao very well, but I do know that he's got to be better company than facing my uncle right about now. I clamber past him through the doorway and try to find a place to hide before my uncle makes his way to this hallway.

Bao quietly closes the door and walks across the room to a dresser in the corner. "I need you to promise me that you will never show anyone what I am about to show you."

"I promise! Just hide me!" I urge impatiently.

He pushes the dresser over about two feet and taps his foot on the floor. A door pops open to reveal a hole in the boards. I walk over to him, wide-eyed, and look down the hole to see that it's a crudely dug tunnel with a ladder set up against the wall that runs down into the depths below. It's very dark, but I can just make out a faint light at the bottom, far down in the hole.

"Climb down there," he says as he points to the hole. "Follow the light, and you'll find a passageway. There is a fork in the path that you will come to along the way. Stay to the left! The left stays under the house. Do not take the right."

I step inside the hole onto the top rung of the ladder, and it sounds like Uncle Vlad has made it to Bao's hallway. My foot hits the next rung, and Bao is hurrying me so that he can close the door and slide the dresser back across the top. I'm barely to the fourth rung, and my head is low enough now that Bao can close the entry to the tunnel when I hear my uncle's loud footsteps stop outside Bao's room.

"Duck!" Bao whispers to me as he closes the door above me. Everything around me goes dark as I hear the secret door above me latch and the dresser slide back over top. I stay perfectly still as I listen to the knocking on Bao's door. My uncle is there!

I hear Bao walk across the floor and open the door to his suite. I can't quite make out what's being said. It just sounds like mumblings, mostly from my uncle. And then I hear two sets of footsteps walk across Bao's floor. I gingerly climb down the ladder as quietly as I can so that no one can hear me moving under the floor. If my uncle finds Bao's secret door, I don't want to be standing on the ladder right below.

It's hard to climb down a ladder quickly and quietly in the dark. The only light is the faint one coming from the bottom somewhere. I can barely make out the rungs below for my feet as I blindly feel around with my hands. I still hear them mumbling above me, and as I go for the next rung with my feet, my foot slips and makes the ladder clang as I catch myself.

The mumbling above me stops.

I'm barely breathing as I freeze on the ladder and listen, hoping that they didn't hear me, or if they did, that Bao can distract him long enough for me to get all the way down and into the tunnel below.

I hear footsteps walking across the floor, and they sound like they're going to the dresser. Every creak of the floorboards makes another hair stand on the back of my neck. This must be what Miriam was talking about when she was telling me how my mother knew when my uncle was near.

I look up to the secret door in the floor and see light peeking through the crack between it and the floor. It's dim, but it's there. I watch the light as the footsteps keep moving. A shadow moves across part of the light. Someone is standing right at the dresser!

I have to keep moving!

My uncle is smart, and who's to say that he doesn't know about the tunnel that Bao seems to have been digging. I continue down one rung at a time, moving as quietly as I can, and my foot finally hits the bottom. The dirt at the base of the ladder is packed down, so Bao has probably been working on the tunnel for a while. Years even.

I look back up to the door, and the shadow has moved away. There's no way of knowing where my uncle or Bao are in this giant house, and now I need to find my way through this tunnel. What did Bao say earlier? Stay to the left? Or was it the right?

I turn to look toward the light that I saw from the top, and it's just a small flashlight stuck in a wooden sconce on the dirt wall. I wonder if Bao was working in here before letting me into his room. There's a small shovel standing against one of the walls near the flashlight. It would take a very long time to dig this out with a shovel that size.

I walk over to the flashlight and bend to pick it up when my forehead hits something hard on the way down. Ow! That really hurt!

I reach up and touch my head, but it doesn't feel like I'm bleeding. I grab the flashlight and shine it on the wall in front of me as I stand back up. There, on the dirt wall about my shoulder level, is a picture nailed into the dirt. It looks like an old farmhouse in the middle of an overgrown meadow. I wonder if this is a picture of Bao's childhood home. Why is it stuck on the wall so low? I'm much shorter than Bao. Maybe it's at his eye level when he's sitting down here. If I ever get out of here and have the chance, I'll have to ask him about it.

I turn the flashlight to shine down the tunnel and start walking. I'm not exactly sure where this will take me, but I know that I need to hide for now. I don't know what my uncle is, but he's not completely human. And I'm scared to know what he's going to do to me once he finds me.

I walk about ten feet when my right foot doesn't hit the floor when I set it down. It doesn't hit anything, just air, and I start to tumble. There's nothing to hold onto as I roll and bump down piles of dirt and gravel. I reach out, trying to grab onto something to slow my descent, but all I get are handfuls of dirt. I finally come to a stop on something that feels like a landing. I shine the flashlight up toward where I fell from and find that Bao dug out about twenty stairs out of the earth, which makes the tunnel system weave much farther underneath my uncle's estate than I thought.

I turn to shine the flashlight down the tunnel and see unlit torches lining the walls ahead. There must be matches around here somewhere. I shine my light to the left along the wall and find nothing. I stand up and brush myself off, thankful that my tumble didn't give me more than a few bruises, and shine the light along the right side. I see it.

It's a hole about a foot wide, a foot deep, and a foot tall; it's dug into the wall. I walk up to the hole and look inside to find not only matches but more pictures … and a key.

Twenty-Seven

What a strange-looking key! It reminds me of something I saw recently … where was that? I pick up the key and roll it around in my hand, touching the curves of the head of the key until I finally remember. This looks just like the keys that are in one of the coffee tables in Uncle Vlad's room that has the lion head. He has three keys in there. I wonder if this key goes with those.

I put the key into my pocket just in case I need it later and pull the pictures out of the hole. There are quite a few, mostly of people and places I don't know. But one catches my eye. It's of my parents holding me as a baby just outside Uncle Vlad's estate in the front where the giant fountain stands now. How did Bao get this? And why didn't someone give me a copy? I place the rest of the pictures back in the hole but slide the one of my parents into my pocket next to the key.

The flashlight in my hand starts to flicker like it's going to go out. There's no telling how long it's been on because it was on when I got down here, so I grab the matches and set the flashlight down in the hole so that it's shining on the matchbox in my hands. I look around and see that the nearest torch is about three feet away from me. I take out one of the matches and strike it against the box. After a couple of times of striking it against the grainy strip on the side, it finally catches on fire, and I cup my hand around the flame as I carefully walk to the torch. I touch the flame against it, and it catches right away, lighting up the long tunnel that is before me. I turn off the flashlight and stick it in my back pocket. A flickering flashlight is better than no flashlight, and who knows how long these torches will burn. I don't even know how long I'm supposed to hide down here or where this tunnel goes. The only thing I do I know is I don't want to be face-to-face with my uncle right now. Maybe he'll calm down in a while.

I take the torch off the wall and walk to the next one, which is about ten feet away. There's another torch ahead of that one. The torches go on for quite a ways ahead of me. I strain my eyes to look as far as I can, and it looks like the torches split up ahead. Maybe that's the split that Bao mentioned.

I start lighting every other torch, instead of each one, working my way to the split ahead. Once I get there, I am faced with a V ahead of me. I can no longer go straight. I go either left or right. I was in such a panic earlier that I don't remember which way Bao said to go. I'm pretty sure he said left. I wonder where the right split goes. I look down the right side of the V and walk in a couple of feet. I feel a breeze that I didn't feel in the other split. I wonder if this side goes outdoors somewhere. Even though I would love to explore the right split, I feel like I need to find Miriam. I'm sure she's already aware of my uncle's temper tantrum this morning.

I walk back to the split and continue on down the left side. It would be nearly impossible to maneuver through the tunnels without the torches because when I light every other torch, the dome of light that it casts doesn't quite reach the next dome of light, and there's a bleak darkness in between. Without the torches, I don't think I would even be able to see my hand in front of my face.

The tunnel up ahead of me splits off again. I don't remember Bao saying anything about another split. This one splits again like a V, except the left side goes to a set of steps dug out of the dirt leading up to another landing like the one I so gracefully found earlier. Might as well see where this leads, seeing that I'm going to be hiding for a while.

I climb the steps upward, and at the top of the landing is a wall that the dirt had been dug away from. I'm pretty sure that I'm under the house, and this wall is probably an outer wall of a room inside the house, but which room it goes to is a scary thought. I stand next to the wall and lean my ear against it. I listen for a few minutes and don't hear anything. There's an empty holder on the wall like the ones I've been passing along the way that held the torches. I slide my lit torch into it and look around the wall. Why would Bao dig right up to the back of a room?

I run my fingers over the wall and feel a seam that runs down it in the middle. This reminds me of the garden door and the door in the back of Miriam's closet. Miriam's door had a hidden lock or button that when she hit it would pop open the door. The garden door has a lock I can actually see but no doorknob, so you have to have a key to get that door to pop open. Or be able to unlock it with a gift.

I look around and don't see a lock anywhere. It just looks like a wooden wall. What was it that Miriam pushed that made the door pop out?

I keep looking at the wall and find various knots in the wood. Some are bigger than others, and some are more oblong in shape than others. And then I see it. One is a different color than the rest. It's glowing like the paradise door did when I was close to it, but because of the golden light given off by the torch, I almost missed it.

I touch the lit-up knot in the wall and push. It releases a latch hidden deep inside. I feel the seam and can tell that it's no longer just flush with the wall that surrounds it. Now there's a lip sticking out like the garden door does when it's been unlocked. I wedge my fingertips around the edge and pry it open.

It opens into a green room. It's some kind of storage room with one of those lights that has a cage over it. It reminds me of a bomb shelter that I've seen in my books. The walls are lined with shelves that hold boxes of different shapes and sizes. Why would my uncle have a bomb shelter? Or is this a secret storage room?

I look around at the shelves and see a bunch of random stuff. He has books about war next to what look like finance ledgers. There's something on the floor under the bottom shelf. It's just barely sticking out. I walk up and pull on it. It looks like a canvas. I've almost gotten it out when I realize that it's the painting of my father! So this is where it went! I hold it up to the caged light so that I can look at it better. There's a long gash that splits the canvas in two, severing the right side of my father's face from the left side. I pull the edges together to have a better look at him. My father was a handsome guy. His eyes are kind, like my mother's. I do see a resemblance to my uncle, though it isn't much. Just a little in the shape of their faces and the strength in their shoulders.

As I'm looking at the painting of my father, I can hear voices coming from the other end of this room. I look and see that there's another seam in that wall, like what I just found that led into this room. This house seems to be full of secret doors.

I set the painting down against one of the bookshelves and tiptoe over to the seam I just found. I quietly place my ear against the cold wall and can just make out the voices on the other side. It sounds like my uncle is talking to someone … a woman. I think he's talking to Miriam!

"Where were you this morning? I put you in charge of that girl, and you are off doing things that are leaving her to get into trouble! And now that she knows how to unlock doors, thanks to your poor judgment of which gifts she should learn first, she's seen something she should not have seen!" My uncle is still angry, and he's blaming Miriam for my disobedience earlier. I knew I was supposed to stay in my room, but I wanted to see what was going on.

"What did she see?" Miriam asks calmly. I am amazed at how calm she remains in the face of such anger.

"We had an intruder, and I took care of it. That's all you need to know. I need to find that girl before I lose her!"

"I haven't seen her since before you went up there to her room. Why do you think you're going to lose her? Please, I'm just trying to understand. I can't help you until I understand how to help you." Miriam's voice is calming even to me, and I'm on the other side of the wall in a hidden room that I got to by using some random tunnel that Bao's been digging.

I can hear my uncle's footsteps as he crosses the room. I'm dying to see where this room leads to, but there's no way I can come out now, not after I promised Bao that I wouldn't let on about his secret tunnel.

"I think I scared her." My uncle sounds much calmer now, almost sad.

"How did you scare her? She's been learning a lot lately. Maybe you didn't scare her as much as you think you did."

"We were up on the roof, Patrina and I, when she spotted a man on the outskirts of the maze. It was that nine-foot giant that we've had poking around here, the one that broke into the arboretum years ago. He was back. I told her to go to her room and lock it while I headed off to take care of this guy once and for all."

He pauses for a moment and then says, "She saw me."

"What do you mean she saw you?" Miriam asks. "What exactly did she see?"

I can hear footsteps moving away from the wall. The voices are getting quieter. Yes! What exactly was it that I saw? I want to bust in and scream it at my uncle in hopes of him telling me, but the voices are too quiet, and I can't make out what he says back to her. Where are they going?

I turn around and decide that since this tunnel goes under the house, maybe it will pop up somewhere else and I can listen more. I go back through the door so that I'm back in the tunnel by the torch I've been carrying around. I push the secret door shut and hear it latch. I grab the torch from the holder, turn to the steps that led me up here, and make my way back down into the tunnel below.

I walk out to the split in the path that led me here and go to the right and continue lighting every other torch along the way. I finally find another set of dirt steps that lead up to another landing. I bound up the steps two at a time until I'm at the top, standing next to another torch holder and a long wooden wall. I flash my torch ahead of me to take a look at the new wall. This wall is different from the last one. It's not made out of nice wood but rather a rougher, cheaper wood.

It takes me a moment, but I find a seam in the wall just like the other one. I search until I find the knot that is the button to unlatch the door and push it. I realize that I'm still holding the torch, and I don't want to take that inside with me, so I set it in the holder that's hanging on the dirt wall. I use my fingertips to pry the lip of this new door open, and it opens up to a dark room. When I step inside, it doesn't feel like a room. There's a wall nearly two feet in front of me, but when I put out my arms to feel for the side walls, they aren't there.

I take out the flashlight from my back pocket and turn it on. At first it just flickers, and then it comes on fully for just a moment. Long enough for me to realize that this isn't a room ... it's a hallway.

Twenty-Eight

The flashlight flickers out again, and I'm left in the dark wondering if I really saw what I think I saw. How did I end up in a hallway?

I bang the flashlight against my hand, and it flashes on long enough for me to see a light switch off to my left. It blinks off, and I bang it again, but it doesn't come back on. I feel around in the dark trying to find the light switch I saw, and just as I'm about to give up, I finally find it and flick it on.

The walls are lit up by a row of lightbulbs that line the hallway. It looks familiar … like I've been here before.

I tuck the dead flashlight into my back pocket, planning on returning it to Bao, and decide to walk to the left to find out where this hallway ends up. It's a skinny walkway, and as I'm looking at the walls, I can tell that these aren't just normal walls. I am on the inside of a wall …

This is the hallway that goes from Miriam's closet up to my tower!

I keep walking until I finally end up at the seam in the wall that I believe will open up to Miriam's closet. Now where's that button? At least these secret doors are consistent.

I run my hand across the wooden wall until I find it and push it in. As it releases the latch, the door pops open into the room on the other side of it. I don't open it all the way just in case I'm wrong with where I think I ended up, but once I peek inside, I can see Miriam's clothes hanging in front of me. This is her closet!

I strain my ears to listen to make sure nobody else is in there. I don't hear anything. It seems like it's empty from the sounds of it. I push on the door, and it hits the clothes that are in front of it, making the hangers clang on the rod. I stop and stay still, waiting to see if anyone is going to come running in here. Those hangers made a lot of noise!

When nothing happens, I reach my hand in through the opening and push the clothes out of the way so that the door can glide clear of the obstacle set before it to keep it hidden. I push open the door, walk inside, and I can see now that the closet door to her bedroom is ajar. I tiptoe over to it and peek out, but it doesn't look like anyone is in there. I don't hear anyone either.

I slowly start to nudge open the closet door when it's snatched open by someone on the other side! I scream and duck, covering my head with my arms. I see a figure standing over me with a baseball bat.

"Patrina! What are you doing in there?"

I look up from behind my arms to see Miriam standing there.

"You scared me! Why do you have a bat?" I yell at her, and then realize that I probably scared her first and have no right to raise my voice to her. "I'm sorry."

Miriam reaches down and offers me her hand so I can stand up. I grab it and pull myself up and then brush my clothes off. She sets the bat down against the other side of the hidden door and then pushes it shut.

"You're a mess," she says to me. "How did you get in there?"

I quickly remember that no one is supposed to know about Bao's secret tunnel and just say, "I took the passageway from my tower to your room. I'm hiding from Uncle Vlad. He's a bit upset with me."

"Oh, believe me, I know," she says as she looks behind her into her bedroom. "You aren't safe here. He's very upset that you saw him use his powers."

"How could he move the hedges in the maze like that? Wait, what powers? Is he like us?"

"No …" Miriam has the strangest look on her face like she's afraid to tell me who or what my uncle really is. Just as she's about to utter another syllable, there's a loud banging on her door.

Miriam's eyes grow as big as dinner plates as she hurriedly opens the doorway to the secret passageway. "You have to go back to your room," she whispers as she grabs my shoulders and turns me back toward the barely lit hallway.

"My flashlight doesn't work! I can't see in there!" I try to resist her as she continues to shove me back into the hole from where I came. Then I hear another knock at the door, louder than the first, and Uncle Vlad calls out, "Miriam, are you in there? Open this door!"

Miriam grabs a tiny flashlight from the top of a shelf near the door, shoves it into my hand, pushes me through the doorway, and closes the secret door behind me. I can hear her sliding the hangers across the rod, hiding the door, and then quickly shuffling across the floor to open the door that Uncle Vlad has been pounding on.

I lean my ear against the door to listen to what he has to say to her that is so important. I can feel his heavy footsteps pounding across her floor as he says, "Where is she? I know she was in here. I heard you talking to someone. Now tell me where she is!"

"She's not here—I swear. You just heard me talking to myself. I was trying to find something and sometimes I just talk to myself." Miriam must be very convincing because he seems to calm down. I hear the bed squeak and think that he must've sat down.

Uncle Vlad starts talking, but he's much quieter than he's been before. "I thought maybe she came to you and you found her after we split up from the great room. This wasn't supposed to work out like this. It was supposed to be easy. That's what they told me when I agreed to do this."

"Sometimes they don't always tell you the whole deal, Vlad. I tried to warn you."

I'm puzzled. Who are "they"? What did he agree to?

And why am I such a big part of this deal?

I hear the bed squeak again; he must've gotten up. His footsteps are moving away from the secret door, followed by the shuffling of Miriam's feet.

"Let's go look in her room again," Miriam says. "Maybe she came back. I think you should tell her that you didn't mean to scare her. That's the only way I think you're going to mend this and get your plan back on track." Miriam keeps talking as the door closes behind them. Their voices are gone, swallowed up by a part of the house these passageways don't seem to go. It sounded like Miriam was helping him. She wouldn't really be in on his plan, would she?

Twenty-Nine

I'm left standing in this passageway with instructions to go back to my room, but I don't know if I want to go back there. If I go back there and he's still angry with me, I don't know what he will do. It's not like a bunch of outsiders know that I'm here. I could easily disappear, and no one would know. But now I want to know who "they" are and what he thought was supposed to be easy. Is he really going to apologize?

I decide to take my chances and go back to my bedroom. Miriam will be there, and she won't let him hurt me … at least I don't think she would. But then again, I didn't think she was working with him either. Or is she just making him think that she's working with him? There are so many questions running through my mind, and none of them are getting answered by me hiding in these tunnels.

I take off, running through the passageway between the walls, trying to be as quiet as I can. I need to beat them to my room if I'm going to keep the passageway a secret. I finally find the tiny steps that lead up to my tower, and I think I can hear Miriam and my uncle talking. They must be in Bao's wing. At this point, it's all about who can make it up the stairs the fastest.

I take the steps two at a time and fly up the staircase,

165

reaching the secret door in a matter of seconds. I listen again as I push it open, and I can hear them on the stairs. I have no way of knowing just how close they are to the top. I slide out of the passageway, gently click the door back into the wall, and jet to my door. Fortunately my door was left open, so I don't have to try to open the lock. I make it into my room and barely close the door when I hear Uncle Vlad's steps hit the landing at the end of the hallway.

I race over to my reading nook, remembering to make sure the diary is hidden, and sit down in a corner next to the bookcase. I quickly grab one of the books that my uncle brought back for me and open it to a random page. I don't even have enough time to catch my breath before they are both coming through my door, my uncle leading the way.

"Patrina! I've been looking for you everywhere! You and I have some things to discuss, young lady!" My uncle is booming at me as he makes his way across the room, but when I look at Miriam, she doesn't look too concerned. Maybe she was able to calm him down on their walk through the house.

I close the book that's in my lap and wait silently as he reaches my reading nook and sits in the armchair across from me. His normally pristine suit is a bit disheveled, and the crazy look in his eyes lets me know that he's not that calm. This might've been a mistake coming back up here.

"Young lady, when I give you an order, you are to follow it—not sneak out to spy on me!"

This isn't starting off very well. I look up at him. There's nowhere to hide now.

Uncle Vlad sits back in the chair and rests his back into the cushion. I can tell he is weary from running all over trying to find me. His exhaustion probably won't work in my favor though.

"Yes, I saw you," he starts as he folds his hands in his lap. "I know that you watched the whole show down there in the hedge maze. And while I am furious with you for disobeying me and then hiding, Miriam," he says as he motions in her direction, "has convinced me that instead of punishing you, we should have a talk."

I'm dumbfounded as I sit here, motionless, in complete silence. I mentally check to make sure I'm still breathing. This is definitely not what I expected when he was booming through the house, hunting for me.

"Ta-talk?" I stammer. I clear my throat as I wait to hear what he really has in store for me. A talk doesn't seem very truthful.

Just listen, dear one, The Guide says. *What he is about to tell you is true but is also missing a lot of the information. He fears the risk of losing his prized investment by you knowing too much.*

What prized investment? I ask in my heart.

You, Patrina. You are more powerful than you know, and a lot more powerful than what you've witnessed. He considers you an investment because of what he knows you can do for him.

Do for him?

This doesn't make any sense to me. I can't do anything for him that would be worthy of being called an investment.

"Patrina!" Uncle Vlad is snapping his fingers in front of my face, and when I look at him, he's not as calm as he was a minute ago. Did I miss something? I must look like I'm spaced out when I talk with The Guide because my uncle seems upset.

"Pay attention, child! I do not have time to hunt for you all day and then have a talk with you when you aren't even listening." He sits back in his chair and continues from where he left off, except I didn't hear the beginning part, so I'm having a hard time figuring out what's going on.

"That man was coming here to take you away from me. He's been an enemy of mine for a very long time. You don't need to worry about him anymore because he's gone," he says with a smile.

"But who was he? And how did you move the hedges? And why were you glowing red, and he was glowing a different color? And why—"

"Patrina," Miriam interjects, "let your uncle talk please."

"Colors? What colors? Nobody was glowing any sort of colors. You must've imagined it or saw the sunlight reflecting off of something. You were very high up, after all. I can move the maze because I have the codes. It is my maze after all. When I had it installed, I had multiple codes for different parts. You just saw me using the codes to open it up."

"How could that man open the maze then?" I'm getting irritated. Where is the truth in this mess?

"He was not a man, Patrina," my uncle starts.

"What do you mean, he's not a man? I saw him! He was huge!"

"Patrina ..." Miriam gently reminds me by putting her finger to her lips that I'm not supposed to interrupt, but it's so hard when he's not telling me all the facts!

"Do you remember Miriam and I telling you about your ancestors? And how there were the original ones that started your line? He's one of the originals."

"How can that be?" I can't help but interrupt now. "Something just isn't adding up. Something—as in years! That was a couple hundred years ago! How can he still be alive?"

Miriam looks at my uncle, and they pass this look to each other. It's a look that communicates something that I want to know. That I need to know!

Miriam looks at me and then looks down at her hands that she has folded across the front of her apron. She draws in a deep breath as she says, "Patrina ... we don't die."

Thirty

"Ummm ... what?" Everybody dies. In fact, pretty much every*thing* dies. How can they just not die? Isn't that like breaking a code of ethics in the universe somewhere?

"Angels and nephilim, like you," Uncle Vlad starts, "all have the immortal quality. Angels are made with the immortal quality, and through breeding, the nephilim have it too. That was a trait that passed down, whether they wanted it to or not."

"Then what happened to my mother? I thought she and my father died in that fire."

I can't believe what I'm hearing. Could they really be alive?

"Your genesis of nephilim can disappear. Nobody knows where they go, but if they're in danger, they just vanish. There's no trace of them ... and I'm not exactly sure they have control over that little quirk," Miriam says as she cautiously darts her eyes at my uncle. Now it's becoming clear. He wasn't afraid I would run away. He was afraid I would disappear!

"Where do they go when they disappear?" I ask, thinking that if they can pop out of places that maybe they can pop into places too.

Miriam moves to the edge of the bed and sits down. As she does, she shrugs and says, "We aren't sure, dear. And being that I've never disappeared, I honestly don't know what happens. I do know that, over the years, your mother and I witnessed other nephilim disappearing, but we never saw them again." Miriam readjusts herself, and that's when Uncle Vlad decides to pipe in.

"Regardless, you should know that I was protecting you from that giant who was trying to get in here," he says, trying to make me think he's the good guy in all of this. "I have made sure that this estate is a protective fortress for you so that you never have to worry about people using your powers for the wrong reasons."

I just sit and listen, still pondering the disappearing thing, and I know in my heart that Uncle Vlad is not the good guy in all of this. But was the nine-foot giant a good guy? And why did he risk coming here for me?

Before I can ask, Uncle Vlad continues, "Well, I have a meeting to attend to before it gets much later. I'm glad we were able to have this talk and you know that I only have your best interests at heart." He presses his hands onto his knees and stands up. He runs his hands over his jacket and then turns to walk toward the door.

It feels like he was just telling me this to make me stop asking questions … or maybe to keep me from disappearing. I know that I can see things that others can't, but something isn't right. When he leaves and closes the door behind him, Miriam is still sitting on the edge of my bed and looks at me as she folds her hands in her lap.

"I don't believe him," I say.

"What don't you believe?"

"I don't believe that he's the good guy in all of this. I don't believe that he has any of my interests at heart, let alone my best ones, and I don't believe that he's trying to protect me. *And* I don't believe that he has 'codes' to the maze. After he did whatever he did to the giant, he just threw down his arms, and the hedges flew apart like he was parting a sea. He didn't type in any code anywhere!"

Miriam puts her hand up as she motions for me to be quieter. She looks at the bedroom door and walks closer to me. She sits on the floor next to me, which she hasn't done since I was very little, and says in a hushed tone, "You have to pretend that you believe him. He doesn't want you to be afraid of him because if you're afraid of him and you feel like you are in danger, then you might disappear like the other nephilim, and if that happens, even I can't help you. I don't know where they go or if they can come back."

I'm so confused, and I just feel like I'm never going to know the truth if I stay here. And then it hits me. I get what happened to my mother with the fire, but where did my father go?

Dear one, The Guide says, *if you ask that, you may not like the answer.*

I have to know. I just need to know where they are and if I can find them again.

"Miriam, with the fire … if my mother disappeared, where did my father go? He wasn't a nephilim, right?"

She sighs as though she knew this question was coming; she looks like she doesn't want to answer it. Is it really that bad?

After what seems to be an eternity, she finally starts telling me what was found at the scene of the burnt remains that used to be my house. "When the firemen and police arrived, all that was left was a shell … a charred shell. Except for you room. Your room, strangely enough, was intact, with only minor scorch marks on the walls from where the fire tried to get in. Nothing was left outside of your room though. The report said that there wasn't any evidence of anyone who may have died there either, but there was one side note in the report that said something about how it looked as though someone may have been dragged out."

"Do they know if that was my father? Maybe he's still alive

somewhere! Maybe he's had amnesia this whole time! That can happen, right?" I'm suddenly filled with hope that I might be able to find my father out there somewhere.

"Nobody knows, Patrina. There was never a report of a death for either of your parents, but they've never been seen again either. For a while, the police issued a missing person report for both of them, but nothing ever came of it. I believe your mother disappeared, probably not of her own will but because she was very afraid of something, though I don't believe a fire could cause that kind of fear in a nephilim with the power she had."

That was a good point. If she had almost the same gifts as me, then why couldn't she just control the fire or put it out? That wouldn't be enough to make her so afraid that she disappeared. And where did my father go? Was he the one that was dragged out?

"I don't know," Miriam says, as though she knows what I'm thinking. I didn't say all of that out loud, did I?

"I wish we knew what happened to them. I really do," Miriam continues. "I searched for them myself for years and never found even a trace. I went back to your house to search among the ashes, and I don't know if the footsteps I saw were from the firemen, the police, or someone else. It's so hard to tell. I did see a set of footprints that I thought were strange, but at the time I didn't really think anything of it. Not until the giant, as you call him, came around here. If he was truly nine feet tall, it would match the footprints that were abnormally large that I found at your old house. Though I don't know when they were put there."

"Wait—the giant was at my house?" Suddenly I realize that he's been searching for me my whole life. What does he want with me? Why me?

"It seems as though a giant was, but I don't know if it was the one we saw today. Or even if the one we saw today was the same one that you saw in your doorway. Remember, there's more than one."

It feels like I'm discovering a whole other world than the one I've known or even read about in all of those books. Other than in the *Ancient Letters*, I've never heard or read anything about nephilim, nor have I seen one.

"So if that giant today was one of the original nephilim, who do you think he was? And why do you think he was here?" I ask. I'm not sure if I want to know, but somehow this mysterious giant is a link to my past, and maybe he knows something about my parents and what happened to them.

"I'm not sure," Miriam says. "There's no way to know who survived all of these years. Many were thought to have been destroyed in the Great Drowning thousands of years ago. That's in the *Ancient Letters* too. Have you read about that?"

"Is that the part about the big ship that could only hold a certain amount of animals, and only one small family was spared?"

"That's the one," she says with a grin. "But if they could disappear when they were afraid too, then that makes me think that they probably didn't drown."

"But if they did disappear, how did they come back?"

Thirty-One

I glance out the window and see that it's getting dark outside. It has been a very intense day full of mystery and new details about my life and my parents. I suddenly feel the weight of the day on my eyelids, and it must show because Miriam starts to get up off of the floor. I can hear her knees and joints creak and crackle, and I realize now why she doesn't sit down here with me anymore. She finally gets up, straightens her clothes and her tattered cotton apron that has seen better days, and lowers her hand to me. As I clasp my palm against hers, she gives me a yank, and I'm suddenly standing next to her.

"I do believe it's time to put today to bed, and you should get to bed too. You're looking sleepy."

"I feel sleepy! Today was a lot." I think back and can hardly believe that everything that happened today could actually fit into one day. I climb out of my clothes that are covered in the dirt from Bao's tunnels and realize that nobody asked me how I got so dirty. My clothes end up piled in a heap on the floor, and Miriam bends down to scoop them up as I wiggle into my pajamas. There's something comforting about pajamas after a long day. I hop up onto my bed and tuck my toes under the blankets, and I realize that although I've been locked up here my whole life, Miriam has really made me feel protected and loved, even if that wasn't my uncle's true intent for raising me.

Miriam has tossed my clothes into the hamper in my closet and comes to tuck me in. As she stretches the blankets up to my neck and they flutter down around me, she asks, "Have you looked in your mother's diary lately?"

I don't think she knows that it's mine now. I never told her that my mother's name isn't in it anymore. I guess there's been too much going on to remember. I reach down to where I hid the diary earlier and pull it out. I know that I can trust Miriam. She did help me find it after all. "I guess I forgot to tell you," I say as I unwind the leather string that holds it closed. "The diary wrote my name in it where my mother's used to be." I open the diary and flip to the first page where it now says "Patrina Palinski" and turn the book so that it's facing her.

She pulls it closer as a look of amazement crosses her face. "It's yours now," she says quietly. "I knew it was meant for you, but I never thought it would declare you its new owner."

"Why not?"

"I guess I didn't know it could do that. I thought it was a book that your mother wrote in, but it looks like it's more than just a book … it seems to be something more," she says as she turns it over and looks closer at it. "I never had anything like this, and I've only seen your mother with it. It looks like it's a mystery—just like you, my dear." She lays the diary back down on my bed and reaches in to give me a hug. As her arm wraps around my shoulder, I feel a twinge of pain.

"Ow!" I exclaim as I pull back.

"What's the matter?"

"I don't know. When you're hand brushed my shoulder, it felt like a pin pricked me. Do you have a pin in your sleeve? Maybe from sewing or something?" I grab her sleeve and turn it over to see if I can see or feel anything.

"I didn't sew today. I haven't even sewn anything lately. Let me look at your shoulder."

She turns me a little so that my back is almost completely to her. She pulls the neck of my shirt down so that she can see the top of my shoulder and gasps.

"Oh no ..."

"Oh no—what? What is it?"

"We aren't ready yet. You aren't ready yet. This is so much sooner than I thought it would be."

I pull away from her hand and turn to face her. "Miriam, what are you talking about?"

"It's your feather ... it's starting."

"What!" I throw back the covers and jump out of bed. I race across the room to the mirror on top of my dresser and try to turn and pull my shirt down to see it in my reflection. I'm twisting and turning, but I can't see anything. There's not even a red spot on my shoulder where it was hurting.

"I don't see anything. There's nothing there. It's not starting yet. You're freaking out over nothing," I say, trying to calm her down while I'm panicking on the inside.

Miriam gets up off of my bed and starts walking across the room. "You probably can't see it from a distance. I was really close to it," she says as she nears my dresser. "Let me look again. Maybe it was something else."

"Okay," I say as I turn my back toward her. She gently pulls my shirt to reveal my shoulder. She must be very close because I can feel her warm breath on my skin. I glance at the reflection in the mirror and see her slowly moving her finger toward my shoulder. She barely presses down onto my shoulder, and it sends a streak of pain through my back.

"Ouch!" I yell.

"Ssshh! You don't want your uncle to hear you, and you certainly don't want him to know about this. It's just starting. It's barely there. Just the very tip of your feather is starting to break through the skin. It's not noticeable to anyone who would be looking at you, but that will change."

"How am I supposed to keep it hidden when it hurts to have even your fingertip rub against it? And why aren't my clothes bothering it?"

"It's just starting, so your clothes aren't going to catch on it yet. I'm able to actually press down and touch the tip of your feather, and that's why it's hurting. Wait here," she says as she goes to my bathroom. I have no idea what she's doing, but I can't believe that this is happening already.

She comes back out with something in her hand that she's opening up. "Bandages are wonderful for feathers," she says with a grin. "Not only do they hide them, but they also keep them from catching on clothes."

She turns me so that my back is facing her, pulls my shirt down again, and then I feel the bandage stick to my skin. She's right. It does feel better.

"Tomorrow will have to be a crash course in your gifts, Patrina. Somehow, we are going to need to get you ready to go because you're going to need to get out of here soon."

I can see the tears welling up in her eyes as she says this, and I realize that she's right. Everything I knew up until now is about to change. And then it hits me. Wherever this adventure takes me, I can't take her with me.

"But what about you?" I ask with tears in my eyes.

"Now don't you worry about me, dear," she says as she wipes her eyes and fakes a grin. "This is only the beginning. We will have a little longer to work on a few things. And I will be with you in your heart. We never know what tomorrow holds. Who knows? Maybe someday we will be able to be together again. That's the least of our worries right now though. You, my sweet, need to get to bed and get your rest. We will have a busy day tomorrow. I don't know what your uncle has planned, but we will have to work around him and get you ready."

She spins me around on my feet so I'm facing my bed, and then she urges me toward it with a nudge. I reach the side of my bed and climb into it again as she pulls the covers up and over, and they flutter around me once more. As they land around me and encase me in my soothing cocoon, I again realize that this too shall not last. Miriam has been my whole world. How can I just walk away and leave her here?

"I love you, my Patrina. I love you as though you were my own. Your mission in life is much bigger than this little tower and much more valiant than doing your uncle's bidding. Please try to sleep." She taps the end of my nose with her finger, gives me a quick grin, and heads out of the room. I hear the door latch, the lock click, and I'm left in my bed … alone.

You're never alone, dear one, The Guide says.

I feel alone. And now I have to leave the one who has been there for me my whole life, and for what? So my uncle doesn't have my feather?

It's much bigger than that …

Thirty-Two

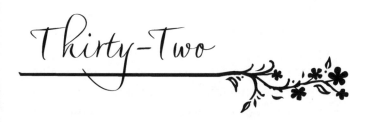

It's so dark … I reach out in front of me and feel something hard … and smooth … like glass. Where am I? I reach next to me, and it's the same cold, glassy wall that meets my hand. My feet keep sliding underneath me, almost like I'm standing on the top of a funnel. I try to get my eyes to adjust to the light, but it's too dark in here. Suddenly I see a small sliver of light off to my left. It's so far away. What is that? The sliver of light is tall and straight, and it starts to get wider the longer I stare at it. I watch as the light grows and realize that a door is opening, and the light is piercing its way through the crack. There's a dark figure edging the light out of the opening doorway. Who is that?

Whoever it is has broad shoulders and fills the doorway, blocking the light for a moment until I see a hand reach over and flick on a switch that blasts the room in a blinding white light, and I can't see for a moment. Once my eyes readjust, I can see that I'm standing inside a glass case … I look at my feet, and the funnel isn't a funnel; it's a point. The dark figure is now illuminated with the glowing bulbs from the ceiling, and I can see that it's my uncle … but he's so big!

As he gets closer to me, the size of him is enormous. I look at the furniture in the room and the surrounding walls, and it's then that I know it's me that's not normal size. He finally reaches where I am encased in this glass prison, and he stretches out his hand. His hand is so huge that I could easily sit in his palm and not fall off. What is he doing? He closes his hand so that only his pointer finger is aimed at me, and he gives my glass case a flick. As I'm swinging back and forth, I look up and see that my prison is dangling from a chain. And that's when I realize … this is the glass pendant like the one Miriam and my mother wore—except I'm not wearing mine. I'm inside it!

My uncle has me on display, locked inside, dangling and swinging, totally trapped and forever imprisoned. I bang my fists against the glass, trying to break it open, but it doesn't even budge. He sees me and starts laughing, and when he stops, he looks at me, his eyes glowing red and the scar on his neck looking as though it's on fire. He leans in toward me and says, "You are mine now, Patrina."

"Patrina! Patrina!"

My shoulders are being shaken, and when I open my eyes, Miriam is right in my face. What a strange dream. I don't know what that was, but I think it's safe to say it wasn't a vision from my mother or one of my other ancestors.

"I've been trying to wake you. You were mumbling about being locked somewhere, and you were punching the air. I almost got knocked out when I got too close."

"I guess I'm a little stressed … So what are we going to do today?" I ask eagerly, trying to change the subject. That dream left me feeling so awful it makes me cringe just thinking about it. I want to move past it and let the memory fade of my giant uncle locking me in a glass pendant.

"Well, first thing this morning, your uncle wants to have breakfast with you."

"Do I have to dress up in those dumb nylon things? I really did not like those." I sit up in bed, not wanting to get out of my warm, comfy cocoon to go have a stuffy breakfast with my uncle. I stack my pillows behind my back so I can flop against them in an attempt to stay in bed a little longer.

"No, it won't be like that. You can wear your jeans and tennis shoes. But you do need to get up, so no getting comfy. C'mon. Hop to it," she says as she snaps her fingers. I don't feel like doing anything today. I wonder if it's possible for a dream to make you even more tired.

She comes out of my closet with a pair of dark blue jeans, a bright pink T-shirt, and a pair of socks that matches the shirt. I guess there's no time for stalling. Maybe the sooner I get this done, the sooner I can get to learning what I need to know so I can leave here. Just as that idea forms in my head, I get a twinge from where my feather is starting to grow out. That wasn't a dream either, I suppose.

Miriam tosses my clothes on the bed, and I finally crawl out of my encasement. It's a cool morning, and I can feel it in the air. As the goose bumps rise up on my arms, a shiver runs through my whole body, and Miriam says, "I'll get you a jacket," as she, once again, walks into my closet. What am I going to do without her?

I put on the clothes she set out, careful not to bump the bandage covering the needle-like feather trying to poke its way through my skin, and slide on my shoes that are just under the skirt of my bed. When she brings the gray sweatshirt jacket from the closet, I ask, "What does he want?"

"I'm not quite sure. I think it might have something to do with his business and the manner in which he plans on you helping."

"Where are we eating? Do you think he will show me the maze?"

"I believe you are eating out by the maze, so it's possible.

There's a little patio out back where he likes to have his morning coffee while he reads the paper, so it wouldn't surprise me if that's where he intends on having breakfast this morning. He just told me to get you ready for a meeting with him this morning and do it quickly. Fortunately for us, he has a rather busy day today and should be gone for most of it," she says as she holds out my jacket so I can slip in my arms. I already feel warmer, but if it's this chilly in my room, what's it going to be like outside?

We quickly walk out of my room, through the hall, and down the stairs, leaving my tower behind. As we pass by Bao's room, his door is opened just a little, and I try to glance inside, but it's not open far enough, and we're walking too fast for me to see anything. We pass the paradise door, the great room, and the kitchen. Where is this patio anyway?

We walk into the glass room, take a left to the arboretum, and walk inside. This room feels so good! The warmth moves its way from my skin all the way down to my bones, and for once this morning, I am finally warm. Miriam is walking ahead of me when I see a butterfly flit across the path between us. I slow down, and she says, "We need to get you out there. He was quite insistent this morning."

"Okay … okay," I mumble.

I've never seen the whole arboretum before now. I didn't realize how massive it was in here. We take the path to the right and come to another glass door. She holds it open for me, and when I step through into the brisk morning air, I see him sitting at a small table on a brick patio nestled among the shrubs and flowers of a garden. All the warmth inside of me goes rushing out with the greeting from my uncle.

"Good morning, Patrina," Uncle Vlad says as he lowers his newspaper and unfolds his leg so that both of his feet are now on the bricks under his chair.

"Good morning," I say. As I walk toward the chair opposite

him, I hear the click of the glass door behind me. I glance back to see that Miriam went back inside. I really do wish she could stay out here with me.

"I thought maybe we could have a quick bite this morning and I could tell you more of what I do and what I'd like to see you do. How does that sound?"

"Good," I say, careful not to give him any reason to be upset with me. He seems to be a very determined man who wants to have things go according to schedule, and if his agenda gets interrupted, he doesn't seem to like it very well.

"Great! Have a seat, and we can get started. I have a full day, so we can't take too long. Where is she with our breakfast?" He looks back at the glass door and tosses the newspaper onto the table. Just then, the door flies open, and Miriam pushes through with two covered plates on a tray.

"Finally! Just set it down. We can serve ourselves," he says as he waves for her to leave. "Patrina, set those plates out," he orders while sticking a rolled-up napkin full of silverware by my glass of orange juice.

I set his plate in front of him and remove the cover to reveal biscuits smothered in a spicy sausage gravy, with a small glass bowl brimming with juicy berries of every color. The smell is amazing! My stomach rumbles to life as I set my plate down in front of me and release the aroma trapped by the cover. I quickly unroll my napkin, throw it across my lap, and grab my fork to start digging into this glorious breakfast that's before me.

"Ahem."

Why is it, just when I'm about to enjoy something wonderful, he has to shove his way in and destroy it?

"Has Miriam taught you nothing? A lady doesn't attack her meal. You look like one of those African lions about to pounce on a gazelle. Now before you cover us both in gravy with your frenzy, compose yourself and eat it like a lady."

I know he doesn't love me as one of his own family, but I never thought I would see such a look of disgust coming at me from his stare.

"If you are to be a part of my company, you must hold yourself gracefully. A pig is not graceful," he spouts as he cuts one of his biscuits with a knife.

My heart feels as though he just sliced it with the knife he is using for his biscuit. A pig? What an awful thing to say! I no longer feel like eating anything in front of this man whom I must call my uncle. I have no doubt that I want to get away from him now. I set my fork down as gracefully as I can.

"Aw, come on now. You can eat. You just can't shovel it into your mouth. You must eat daintily, like a lady. Even I eat more like a lady than you do," he says as he laughs. I, however, do not find it amusing, but I do pick my fork back up and start to eat slower than I want in hopes of moving along this breakfast meeting.

"There ya go! Now we can get back to what this breakfast is all about. I am the main importer and exporter of Poland. This means that I have to make sure that what needs to get to the States or somewhere else actually gets there in the time necessary. My goal is to get the appropriate amount of money, if not more, that I'm supposed to receive without penalties. That's just the exporting portion. The importing portion is where I want to get the best deal possible, as fast as possible, and in the best condition it can be so that I can turn it around and export it for more. Anything like weather, wars, or even pirates can interfere and cause me to lose money."

"Pirates?" I nearly choke on my biscuit. Aren't pirates only in fairy tales like *Peter Pan*? Maybe I shouldn't have said anything. He stops midslice with his knife, calmly sets his silverware down, dabs the corners of his mouth with his napkin, and sets his steely blue eyes on me.

"Yes, Patrina. Pirates. They aren't the kind you read about

in your storybooks. These are real. They board the ships, hurt the crew, and steal the goods, which means people like me lose a lot of money. Can I continue without any interruptions now?"

"Yes, Uncle Vlad," I say as I look down at my plate. How is it that he can make me feel so ashamed of asking a question?

"Very good! Now comes the part that you need to know. Since you are a virtue and can control many things like your ancestors could, that means that you can control the weather, wars, currency fluctuation, even the timing of the seasons for fruits and vegetables! With you, I'll be able to—"

"Wait! I don't know how to do any of that!" He's starting to freak me out with what he thinks I can do because I can't seem to do any of what he just listed.

"But you will! Miriam is training you, and with a little nudge here and there from me, you'll be able to do all of that and more. You don't even know what all you can do. I don't even know what all you can do!"

He excitedly tosses his fork onto the table, throws his napkin into the air, and stands up so fast that his chair is knocked down behind him and clangs on the brick patio.

"You are going to make me millions, and you don't even realize what that means! With you controlling the variables, I will dominate the world of import and export. That's why it's so important that you learn how to use the gifts we know about because there's so much more that we don't know, and I can capitalize on those too."

I don't even know what to think as he's rambling about me controlling variables and him dominating the world. As I sit there dumbfounded, he seems to gain his composure. He smooths his suit, looks up at the sun, and pushes the chair farther across the patio with his foot. He suddenly says, "Time is of the essence, Patrina, and I do need to cut this short as I have a day full of meetings. You and Miriam need to get working on those gifts. Your birthday is soon, and that's when I intend to make you an employee. You and I will meet for dinner tonight, so I expect to hear something that you've learned." And with that, he spins on his heel and is walking out of the door before I can utter another word.

Thirty-Three

"Oh, Patrina ..."

I'm not sure where she came from, but when I look up, I see Miriam standing next to me.

"Did you know," I stammer, "did you know the whole time that this is what he wanted me to do?"

"I ... yes ... yes, I did ... I'm so sorry," Miriam starts as she tips the fallen chair back onto its feet and takes a seat across from me. "He has planned this from the day you were born ... he just needed to get you away from your parents."

"Wait—what do you mean to get me away from my parents?" She's starting to fidget, and small beads of sweat pop out on her forehead with every increasing breath. "Miriam, what's going on?"

The Guide says, *Listen to her, dear one ... prepare your heart.*

"Patrina, I love you as though you were my own ... I always did. Your mother, she wasn't going to teach you about your gifts. She wanted you to be free ..."

"I thought you never saw my mother again after she broke your pendant." I'm so confused, and yet if The Guide is here with me, urging me to prepare my heart, something isn't right ... something must be very wrong.

"I saw her when they visited here years ago ... when you

were born. I helped her deliver you. I was here through it all. The thunder and lightning, the winds, the storm—it was all from her laboring to have you. She was causing it, Patrina. In the midst of her pains, she vowed to me that she would do whatever it took to keep you from experiencing all that she had with these powers. That's why they didn't stay. Vlad promised both her and Konrad to give them their hearts' desires. Anything they wanted they could have if only they would keep you here so that he and I could train you to be the most powerful virtue that ever lived. When they left, they promised that we would never see you again, and they would never allow you to know who you really were to protect you from people like him … and me. I was the one, my sweet. I never wanted you to know, but I fear if you don't find out from me that your uncle will one day use it as fuel against me to bury a wedge between us once he has you how he wants you. I regret it every day, truly I do."

"Regret what? What are you talking about?" My insides feel like they are on fire with nerves. The very pit of my being knows … I suppose I always did … I start to scoot my chair away from the table. I feel as though I can't be near her when I hear the words come out of her mouth. Yet the farther away I go from her, the closer she leans to me.

"The fire … oh please, don't hate me! Patrina, I love you," she exclaims as she tries to grab my hand. "Vlad told me I had to make it so that your parents didn't have a choice and you had to come here. But there wasn't any other way to get them to let you come here, so I did it. He threatened me with locking me in that tower, to live out my days alone. He said that if I did what he wanted that he would make my life here tolerable, and that was more than I had back then.

"Your parents didn't see me there on that afternoon. I used one of Vlad's lighters he had gotten on one of his trips. He told me to use it because it was special and would get the job done the way it needed to be done. Your house was so old that it was like kindling waiting to ignite. Once I lit the lighter, the fire leapt from it as though it had a mind all its own and jumped to the back corner of the house. I couldn't do anything after that because it was too late. It started up and took over before I knew it. I don't know what was in that lighter, but it wasn't normal. It was something much more evil. Something that your mother knew she couldn't contain or control. That's why she disappeared.

"I hid in the woods near the house and cried while I waited until it died down. I watched it swell up and engulf your tiny house. I watched it slither like a snake around the edges, but when it got to your room, it snapped back as though it was being repelled. I've never seen fire do that. Once it was done, and all that was left were charred embers surrounding your room, I saw movement in the doorway to your bedroom. I walked up to it and found your father lying there, barely alive. I was the one who dragged him out. I brought him out to the car by the edge of the woods that surrounded your house … where your uncle was waiting for me. I helped him put your father into the car, but then Vlad yelled at me because he wasn't supposed to survive the fire, and he had to take care of your father, and I had to finish the rest. He knew you'd survive it … I don't know how … but he knew …

"He drove off with your father. I don't know where he brought him, but I made my way down to Old Miss Latterly's house. I knocked on the door and left a note, letting her know that someone needed help … that there had been a fire. The rest … the rest you know. I'm so sorry …"

I can't help but stare at her as she sits across from me, tears rolling down her face. How could she? How could she do this to me? Or to my parents? I don't even know what to say to her, so I get up from my chair and contemplate running. I'm right by the maze. Maybe since I can make plants move I can make the maze move out of my way like my uncle did. But the thought suddenly occurs to me—I don't know if I want Miriam knowing when I leave now. She has been kind and loving to me all these years, but ultimately she is owned by my uncle, and if he wanted her to do something, she would have to do it … like setting my parents … like setting *my* house on fire. I was there too. She couldn't have known that something would protect me. Could she?

I look at her and see her staring at me, tears flowing down her cheeks, wringing her hands in her old apron, and I can't help but feel sorry for her. I'm not sure what I would've done had I been in her position. I slowly walk over to her, lean down, and wrap my arms around her.

"I still love you," I whisper in her ear. Her whole body starts heaving uncontrollably with every sob that releases from her, as though she had buried them deep within, and they are just now coming to the surface.

"I am so sorry, so very sorry," she sputters through her tears. Even though part of me wants to distrust her and never let her back into my heart, part of me knows that she was trapped, like me.

She does love you, The Guide says.

Why did you tell me to prepare my heart then? I ask in my head. The Guide is always there, but sometimes I don't always understand what's really going on.

Because it's too easy to shut someone out who has hurt you. You needed to be prepared to choose to love her even though she took away your chance to grow up with your parents.

How can I not love Miriam when she's loved me all these years? Maybe the reason why she loved me so much was because she was trying to make up for what she did all those years ago.

I let go of the hug we are wrapped in and pull back to see her face, red and blotchy from crying. "Can we move on with today? It's kind of been a rough start," I say, trying to get her to realize that I still want her to be in my life.

"I would love that," she says with a sniffle. She stands up, and we pick up the dishes from breakfast. I follow her back into the house.

"What are we going to learn today?" I ask as I clear the arboretum door and start making my way through the glass room.

She stops in the doorway to the main hall, turns to face me, and says, "Everything …"

Thirty-Four

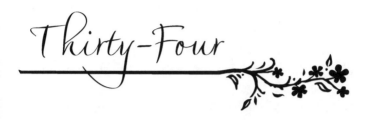

I stop midstep as the word "everything" resonates through my head, and I realize that covers a lot … a whole lot.

"What do you mean *everything*?"

"Some things will come naturally to you, like the grace you've just shown me. But there's a lot that your ancestors could do, and you will need to know how to do all of that. And then there's more that you can do that they couldn't because you're the tenth, but I'm afraid you might have to discover those on your own. I have never been around the tenth genesis of any of the nephilim. Yet there must be something amazingly special about them because they are the ones that are being hunted." Miriam turns around and starts walking away, as if what she just said was common knowledge. I knew there was one that seemed to be trying to get to me, but they were trying to get to the entire line of tenth genesis? Why?

I follow Miriam to the kitchen where we drop off the dishes from the patio. Bao is in there working on something in the corner, but we don't say anything to him, and he doesn't say anything to us. Miriam and I walk back up to my tower bedroom in silence, and I don't know if it's because she doesn't want my uncle to hear her talking to me or if it's because she doesn't know what to say after divulging the fact that it was her that caused me to have to live here.

She opens the door to my room and steps aside so that I can go in first, and then she closes the door behind her. I walk over and climb up onto my bed and wait to see what she's up to. She's not normally this quiet.

She crosses the room to my windows and pulls the curtains closed, making it fairly dark in here. Why would she close the curtains?

She starts to walk across the room toward me, and just as she nears my bed, she stops, turns toward the door, and quickly walks back over to it and locks it. What is going on? She glances around the room and seems to be checking off items on a checklist in her head. Has she lost her mind?

She walks back over to where I'm sitting and climbs up onto my bed across from me. She pulls her apron across her lap and then leans in so that her face is within inches of mine.

"You will have to learn some things in private because if I know all that you have learned, your uncle will force me to tell him. In fact, I shouldn't have told you that because then he'll find out that you know how much of a hold he has on me. Whatever, he's going to reprimand me and punish me for all that I'm about to teach you anyway, so here's what you need to realize: you can't tell me all you know, you can't tell me all you can do, and most of all, you can't tell me when you're going to leave or how. He will make me tell him, and then when he gets you back here, against both of our wills, he will never, ever let you go again. I thought maybe I would be able to help you out there," she says, pointing toward the closed curtain, "but I know that's just a dream of being free, and I'll never be free of him. What you've seen of him is the nice side. You've heard Bao's stories. And you saw what he could do when that intruder was here. He has powers, Patrina, powers from something … something evil, and I don't know from what."

Suddenly, the red scar on his neck flashes into my mind. "Does his power have anything to do with that scar?"

"The one on his neck?" Miriam is talking much quieter now.

"I first saw it that day we were on the roof," I whisper. "I saw it in the reflection of the pond up there. It wasn't until I saw it peeking out from under his collar the other day, and how he was so quick to hide it, that it made me wonder if there was something more to it."

"There is," she starts, "but I don't know what it is or how he got it. All I know is that somewhere along the line, something happened that made that scar, and it looks like it was pretty bad. He hides it well. You've only seen a tip of it. I've seen it when he wasn't looking, and it wraps all the way around the back of his neck. That's why he always wears shirts with collars like that. The only one who really knows what happened is his brother, your father."

I have all sorts of books in my room, and one of them is about the human anatomy. If something cut his neck … "That cut would've been deadly," I say aloud, finishing my thought.

"Yes, that's what I thought too."

"How could he survive that?" I ask, not knowing if I want the answer.

"I don't really know …"

He didn't, The Guide whispers to my heart. *But you cannot tell that to Miriam. This is only for you to know because you need to realize what you are up against.*

I am in shock, but if I am not supposed to tell Miriam, I need to go to another room because the gravity of this new information is going to be written across my face, and she's going to know The Guide said something to me.

"Uh, I need to go to the bathroom," I say as I start to get off of the bed. "I want to be ready to focus, so I should go now before we start learning everything."

"Oh, okay, that's probably a good idea."

My sudden change of subject seems to have taken her off guard, but she acts like she accepts it as I watch her adjust herself on the bed. I turn and quickly walk into the bathroom and shut the door. At first I just stand there, looking at my shocked face in the mirror. It was a good idea to come in here because even I can see it all over my face that I know more. I look into my deep blue eyes and see my mother's eyes. The shape of my face resembles the oval shape of hers. Our hair color is very different though. Hers was the color of the sun, and mine is more the color of the red sky in one of my first visions of Arcadia. I smooth down a strand of auburn hair that has a mind all of its own and decide to flick on the fan and go sit on the edge of the bathtub as the image of my uncle's scar comes barreling back to my mind.

How? I ask in my head. *How did he … and how can he be alive now?*

"It was a long time ago, Patrina. He's not who he used to be and hasn't been for the entire time that Miriam has known him."

Did Bao know him before … was it an accident? What was it? I don't even know what to call this thing that happened to him.

No, Bao didn't know him before the accident.

The Guide seems to give me only bits and pieces sometimes, and I really wish he would tell me all of it.

Are you ready to know all of it, little one?

I forget that he can hear my thoughts even when I don't direct them to him. *Yes … please …*

There's a lot to understand. He was already hungry for power. He always has been, ever since he was a young boy. When he got to be a little older, he fell in with a crowd that was not your typical teenage group.

"Patrina? Are you okay?" Miriam knocks on the door and starts to turn the knob.

"Yes, just fine. I'm almost done. I'll be right out," I holler to her, hoping to stall a little longer.

She stops turning the doorknob and says, "Okay. I was just getting worried."

"No worries. I'll be out in a second," I say.

Please continue, I say in my mind.

There isn't time right now, dear one. You mustn't keep her waiting.

But you could just tell me real quick. She's okay. She's waiting. How could he start telling me this only to cut it off and think that I'm going to be able to go out there and be normal?

You'll be fine.

Ugh! Why does he have to listen to everything in my head?

I will tell you the rest of it later. She knows that you are able to talk with me, but she isn't able to anymore. Do not forget that. She yearns to be able to open up that communication again, but she made her choice a long time ago. If she knows that you are talking with me, she will want to know what we are talking about, and I know that you will feel sorry for her and want to tell her. That is not a position I want to put you in, so you need to just go out there and work on your gifts. We will finish this story in due time.

Okay, I say begrudgingly in my head.

I decide to wash my hands and sprinkle some water on my face. It feels refreshing, and I am ready to face her when I turn off the fan and unlatch the door. As I come out, I see that she is sitting in her chair near my books, and she is holding something. It looks like a book, but as I get nearer, it's not just any book. It's the diary.

Thirty-Five

"What are you doing?" I ask as I wipe any remaining water off of my hands onto my jeans.

"I found it. When I sat down, I saw it peeking out from behind your nightstand. It's warm," she says as she runs her hand across the top of it. There's a look of love on her face, and I think she's holding it not because she wants to know its secrets but because she misses her old life.

"Yes, sometimes it's warm. Sometimes it's just like a normal book. You miss it, don't you?"

She stops rubbing the book and looks up at me. "Miss what?"

"Your old life ... your old job."

"I miss being free," she says quietly.

"There is no free, as you call it, because you pick sides one way or the other ... don't you?" I ask. I can feel my forehead wrinkle up into a scowl that forms when I'm confused or don't believe what I'm hearing. It really is hard to hide what I'm thinking. It just seems to show on my face whether I want it to or not.

"Yes ... and no. Yes, you do pick sides, because if you don't pick the Monarch, then you pick the Fallen. But if you do pick the Monarch, there is freedom there that you won't have if you pick the Fallen. The Monarch allows you to grow and learn. He allows you to love and be loved, and he allows you to fail and try again. The only thing he doesn't allow is if you decide to pick the Fallen, even for a little bit, to ever come back. That's one mistake that he doesn't let you try again … at least so it seems. The Fallen though … they don't allow you to do anything. You are a slave to that side. The Fallen entice you with riches and promises at first, but once you have chosen to go to that side, it's all over."

"Forever?"

"It would seem so." She looks like she lost herself in her memories as her eyes glaze over and her shoulders slump.

"Have you tried apologizing?" I ask. Maybe she could still get back what she once had, and the Monarch will take her back. Anything is possible.

"He wouldn't want me now. Why would the Monarch want someone who betrayed him? I turned my back on him. I'm the one who picked the other side. It might've only been for a minute but it's over and I've had to accept that. I'm the lost one now." A tear glides down her cheek, and I can't help but feel that she's not really lost. The Monarch doesn't seem like one who would shut her out forever just for one little mistake.

I'm starting to get lost in thought myself, and she quickly wipes the tear from her cheek and turns toward me. "We should really do what we're supposed to do today. Come on," she says as she hands me the book and starts to get up. "You do need to hide this just a wee bit better though. Had your uncle sat there, he would've seen it, and then we would've both been in trouble!"

I take the book from her, and my fingers graze hers. They're so cold. It's almost as if any blood she may have had running through her hands has left and gone somewhere else. She pulls back her hand and puts both of them into her apron pockets.

"You're probably wondering why I closed all of the curtains, aren't you?" Miriam walks across the room, and when she nears the window, she lifts the corner of the curtain and peeks outside.

"Yeah, that had crossed my mind," I say as I reach behind my nightstand to put the diary back. I push it a little farther, and when I step back, I try to find it just by looking, and I can't see even a hint of the brown leather diary.

"Well so far, you've been able to look at what you were trying to influence. Like the locks and the plants, those you could see and then visualize in your head. Today we're going to work on what you can't see. You will need to visualize it in your head from memory … and from what you can see in your mind."

"From memory? How am I supposed to do that? I can't see anything like that in my mind," I interject.

"You will. It might take some practice, and you might not fully get it today, but you will be able to do it eventually." She lifts the curtain a little and looks outside. "Okay, why don't you try to make it cloudy?"

"I don't know how to do that! How am I supposed to just make it cloudy? I don't even know the first thing about doing that." I'm already getting frustrated, and we've only just started.

"You remember your books about the different clouds, right? Why don't you pick one, maybe one of your favorites, and build it in your head." She's a lot calmer than I am, and why wouldn't she be? She's not the one that has to figure out how to do this.

I think back to my books, and there's this one really neat cloud that I saw, but it usually only forms around mountaintops. When I saw the picture in my book, they reminded me of a stack of pancakes that Bao makes for me once in a while. But how am I supposed to make them?

"You can do it," Miriam says as she looks from me to

outside the curtain. She's smiling, and while I'm glad that she's doing that instead of crying, I really don't think I'm going to be able to make a cloud.

I squeeze my eyelids tightly and try to picture it in my head. I clench my fists and grunt. Every muscle in me is tensed. I finally release the tension and look at her. "Anything?"

"Um … no. But good effort! You looked like you were trying really hard!"

"I don't think I can do this! Maybe I don't have this gift. Maybe it skipped me."

"No, you have it. You have them all. That's how they work. Try to remember what a cloud is made up of. It's all elements, just like the locks are made up of elements. These are just different ones."

"Okay." I start going back through what makes up a cloud. Clouds are made up of tiny droplets of water. It's the air that lifts them, and the more droplets of water that are in them, the darker they can become. What are those pancake clouds called again? Lenticular! The lenticular clouds are a little different because they're formed with the way the wind is blowing and if there are any masses to help it. Where she wants me to put a cloud, there's no mountain or hill, and it isn't even that windy out today. At least it wasn't this morning when I was outside eating breakfast. So not only do I have to control the water in the air, I have to make wind and bring it all together. This is so complicated.

I start to picture little droplets of water floating and joining together. I picture them stacking on top of each other but not joining, because that wouldn't make a cloud. That would just make a giant ball of water, and that is definitely not what I'm aiming to do.

I can see in my head more and more water droplets, and I can feel the wind blowing them together. It's almost as if I'm outside looking up at it as it forms. I build one long, stringy cloud, and then I build another and another until I have a stack of five in my head. When I open my eyes to look at Miriam, the look on her face scares me.

"What is it? Is something wrong? Did I make something bad?" I ask as I rush across the room to her.

"I … I've never … you … Patrina … you did it!" she stutters as she pulls the curtain back to reveal a giant stack of clouds just outside my window. "They're beautiful!"

"I did it! I really did it!" I grab her hands and start dancing around the room with her. I can't believe it. I'm overcome with joy, and just as we stop dancing, that's when we both notice that the floor is still moving.

The bed is starting to shimmy across the floor. Books are falling off of the shelf. The floor is rolling under our feet, and we both grab onto anything we can to steady ourselves.

"Stop!" Miriam yells at me over the thundering noises that are bellowing through the room.

"Stop what?" I yell back.

"This earthquake!" she yells as the floor pitches and knocks her off balance. She hits her head on the corner of the shelf, landing on the floor with a sickening thud, and I see her body slump, barely breathing.

Thirty-Six

Earthquake? I know I definitely don't know how to do that! And now the one person who can help me is unconscious on the floor.

Calm yourself, little one, The Guide says.

"How can I calm myself when I don't even know what I did?" I ask aloud.

Your gifts are strong, and if you don't control your emotions, things can happen that you don't know how to handle yet. Take a deep breath.

I do as The Guide tells me, but I'm so scared. How could I have done this? And I hurt Miriam too. Her head is starting to bleed. Oh no—what have I done?

Breathe, little one. Just breathe. It'll be okay.

I close my eyes and focus on my breath, like he taught me to do in the library when I was high up on the ladder. The more I breathe, the calmer I feel, and the floor stops rolling and pitching underneath me. Soon it comes to a stop, and when I open my eyes, Miriam is still unconscious on the floor.

"Why isn't she waking up?" I cry as I rush over to her side. When I kneel on the floor, I see the gash across her forehead, and tears start falling down my cheeks.

You can heal her, Patrina. She can be fixed.

"What … how? No … I can't do that. I can barely make a cloud, and I messed that up, and now look at what happened. Maybe my mother was right. Maybe I shouldn't be messing with any of these gifts."

Don't think like that. You need to learn how to control what the Monarch has given you, not shun it.

"But look what I did! I hurt her, and I didn't mean to. I don't want to be like my ancestors who hurt people. I don't want to be mean or make wars happen. I don't want to do any of this! Can't I just be normal?" I say, wishing that, for once, things could go back to the way they were a few days ago.

You don't have to be like them, dear one. You can choose to be loving and kind. You can be giving and full of grace. You can choose to be who you want to be … as long as you choose to be for the Monarch and not against him. You have to choose to be better than your ancestors and not give in to the temptations of your heart. Do not give up now. Miriam needs you.

"But how? How can I help her?"

Remember the glass, little one … put her back together like the glass …

It feels like forever ago that my uncle brought me the glass that he insisted I put back together. And I didn't know what I was doing back then either. *Elements,* I remind myself, *even we are made up of elements. What were those again … oxygen, nitrogen, carbon … there were six of them. I can't remember them!*

You're getting bogged down with the details. Just let go and remember how she looked before. Remember her before making the cloud today.

I can't stop the flow of tears, and yet I have to forget about that and focus on how she used to look, before she hit her head. I put my fingers on her forehead and close my eyes. I see her kind eyes in my mind first. She's always had the kindest eyes. And then I see her skin, worn with age and years of sadness from dealing with my uncle. I see the edge of her hairline where the white hairs are poking out even though she tries her best to hold them back in a comb. I see her smile, and it makes me feel so much better. In my mind, she's Miriam, the same as she was all those years I saw her as I was growing up.

Suddenly something warm touches my hand, and my eyes shoot open to see Miriam awake in front of me, holding her hand to mine, her head healed of the gash inflicted by my earthquake.

"You're okay!" I squeal as I bend down and wrap my arms around her.

"Yes, yes, I'm fine. What are you talking about?" she says as she pulls away to look at my face.

"Uh, you weren't fine a few minutes ago. Don't you remember?" I look at her and see from the vacant look in her eyes that she has no idea what happened.

"Remember what? We were going to work on clouds." She starts to get up and leans forward, but I stop her and point to the floor where she was laying. There's a spot of blood still on the wooden plank.

"You got hurt." I pull my hand away from her, ashamed that I let my gifts get the better of me.

"What … how did I get hurt? I feel fine." Her kind eyes look at me and are full of alarming puzzlement as she searches my face for an answer.

"We did work on clouds, and I made one …" I start to tell her about what happened when The Guide interrupts me.

You can show her …

What? I ask in my mind.

You can show her what happened. Take her hand and show her with your mind. Be careful not to reveal too much by guarding your thoughts and keeping the ones that only you should know locked away.

"Here," I say as I gently take her hand in mine. "Let me show you ..."

I start to relive what happened. I see her at the curtain, peeking outside, and the clouds in my head. I see the look on her face as she sees them form outside in the sky, and it mirrors the one she has on her face now. She can see what I'm showing her!

As I start to show her the part where we were dancing and skipping around, I see her face change. She's scared, just like we both were when the floor started shifting under our feet. And then I get to the part where she falls and hits her head. She tries to pull her hand out of my grasp, but I hold on tightly because I want her to see what I just learned.

I show her how her body crumpled to the floor and how, even in the dimness of the room, I can see the dark trickle sliding down the side of her face. She's starting to shake and cry. Why is it affecting her so much?

She's feeling your emotions, little one. You're showing her your heart as well.

I continue, trying not to let her fear block what I need her to see, and as I kneel down in my thoughts, I show her how I touched her forehead and put her back together. She's calming down now and starting to relax. And then the biggest grin stretches across her face.

"You can heal!"

"I can!" I squeal.

"How did you learn that?"

"The Guide was with me. He told me how to do it," I explain.

"Like how he helped in the library when you found your mother's diary?"

"Yes! Like that!"

"That's wonderful, Patrina! I'm so happy that he's helping you." Just as quickly, her face changes to confusion. "But I remember something kind of strange now that you showed me all of those flashes of this afternoon."

"What do you mean, strange? Like what?"

She gazes at me with eyes that are show fear as she says, "Vlad … died?"

Thirty-Seven

"Uh … what?" I stammer, trying to remember if I showed her that … or rather, when I showed her that.

"I don't know. It was just there in my head with all of the other stuff you showed me. It was a familiar voice saying it to you. Was that The Guide?" she asks excitedly.

I don't know what to say to her, so I decide to just tell her the truth. Good thing I don't know very much. "Yes, that was The Guide."

"Oh," she says. "Why did he tell you that?"

I can tell by the look on her face that she wishes she was still able to talk with him.

"Because he wanted me to know what I was up against. He didn't tell me much. Just that he had died."

"Is that what his scar is from?"

"Yeah, when we were talking about his scar this morning, that's when The Guide told me. I don't know anything else, but I'm thinking that whatever caused him to die was the turning point in his life and …"

"Whatever caused him to live is how he got his power," she finishes.

"Yes, but I don't know that for sure because The Guide didn't get that far." And it's a good thing that he didn't get that far because then she would know even more of what I wasn't supposed to tell her. This is awful.

It'll be okay, dear one, The Guide says. *Do not fret. She would've learned it eventually. Now is just a little sooner than I wanted.*

You wanted her to know? I ask in my mind.

"You're talking with him now, aren't you?" Miriam asks, jolting my mind back to the room.

"How do you know that?"

"You get a strange look on your face, and if I'm talking to you, you don't seem to notice. It's like you're here but not here. Do you need to finish talking to him or can we move on with learning some more new things?"

You can move on. We will talk later.

"I guess we can move on. What's next?" I ask, wishing that I could talk to The Guide longer, but I guess I do need to learn to control my gifts so I don't accidentally cause another earthquake.

"Well, first we need to put your room back together so that if your uncle comes back, he won't know that you can make earthquakes. And then we really need to see if Bao is okay."

She's right. I hadn't even thought about Bao. We hurry and put all of the books that fell back onto the shelf, and it takes both of us to push my bed back into place. I never considered just how heavy my bed might be until now. We give the room a quick glance over and decide that it looks normal again.

"Shall we go check on the rest of the house?" she asks as she points toward the door that is amazingly still shut and locked.

"Sure. I hope this is the only place that looks this bad."

"Me too, but I don't think we're going to be that lucky," she says with a shrug. She loops her arm around my shoulder as we walk toward the door. Just when we're about four feet from the door, she stops us.

"Go ahead," she says, nodding toward the doorknob. "Try to open it."

"I can only unlock it."

"Are you sure of that?" She has a twinkle in her eyes that makes me think maybe I can do more.

I picture the lock in my mind and quickly unlock it and then I picture the doorknob in my mind. Just like the locks and the clouds, I move them in my head, and I suddenly hear the door unlatch and creak open. This makes me wonder if I can open the door all the way. It's an element too. So I nudge it with my mind, and it swings wide open.

"I knew you could do it!" Miriam exclaims as she gives my shoulders a squeeze.

"How did you know that? Even I don't know these things."

"Because … just because. There are a lot of things you'd be surprised that I know," she says as we near the top of the stairs. When I look down, I see that the rest of the house didn't fare as well as my room.

There's a giant crack along the wall all the way down the staircase. Once we get to the bottom of the stairs, some of the pictures that were on the walls are on the floor, while others are tilted as if someone haphazardly threw them up on the nail. Doors are open that I have never seen open, and I try to steal glances inside, but Miriam rushes me along. As we pass by Bao's wing, I strain to look inside his main room, but I don't see him. He must be in the kitchen … oh … I bet that room is a disaster. I feel so bad. Why did I let my emotions take over and create such a disaster?

We finally make it to the kitchen, and it's just as bad as I thought it would be … maybe worse. All of the cupboard doors are open, and bowls, plates, glasses—everything is scattered or smashed on the floor. The countertops have shards of glass and bits of plates strewn all over them. Even the drawers are open, but those don't seem to have lost anything. They're just messy, as though someone dumped the contents in instead of organizing them.

I look up, and Bao is standing in front of us with his hands full of dishes, utensils, and a toaster. I didn't realize just how big he was until I see him holding all of that. And where did he pick up the toaster from?

"Good morning, Miss Patrina! Quite a shaker we had this morning, didn't we?" Bao says with a little chuckle. At least he seems to be in a good mood. He probably doesn't know that it was my fault.

You mustn't tell him, The Guide says.

Why not? Why must I keep so many things a secret? This gets so irritating.

If Bao knows, then your uncle will know. Hopefully Miriam can keep it a secret for a little longer … till it's time.

Time for what? I ask, knowing the answer.

Time for you to leave. It's very soon, my child. There will be a moment very soon, and you will know.

What do I do? Where do I go? How do I get out of here? You know that he has this place locked down. I can't … I just …

Breathe, child. I will be with you. Smile.

I immediately smile and realize that Bao and Miriam are joking around about how a good shuffle of the house makes it easier to clean.

"Right, Patrina?" Miriam asks as she nudges me with her elbow.

"Right! What can I help with, Bao?"

"Oh boy, I'm not sure, princess. I think I can handle it in here. You must have a million other things you need to get to, right?"

"That's very true," Miriam interjects. "We do have a lot to get done today. We wanted to make sure you were okay, and at least you are. Your kitchen isn't as good," she says as she gently scoots me toward the door.

I wave good-bye to him as I'm ushered into the hallway toward the arboretum. Even the plants in here look a little shaken, and there are leaves and petals on the floor. At least nothing seems broken.

Miriam opens the door to the patio, and once I step through, she closes the door and then gently pulls me so that I'm facing her.

"Patrina, you mustn't feel bad. You didn't know."

"But it's all such a mess … everything is such a mess. How can things be so bad when I was so happy?"

"Strong emotions produce strong results. That's something you need to remember. Fear blocks your gifts, and strong fear seems to short-circuit your gifts, as it did to your ancestors because they disappeared. And apparently happiness can cause an earthquake," she says with a giggle. "But look," she says as she turns me to face the house, "the house is still standing. Yes, it's a mess, yes it will need some repair, but it's still there."

"I guess … I just feel so bad."

Right at that moment, there is a loud bang, and the house begins to shake once more.

"Oh no! I didn't … that wasn't me … did I?" I can't even get the words to form a complete thought because I'm so worried that my sadness and guilt are causing an aftershock.

"No … no, that wasn't you. That's your uncle."

Thirty-Eight

"What is he doing here? I didn't think he was going to be home today. He's going to know!" I'm panicking, and it feels like all of my insides are vibrating. What if he sees all that happened when I made the earthquake? What am I thinking—what if? Of course he's going to see what happened! He's not blind! And when he sees the crack in the wall … is this the sign The Guide was talking about earlier?

"Patrina, calm down! You can't be so afraid or you'll disappear."

"But maybe I want to disappear! Maybe that would be better!"

"No, no it wouldn't. Please, just breathe. Just calm down," she says as she runs her hand up and down my arm. I think she's trying to settle my nerves, but all she's doing is making it worse.

I pull my arm away from her. I start pacing, trying to look in the windows, and say, "I have to leave. This is it. This is what The Guide was telling me. I have to get out of here. If he knows that I did this, and then he knows about that," I point to my shoulder, "then he's going to be mad … or excited … I don't know, but I'm never going to get out of here … ever!"

"It's not time, Patrina! You can't go yet. I haven't taught you all that need to know!"

Yes, special one, The Guide says. *It's time.*

"I knew it!" I exclaim, now trying to make my way through the racing thoughts in my mind.

"Knew what? What are you talking about?" Miriam looks confused and tries to grab my hand as I sprint by her. And then I realize this may be the last time I see her, and I don't want to leave like this. I turn back and go to her and grab her small, warm hand, the hand that raised me through the years. I feel calmer inside now because I know without a doubt that The Guide will be with me, and wherever I go, he will go too.

"The Guide told me that there would be a sign that would let me know when I was to leave. This is it. I love you, Miriam. You're the mother I never had. Really, you're the father I never had too for that matter. I have to go to Arcadia. I know that for sure. I know that I can't be my uncle's slave, and I can't stay here. If I stay, who knows what he will do now that he knows I can make earthquakes. And if he ever knew I healed you … I just have to leave."

"Oh, Patrina …" she says as the tears come to her eyes, "I knew one day you'd leave, but I'm not ready."

Just then, we hear my uncle yelling from inside the house. He's yelling for me. I don't know where he is, but I remember that my mother's diary is upstairs in my room.

"Oh no," I say as I drop Miriam's hands. It's as if she realizes it at the same time.

"The diary," we both say as my shock and panic are mirrored in her eyes.

"I'll try to delay him. I don't know how, but I'll think of something. You need to run! Run as fast as you can and then get out. Don't tell me how because he will force me to tell him everything that I know. And Patrina," the nanny I've had for my entire life gazes at me sadly for what I realize will be the last time, "be safe."

"I will," I whisper as I lean in for a quick hug, and then I run toward the glass room. I try to listen as I run, but my heartbeat is starting to echo in my ears. I reach the arboretum and hide behind one of the tall palms in a corner. I hold my breath long enough to listen, and then I hear him yell.

"Patrina! I know that you're here! And I know what you can do, girl!"

Why does my ability to create an earthquake make him this upset? And how does he know I can do it?

Your uncle has great power too, The Guide says, *and he knows that no other virtue was ever able to do this at your age. You are strong, little one, and he knows it. He knows exactly what he's losing if he loses you.*

I can't even think. It feels as though he's so close. The tiny hairs on the back of my neck are rising as I see him storm into the arboretum nearly six feet from my hiding place. He looks disheveled; his normally perfectly groomed hair is mussed, and his suit jacket is unbuttoned and swinging with every erratic movement. He's so close to me now that I can hear him breathing, and I realize that if I can hear him breathing, then he can hear me too, so I hold my breath and try to stand very still. Suddenly the leaves of the palm slowly and silently move to cover me. Soon I can barely see his head, as only my eyes are able to peek between the leaves.

I didn't make them do that, I think to myself.

Even the palm knows you have great power, dear one.

Just when I think my uncle is going to find me, he races out into the glass room. I tiptoe out from behind the potted palm and lean so that I'm barely looking into the glass room. He's in there looking under the table, and with a huff he storms outside where Miriam is waiting. I decide this is my chance to make a dash up to my room. I fly out of the arboretum, turn the corner, and see my uncle coming face-to-face with Miriam through the giant glass window.

"Where is she, Miriam? I know she's here. She did that!" he yells as he points back to the house. I duck just below the trim around the window and start to creep along the floor, hoping that the top of my head doesn't poke up high enough for him to see me.

"She's not here. Why don't you sit down, and I'll get you something cold to drink. You look like you've run a marathon," she says. I peek over the trim to see her starting to go back toward the house. Why would she do that? She knows I'm running to hide. Why would she redirect him back into the house?

"You're not getting me anything unless it's that girl!" And with that, my uncle lunges at her and clasps his hands around her neck.

"Vlad! Calm yourself! You don't want to do this!" she says as she desperately claws at his hands to release her.

"What I want is that girl! And if you're going to stand in my way, then you leave me no other choice!"

I watch as he starts to lift her up by her throat, and just as her feet start to come off the ground, The Guide urgently whispers to my heart, *Run!*

How can I leave her when he's hurting her?

Run, Patrina, run!

I hunker back down, and even though I know I should run, I just can't leave her in his clutches. I peek back over the trim and see a climbing rose nearby. I concentrate and am able to get one of its thorny tentacles to move toward him. I hear her pleading with him to release her, and I urge the rosy vine to quickly wrap around his ankle, piercing his flesh with each needle-like thorn. I get an earful of him hollering in pain, and just as I pass the window, I stand up so I can sprint down the hallway. I pass the kitchen and see

Bao in there working on putting the last of the dishes back into the cabinet.

"Patrina, what are you …" he starts to say as I dash past. I can't tell him what's going on. Both he and Miriam are totally under my uncle's control, and if I don't get out of here, I'm going to be just like them. Maybe worse.

I take the corner by the paradise door too fast and skitter into it. At the very touch of my hand, the river that is carved into the door becomes actual water, and my hand slides in up to my wrist. I feel the ruby doorknob beneath my hand and use it to push myself back up onto my feet. I regain my balance and start to run again just as I hear my uncle come slamming into the glass room. I don't hear Miriam …

Run, little one. She cannot help you now.

What do you mean she can't help me now? I can't even fathom what might've happened to her, and I feel my heart racing as panic starts to close its grip around my throat.

Just run. Get the diary.

I dash down the hallway, past Bao's rooms, and climb the stairs up to my tower, taking them two at a time. My legs are starting to burn, but I have to keep going. I reach the top, slide around the curved hallway, and bash into my closed bedroom door. Why didn't it open?

I try to close my eyes and envision the lock opening, but there's something in the way, like whatever was protecting the lock to the roof garden. Like an enchantment. I remember that I had to push that out of the way before I could get to the tumblers inside, so in my mind I sweep the enchantment aside like a giant curtain. With part of my mind, I have to hold the enchantment out of the way while the other part of my mind works on the tumblers. One tumbler. Two. Three and then four. Why won't the fifth one budge?

Calm yourself, The Guide urges. *Remember, you have to stay calm; otherwise your gifts won't work the way you need them to.*

I take a deep breath, relax my shoulders, and with a loud clack, the fifth tumbler moves out of place and takes it spot with the others. I reach for the knob, turn it, and barge into my room. And then it hits me. If I'm never coming back here, I will need more than my diary.

I scramble into my closet and look around. There must be something in here that I can use to carry some things with me. I push back some of my clothes that are hanging on a rod and look down at the floor and find a backpack. I grab it. I have no idea how it got in here or why it would be in here, but I'm glad that I have it. I unzip one of the compartments as I race over to my bed. I shove my hand behind my nightstand and accidentally shove the diary farther behind the bed. Why is this happening now?

I sink to my knees and bend over so that I can try to fish it out from behind the headboard. My fingers are barely able to touch the binding. Wait. The diary is made out of elements. Maybe I can move it toward me! Just as I start to think that I can move it, I hear my uncle downstairs slamming open the doors in Bao's hallway. He's way too close!

I stretch my fingers as far as they can go, and I can hear the diary slide a little. I try again, and I hear it slide a little more, but I can't even touch the binding anymore. I'm pushing it away from me! No! I have to get it, and I don't have time to figure out how, so I slam my shoulder into my bed and scoot it across the floor just enough that I can grab the leather strap that wraps around the book and drag it to me. I snatch up the diary and finally shove it into my backpack. I race back to my closet to grab a jacket because if I'm going to go out there into the big, wide world, I'll at least need a jacket.

I hit the threshold to my closet and hear my uncle at the bottom of the stairs. "Patrina!"

I find the first jacket that I come across, which is a little heavier than the other one I have, and shove it into my backpack. I find a blanket sitting on a chest in the corner and grab that too and shove it in. Just as I'm about to run out of my closet, I see the key that I found in the tunnels laying on the floor next to the hamper. It must've fallen out when Miriam put my clothes in there. I quickly bend down and snatch it up, shoving it into the front pocket of my jeans. I don't take any time to zip my pack before I dash out of my room. I quietly close the door behind me and let the enchantment fall back into place as I hear him coming up the stairs. He's coming quickly, too quickly. I remember the secret door in the wall and nudge it open with my mind. I pry it all the way open with my fingertips and slip inside. Just as I'm clicking it closed, I hear him barreling down the hall toward my bedroom.

I start to move away from the secret door and realize that I haven't been breathing and sweat is beading on my upper lip. I take in a deep breath and let it out as I wipe the sweat off of my face with the back of my hand. Now what?

You must get a flashlight, little one.

Thirty-Nine

While I'm thankful that The Guide is giving me cues, how am I supposed to get a flashlight? I'm stuck in the wall with a crazed uncle on the other side.

Miriam's closet, dear one.

Oh yeah! I forgot that she keeps one just inside her closet on the shelf. I turn toward the set of skinny steps and start to go down them. I can still hear my uncle ravaging my room. It sounds like he's turning over every piece of furniture in his search for me.

When I hit the bottom of the stairs, I try to run through the hall that Miriam had built years ago between the walls. I forgot just how tight it was in here, especially with a backpack. Every stride I make causes my pack to hit the wall and creates a thud that I'm sure my uncle will hear. I quickly slide it off of my shoulder and rotate sideways so that I can hold it in front of me. Maybe if I zip it shut, it will take up less space. I start to zip it but stop almost immediately. It amazes me just how loud a zipper can seem when you're trying to be quiet. I decide to just do it quickly, like ripping off a bandage.

Once I get it zipped shut, I stay motionless and listen. He's still throwing things above me, so I'm pretty sure he didn't hear me. I throw my pack back onto my back, turn around so that

I'm facing the right direction again, and start making my way toward Miriam's closet. My pack still thuds if I run, so I take it off and hold it. It's harder to run while I'm holding it, but at least I can run and not make quite so much noise.

Finally I see the doorway up ahead and realize that the lights in here were left on. Did Miriam turn them on for me in case I needed to make my way through here? Or was someone else back here? She didn't know that today was the day I would be trying to escape. Even I didn't know that.

I shake the thought from my head that someone else has been in here because it's not going to do me any good right now. I push the door open that goes into her closet. The hangers on the other side clang, and I freeze in place.

I forgot about those!

I stand and listen for a few seconds, and when I don't hear anything, I push the door open enough to get my hand through to push the hangers out of the way. Once I move those, I push the door open the rest of the way and slip inside the closet.

I start looking around for the flashlight that I know she keeps in here, but I can't seem to find it. Where did she put that? I see a shelf up high above the rod that holds all of the hangers full of her clothes and start feeling around up there. As my hand bounces around on the top of the shelf, my fingers bump into something, and I accidentally knock it from the top of the shelf. It hits the floor with a loud thud. That's when I hear the footsteps in the hallway.

"Patrina!"

How did he get over to this end of the house so fast?

I look down to see that it was a shoe that fell from the shelf and I continue feeling around high up out of my sight. My fingers finally touch what feels like the flashlight, and just as my fingers graze it, I hear him bust in through Miriam's bedroom door. Oh no! Now he's in here!

I jump up and grab at the metal cylinder and pull it down,

thankful that it is the flashlight, but I hear him making his way toward me. I spin on my feet and turn to pry open the secret door just as his foot clears the doorway into the closet.

"I found you! Get back here, girl!"

I quickly slip into the hallway in the wall and pull the door shut with my all of my weight. I nervously latch the door behind me, and before I can stop shaking, I start to make my way down the hallway. It's not going to take him long to find the secret button on the wall to make the door open. Where is the other door? The one to the tunnels that Bao made?

I slide the flashlight into my back pocket and start tracing my fingers along the wall. My uncle is yelling and banging on the wall inside Miriam's closet, and I know it's not going to take long before he busts through. I have to get that secret door open before he gets in here!

I run my fingers all over the wall. Up one way and down another. Finally I find the button and push it. I'm barely inside the door and starting to close it when I hear the button to the secret door in Miriam's closet unlatch that door. I pull to shut the door to Bao's tunnels, but something is in the way. I look down, and there's a rock that must've come in off of my shoe. I glance back at the door to the closet, and he's almost got it open. As I hear Miriam's wire hangers clanging, I nudge the rock inside Bao's tunnels with my toe and quickly shut the door. Within seconds, I hear him running down the tiny hallway, slamming into the walls as he goes.

The realization that I barely made it out of his clutches hits me, and I sink to the dirt floor. How am I ever going to get out of here? How am I ever going to get out of the house?

Not yet, The Guide says.

What? What do you mean not yet? You told me to go, so I did! You need three more things, little one.

I can barely stand it. I hardly got this far, and now I have to go back and get something else? *How important is this?* I ask The Guide in my mind.

Very.

Okay ... what is it? Can you at least tell me where to find it so that I'm not out in the house too long? If he catches me, he's going to lock me up in that tower and use some super-powerful enchantment that I can't break. Just the very idea of going back out there is making my skin crawl and my stomach feel all flip-floppy. This is awful.

Patrina, my special one, there are going to many adventures ahead of you on your way to Arcadia that will make you feel as though you can't do it. You're going to be led to believe by those around you that you aren't strong enough, that you aren't smart enough, or that you're too young to be able to do whatever you need to do to get to Arcadia. Do not believe them. There are many out there who know who you are without you even meeting them. You must be wary of the ones you take as allies because they may not be allies at all. I will be with you through it all to guide you to where you need to go. Sometimes I will ask you to do what may seem like the impossible, but rest assured it is only to get you to the next part of your journey.

Is that why you're telling me that there's more that I have to get out of the house? My adventure to Arcadia seems as though it's going to be much harder than I thought. I guess I thought that if I could get out of here, the biggest trouble I would have would be blisters on my feet from walking so much.

Oh, dear one, blisters will be the least of your worries.

Ugh! I always forget he can hear my thoughts. *Okay, what do I need to get?*

Remember the room that had the lion's head in the table?

Yes. That was a weird room.

Bao's tunnels go right up to the secret door to the storage room that connects to that room. Remember that?

Yes.

Inside that storage room, there was that seam in the wall. That's the secret door into the great room. In that room, there are two tables. One has the lion's head in it, and one has a set of keys, a map, and five stones. You must get those. You will need them along your way.

Uh ... those were stuck inside a table. As in, I can't get them out.

When the time comes, you will know what to do. Do not let your uncle see you. You are right. He will lock you up and never let you go if he catches you.

Great.

I wonder why I need those little trinkets so badly that I have to risk going back into the house. I get back up on my feet, brush the dirt off of my pants, sling the pack back onto my shoulders, and start going down the steps from Miriam's section. I still haven't heard her anywhere. I hope she's okay.

It's so dark in here. I can't make out the next step, and I'm afraid that if I try, I'm going to miss, and then I'll fall down the rest of them. This is no time to get hurt. I dig out the flashlight that I tucked in my back pocket and click it on. I hope these are new batteries. The last time I used a flashlight, it stopped working when I needed it most.

I shine the circle of light onto the steps in front of me and make my way down to the dirt landing below. It's easy to get lost in here, but I picture the layout of the house in my mind, and if I was just at Miriam's room, then that must mean the great room is up ahead and to the right. I see the torches on the walls and wish I had some matches because then I wouldn't have to use up the batteries in my flashlight. And then it hits me. When I was down here before, I did light the torches but never put them out. Yet they aren't lit right now. Someone must've been down here for sure! Maybe Bao was working in his tunnels.

I finally see the steps that go up to the landing that leads to the door inside the storage room that's just behind the great room. The picture of my father is in there. I remember seeing his face in the portrait that he and my mother sat for all those years ago. I also remember the slash through the painting that could only have come out of pure anger and jealousy.

I trudge up the steps to the landing, and I really don't want to go inside. Where do I go once I get the stuff The Guide wants me to get?

Back in the tunnels, sweet one. You need to go back in here and make sure to close the doors behind you.

I guess that's all I need to know for now, otherwise he would've told me more, right?

Right.

Ugh.

I pry open the door with my fingertips and wedge it open. Once I can see inside, I realize that I should've checked first before I opened it all the way. He could've been in the storage room looking for me. I need to be more careful.

I step inside and walk past the stack of paintings that I know holds the one of my father, past the knickknacks and memories stacked in boxes, and finally make my way to the door at the other end. This must be the secret door that my uncle knows about because this room holds all of his treasures.

I stand still and put my ear to the door so I can listen to the room just on the other side of it. I don't hear anything, so I trace my fingers around the edge of the door. How does this one work? Miriam's secret door has a hidden button in the woodwork, but this isn't her door. This is my uncle's.

There doesn't seem to be a button in the woodwork, not like all the other doors I've encountered. And there's not a hole for a key.

Close your eyes and see the door in your mind, child.

I close my eyes, and it's like they aren't closed at all because I can still see the door in front of me, except it looks different. I can see a glow all over it. The door is enchanted! That makes sense! If my uncle enchanted it, then even Miriam and Bao can't get into it.

It's the same color as the enchantment he put on my door upstairs. He must not have gotten to changing it since I was able to move it from my door. I push the enchantment away like I'm pushing a giant, heavy curtain aside, and when I get it out of the way, I open my eyes and see that the door now floats open. I have to keep my back to the enchanted curtain so that I can hold it out of my way as I grasp the edges of the door and slowly push it open just a smidge. I look into the room. I don't see anyone. I don't hear anyone either. I open the door just a little more and begin to step inside.

And then I hear something. Are those footsteps?

Forty

I quickly pull my foot back inside and quietly close the door. I stand there for a few seconds and listen as the footsteps thud away into another part of the house. I take a deep breath and try to calm the jittering I feel inside. I'm sure it's my uncle. I don't know where he's going now, but I know he's not here, so I take advantage of the moment and scramble into the room with the plush carpet and half-circle couches. Once I move out of the way of the enchantment, the door closes behind me. That might be a problem later, but first I have to get those trinkets out of that table.

I rush over to one of the tables and look inside. I almost fall backwards in shock even though I already know what's in there. Why would anyone put that lion's head in a table?

I regain my balance and run over to the other table. There it is. All of it. The keys on the ring that reminded me of the keys to a pirate ship, the folded-up paper that must be the map, and the strange five rocks that don't look like rocks at all—at least not the kind I've seen down in the tunnels.

How am I going to get this stuff out?

I know The Guide can hear my thoughts, and yet he's staying quiet, which means I need to figure this out on my own. I realize he's teaching me stuff, but sometimes I wish he would just tell me what I need to do next.

I kneel down onto the carpet, and my knees are swallowed up by the long fibers. I could sleep on this! It's so soft! As I lean over to feel the top of the table, my pack slides off of my shoulder and flings in front of me. This is not going to work. I slide my arm out and let the pack flop onto my lap, and then I shove it onto the floor.

I run my fingers across the top of the table and then down the sides. There's a lip just under the top, and I run my fingertips under the edge, searching for a seam or a latch, anything that will let me open the top.

This is taking too long!

There's nothing.

I have no idea how he got this stuff in there or how I'm going to get it out. Maybe he had the table made around these trinkets. If that's the case, the only way I'm going to get in is if I break it, but if I break it, he's going to hear me shattering the glass, and then I'm not going to have enough time to get the items and get out.

Suddenly the memory of fixing the glass flashes into my mind. When I touched it, it was as if I could melt the glass back together. I wonder …

I set my hand on top of the glass in the table. At first nothing happens, but then I feel it starting to melt under my touch. I put both of my hands on top, and now it's really melting. I dig my fingertips into the glass and peel it back! When I let go, it immediately hardens, and I'm left with a hole that my hand can fit inside. I stretch my hand in, just past my wrist, and I can get at the little treasures.

As I'm scooping up the keys and pulling them out, I realize that I haven't heard my uncle for a while. I don't know where he is, and if he's this quiet, I need to move fast. He might be watching me from somewhere, but if he saw what I was doing, he wouldn't be watching in silence.

I toss the keys into my pack, grab the map, and toss that in too. I go back in for the rocks, and when I touch the first one, it starts to glow. It goes from a dull brown to a vibrant green. That's weird, but I don't have time to look at it, so I toss that in my pack too. When I pick up the next rock, this one glows too, but this one is orange. Each rock I touch glows a different color, and as I put them into my pack, I take note of the different ones. First green, then orange, then blue, now yellow, and the last one doesn't glow.

At first.

I'm so surprised that this one doesn't glow that I sit back on my heels and just look at it. Rolling it over in my palm, letting the rock catch the light in the room and glitter, it finally starts to change. It's dull at first, just a glimmer of red. And then it starts to get brighter as I hear the footsteps. The closer the footsteps get, the brighter red it glows. This one must be linked to him!

I toss the rock into my pack and sling it back up onto my shoulder. I wanted to put the glass back the way I found it, but I don't think I have time. I zip my pack shut and get up onto my feet and start to scamper across this dreamy carpet that seems to keep every step a quiet whisper. I finally get to the door and try to pry it back open, but it won't budge, and the footsteps are getting closer!

I don't have time to keep trying! I have to find a place to hide! My eyes dart around the room, and I see the bar. Maybe I can hide behind it. I race to the end of the countertop, brace my hand on the end, and use it to slingshot myself behind it as I hear the footsteps nearing the entry to the room.

I hunker down so that he can't see me, but that also means that I can't see him. I can only listen to the sounds in the room, and the beating of my heart is drowning them out. I crawl to the farthest corner and try to cram myself under the counter, but there are glasses and bottles in the way. If I get too close, I'm sure I'll bump something, and then he'll know exactly where I am. I ball myself up as tightly as I can and hope he doesn't look behind the bar.

"Patrina, come on. You can come out. I just want to talk," Vlad says from somewhere in the room.

He sounds calmer. Maybe it'll be okay?

"I promise I won't get mad. Come on now," he urges. He must be close because I can smell his musky cologne.

Should I go out there? Where's The Guide? Why isn't he telling me if I can go out or not?

"Patrina! This is enough! You get out here right this minute!" His voice is rising, and it sounds as though he stomped his foot or threw something down.

"Girl!"

Something crashes on the other side of where I'm hiding, and I start to shake. It sounds like he's throwing the furniture around the room. It's like the noises that were coming from my room earlier but much, much louder. I hear something slide and then bang against a wall. What if he looks back here?

"Girl, if you do not come out right this minute, you will never see the light of day!" he screams as something slams into the other side of the bar.

I must've jumped because the glasses that are right by my elbow clank together and teeter on the verge of crashing down all over the shelf I'm nestled up against. And then there's just eerie silence … the kind of silence that only happens when someone stops what they're doing because they've found something else.

"What is this? You *are* in here! Only you could do this to my table! Girl! I know you melted this glass! The only other one who could do this was your mother, and she's gone. You will never see her again, so you might as well give up. You won't find her in Arcadia. Don't even bother going there. I know that Miriam pumped your head full of lies about how if you go to Arcadia, you'll be free, but you won't be. You'll never be free, and you'll never find your mother. Or your father. I took care of him myself. That's right, little one! Daddy's never coming home! I'm all you've got!" He throws something else across the room, and it smashes into the wall.

I hear his footsteps shuffling my way. A wave of cologne makes its way to my nostrils, and I cringe at the smell. And then a loud thud comes from the top of the bar. He must've slammed his fist into the top because a rain of splinters falls around me.

And then he stops.

"Patrina?"

Oh no … did he see me? He could've easily looked over the edge and seen my foot or something.

I hear him dragging his hand down the top of the bar, and as it nears the end, I see his foot peek out from behind it. He's going to see me—and then what?

"Patrina?"

Forty-One

His other foot makes its way around the end of the bar, and suddenly he's standing in front of me. Why isn't he saying anything? He's not even looking at me, and I'm right here. I'm right in front of him.

He leans over and sets his elbows on the bar and then lays his face in his palms. What's he doing, and why isn't he coming at me? Can't he see me? I look down at where my feet were, and all I see is carpet. I can feel my legs resting against the back of the bar, but all I see are the shelves that hold the glasses. What happened? Even my pack that I'm holding is gone, but I can still feel it. Am I disappearing from fear? I don't want to disappear because nobody knows where they go, but if I become visible again, he's going to see me. How can I stay invisible until he leaves so I can get back into the tunnel?

Dear one, you're overthinking it again. Keep it simple.

Can I just stay invisible? He's right there! The panic inside is engulfing every cell in my body and taking over. How can I be overthinking this? As I sit here freaking out, my uncle stands back up and starts looking around the room again. He doesn't know how close he is to me.

I know you've been told that when others like you have gotten scared, they disappear but because no one was able to see them,

241

they didn't know where they went … or if they ever reappeared, The Guide says. *Sometimes only half of a story is just that … half of a story. And when people don't know the other half or don't understand it, they tend to fill in the rest with the wrong information. You will not disappear and end up lost somewhere, my child.*

What? But I thought … then where did my mother go? She disappeared, didn't she?

Did she?

That's what Miriam told me.

That's just half of a story, special one. Right now, you have other things to concern yourself with though. You will learn more about your ancestors and your mother at a later time. Controlling this new gift is definitely linked to your fear. Miriam was right when she told you that. You can control it without being afraid too. This is one of those gifts that will be very important in your journey.

Great, but I'm never going to get to this journey at this rate. How am I going to get out of here? He's still looking for me in here.

You can create a diversion, but it's going to take some work.

What kind of diversion? What do you mean? My mind is racing as my uncle steps away from the bar, and I hear him rustling around in the room.

"You really are strong, Patrina," my uncle mutters from somewhere behind the bar.

The Guide says, *You can make something make noise …*

… Somewhere else in the house! I finish as the idea comes flooding into my head. I just have to see it in my mind, that's all. There was a tall vase by the arboretum. Now if I can just tip it. I remember how it was nearly up to my waist, and it had all of these little pictures on it painted in blue and white. I start to see it wobble in my mind, first one way and then the other. I push it harder in my mind, and then my ears are filled with a shattering crash from the other end of the house.

"I found you!" my uncle yells as he storms out of the room and down the hallway. I look down and see my legs and feet start to reappear again. It would be nice if I could control that gift, but for now I can at least make my escape back into the tunnel.

I stand up just high enough that I can peek over the top of the bar, and when I see that the room is clear, I swing the pack up onto my shoulder. As it lands with a thud against my back, I mentally make sure I put everything into it that I needed to get: the map, the keys, and the five stones. I can hear him racing down the hall. He must've slid to a stop because it sounds like glass skittering across the floor. I fly around the end of the bar and dash over to the hidden door. How can I get it open again? This one had that weird veil of enchantment over it. I close my eyes even though I'm freaking out inside and quickly push the veil aside in my head. The door pops open just enough that I can pry my fingertips under the lip and open it up so that I can slip inside. I let the veil slide back over the door, but something is wrong. It's not falling back into place, and the door isn't shutting. If the door had opened the other way, I could've propped something against it from inside the storage room to keep it shut.

"Patrina!"

My uncle bellows my name down the hallway, and it sounds like he's coming back this way. I have no idea how to get this door shut. I decide that I have to just leave it. I don't have time to try to get it shut because what if I can't, and then he finds me in here—or worse, what if he sees me going into the tunnel?

I pull it closed as much as I can and turn on my heels to run to the back of the storage room. Just as I'm about to unlatch the door, I hear him. He's in the room again. He's right there.

I can't breathe. It feels like my whole world is crumbling around me, and I'm suffocating. I'm fumbling, trying to trace my fingers around the door to find the switch, but I can't get this door to open!

"Patrina … are you hiding in my storage room? Come on out, girl. I know you're in there."

Oh no … my fingers crazily skitter around the opening, and they're feeling raw. Ugh! Why won't this door open? I finally feel the switch and push it. The door pops open, and I try to slip inside, but something is in my way.

"Patrina. Come on out. Let's talk."

He's pulling the door open.

I can't get out.

I look to my feet, and see it's a painting. My father's portrait has fallen in my way. I flip it back, not really caring if it makes any noise, and now I can shimmy behind the secret door and latch it as quickly and quietly as possible.

Did he see me?

Should I wait and listen?

As much as my curiosity wants me to wait and listen, I know I have to move. I have to get out of here. I secure my pack onto my back by slipping the other strap over my right shoulder and start to go down the dirt stairs to the landing below. It's so dark in here that I can't see anything. I feel around with my toes, but it's just too hard to tell if I'm finding the stair or not. I reach back to my pocket to pull out the flashlight, but it's not there. Where could it be? Where did it go? Did I drop it?

I'm panicking as I mentally trace my steps and try to think of where it could've possibly fallen out. Maybe it fell out onto that plush carpet by the table? If that's the case, there's no way I can get it now. I can't go back in there. I'd be walking right back into my uncle's arms and imprisonment for the rest of my life.

What did I do with it?

I walk back up toward the secret door. I can see a small,

thin line of light peeking through the seam, and I hear him throwing things around inside his storage room. Just as I get right up next to the door, my foot kicks something, and it rolls away. I kneel down and begin to feel around in the dirt, patting all over in hopes that what I kicked is what I think it is. I pat around in front of me toward where I think it rolled, and just as I'm about to give up, my fingers touch something cold and metallic. I grab the familiar cylindrical body. As I trace the edges, I slip my thumb over the end and find the button. It's my flashlight!

I breathe a sigh of relief as I push the button and stand back up, now able to see the steps leading downward. It would've been a nightmare trying to find my way around without any light, and I don't know if Bao has any other packs of matches down here to light those torches. Speaking of Bao, I haven't seen or heard him in all of this. I hope he's okay. I know my uncle is an evil man, but would he hurt him? Could he hurt him? Bao is pretty big.

I stumble down the crude dirt steps, and when I reach the bottom, I start to make my way back to the tunnel. I don't really know where to go from here. I can't stay down here the rest of my life.

Just as I near the opening to the main tunnel, I see something flickering. Is my flashlight dying already? I hope not! The very thought sends a chill over my skin, and goose bumps radiate down my arms.

I click it off just to see if the strange glimmering stops, but it doesn't. What is going on? I strain my eyes as I turn to look down the tunnel a little farther. What is that? Is that …
a torch?

Forty-Two

I throw myself against the wall and try to hide. He couldn't have gotten down here this quickly, could he have? Last thing I knew, my uncle was tossing around the storage room.

The light is getting closer and brighter. The brighter it gets, the more I'm lit up, and my hiding spot against the wall isn't good enough. Whoever it is, they will find me here soon. Why can't I become invisible now? What good is a gift like that if you can't use it when you want to?

I close my eyes. Whoever is down here with me is so close that I can hear their footsteps plodding in the dirt. The steps aren't the same as my uncle's. They have a longer stride. Like someone who is bigger than him. The memory of the nine-foot tall man flashes into my mind and scares me enough to open my eyes. If it's him, I want to see his face.

"Patrina?"

It's a man's voice but not my uncle's. Someone familiar though. I can't see who it is because he is holding the torch by his head, and the light is too bright for my eyes. I shield my eyes from the light as I cringe away from the man standing before me.

"Patrina? Is that you?"

That voice … I know it.

"Bao?" I ask.

"Oh, princess! What are you doing down here? Yes, it's me. Why are you still here?" He quickly lights a torch on the wall near me and finds a holder on the wall to place his torch. Once his hands are free, he grabs me into the biggest bear hug I think I have ever encountered. His massive arms wrap all the way around me, and I feel like if anyone were to look at this man, they wouldn't even see me inside his embrace.

"I'm trying to get out, but I had to get a few things."

Be careful what you say, little one, The Guide warns me. *Enemies can seem like allies for a time.*

"What did you need to get that you had to go back in there? He's so angry! I came down here to hide!" He lets go of me enough that I can feel the cool air of the tunnel on my skin again.

"Just a few things that I couldn't leave without. You scared me! I thought you were my uncle when I saw the torch."

"Oh," he starts, "you're uncle does not know of my tunnels. He knows of Miriam's passageways because he watches her very closely. Even she doesn't know."

"Know what?"

"Your uncle has cameras all over this big mansion. He has a whole wall of monitors in his wing, and he watches us all. I found them one day when I went into his wing to bring him something to eat, and he got really angry … though not as angry as today."

"So that's why …" I'm putting things together in my head.

"That's why what?" He lets his arms drop from around me and shoves his giant hands into his front pockets. I'm surprised his hands can fit in there.

"That's why Miriam was so upset when I almost went into his wing the first time I was able to make my way through the house."

"Oh, well, she doesn't know about the cameras. But Vlad

has gotten very upset with her for seeing other things that he's hiding in there," he says as he kicks at the dirt between us.

"There's other things?" The feeling of dread is welling up in my throat. I'm not so sure I want to know what these other things are now that I think about it.

"We don't know for sure all that's in his wing because he's very explosive when he finds us in there, like that day I tried to bring him some breakfast while he was working in the office in his wing. I had a tray filled with all sorts of delicious treats, but when I got in there and saw him sitting at the desk, looking up at the monitors, it was as though he had eyes in the back of his head! I swear I didn't make a sound, and he whipped around and yelled at me to get out. The booming of his voice scared me so badly that I dropped the tray and ran. I've never been back in there since."

"But what else did you see? You said there were other things." I have to know all that I can about this uncle if I'm ever going to get away from him.

"Oh yeah! There was this strange, old, medieval-looking goblet."

"A goblet?" *What's so bad about that?* I wonder.

"Yeah, it was silver and had these stones on the sides of it that were all different colors. But that wasn't the weirdest part. There was something inside the goblet that was glowing red!"

I think back, and the only things I've ever seen glow red was my uncle's scar and that rock I put in my pack. I wonder what the goblet has to do with anything. And where did it come from? I know he collects a lot of strange things from all over the world, but the fact that it glows red makes me wonder if it has more to it than just being a medieval-looking goblet.

I look up at Bao and see him staring back at me.

"Lost in thought, tower princess?"

"I'm just trying to make sense of it all. And get out of here. Do you know how I can get out? I can't go back into the house, obviously."

"It is a lot to try to put together. I know. I've been trying to understand it all for years, and I still haven't figured it all out. Miriam has secrets too. Well, at least she did," he says as he looks away.

"What do you mean *did*?"

"The last time I saw her was this morning when she was out on the patio and he was yelling at her. That was my cue to hide. I haven't seen or heard her since then, and with how angry your uncle was … I'm not sure we ever will. He has a way of making people disappear."

Does he know about my mother? Just as I'm about to ask, Bao changes the subject.

"You needed to get out of here, right?"

"Yes. Do you know a way out?"

"Well, sort of," he says hesitantly. "I just finished it the other day. I was a bit surprised at the outcome myself, and I don't exactly know how to escape necessarily. Do you remember when I told you to stay to the one side of the tunnel and not to go down the other tunnel?"

So much has happened since then that I have to think back and replay it in my head.

"Yes … yes, I think I do." I look down toward where that tunnel was and remember that I really wanted to go down it at the time, but I had to stick to the tunnels under the house.

"I've been working on a way out of here. I thought that maybe someday, when your uncle was away on a trip, I could escape through the tunnel I dug. You know, escape without being caught on camera. So the other day when I finished it, and I popped out on the other side, I was disappointed. I think my calculations were off a little."

"Where does it go?" I ask, even though this doesn't sound like it's going to work.

"It ends in the maze."

Forty-Three

"Oh no ..." Now it seems that my way out, my only hope for escape, just got thrown out because that maze shifts and turns. "Anyone going in only gets turned around to end up in the same spot they started."

"I know," Bao says. "I could keep digging and shift over a bit. Maybe then I could get it to come up beyond the maze. It would take a while, and I don't know where you could hide that long." The look on his face is depressing.

"I don't have that kind of time, Bao. He's hunting me, and it's only a matter of time before he finds your tunnels, especially now that the end is in the middle of his maze. He will know that someone has been digging, and then he'll find me ... and probably you." I rub my hand over my face. I feel the grit on my skin, and I know that I am covered in the filth of the underground.

I close my eyes and lean against the dirt wall. I'm tired. I'm so tired of running. If I give up now, what will he do? Will he be thankful that I decided to stay? No, my inner conscious butts in to remind me of all the threats he has vehemently spewed in his hunt of me just today. I either get out or I stay as his prisoner. I roll to my side on the wall and feel the prick of the impending feather as it sends a spike down my spine to foretell of its coming. There's no other choice.

I slide the flashlight into my back pocket, reach up, and take the lit torch from its holder as I look up at Bao.

"Neither one of us has any choice but to try to get out of the maze. Let's go to that tunnel, Bao. Let's see what we're dealing with."

"Yes, Miss Patrina!" he says with the excitement of a little kid as he grabs one of the other torches off of the wall.

"The tunnel is long," he warns, "and there are some things along the way that I found … things that surprised even me."

"What kind of things?" I ask. He's starting to scare me. What have I gotten myself into?

"I'm afraid it would be best if you saw them. Maybe you know what they are since Miriam was teaching you. Maybe she told you the history of this place. She was here long before I was, and I don't know very much about the building of the mansion."

I nod my head, and he turns to start leading the way to our escape. Miriam didn't tell me much about the history of this place. The only thing she ever mentioned was how she helped to make sure everything was built according to plan, and she added her back passageways at the very beginning. What could he have found anyway? Whatever it is must've been buried at the time of the building or was here long before the mansion was built. I'm not sure Miriam would've known about it anyway.

We make our way down the tunnel toward Bao's entrance from his room, and we come to the split. I feel the cool breeze coming from it like I did when I first saw it. He must've finished this before I came down here the first time.

I follow him as we enter this new tunnel, and there are torches in here too, though not as many as in the main tunnel that goes under the house. He lights them as we go, and each one casts a yellow glow on the dirt walls ahead of us. We walk for quite a while before we turn to the right. I feel a little disoriented, but it seems like this is going back toward the house. Why would he do that?

I start seeing strange marks in the wall. They look like claw marks, dragging their way down this long corridor. I look up ahead, and Bao is still walking with his back to me and doesn't pay any attention to these marks. Does he know how they got here? Did he do this? Is this how the nine-foot giant got in?

Suddenly the light from my torch catches the glint of something to my left. Bao is still walking and doesn't see that I've stopped. I slide my torch back and forth in the air, trying to find the glimmer that caught my attention moments ago, and I finally see it light up again. I strain my eyes and try to see what it is when it vanishes. What is that?

"Oh, you stopped. I'm sorry. I didn't realize. I just noticed that I couldn't hear your footsteps anymore." I look up toward his voice and see that he has turned around and is starting to make his way back toward me.

"I saw something … something shiny," I say, moving my torch to see if I can locate it in the dirt.

"Yes, there are many strange things down here," he says hesitantly. He doesn't come too close but just watches me.

My torch flickers in the wind that is coming from somewhere at the end of this tunnel, and when it does, the thing in the wall lights up again, and I can see that it's long and thin. I hold my torch still and walk toward it, now focused on where it is, and when I get up close to it, I reach out my finger.

"I wouldn't touch it," Bao warns.

"Why not?" I stop with my finger in midair.

"I've just found some things down here that I wish I hadn't touched is all. I don't know what it is you've found, but you should be careful."

That makes sense. I get as close as I can with my torch

and just look at it. It's hard to make it out, even with the light from my fire. I decide to touch it anyway, and I stretch out my finger, tracing the glimmer from my torch. It's a little rough, but there are tiny specks of something that shine when light hits it. I use my fingers to brush away more of the dirt around it and find that it's really close to something that's very similar. I brush some of the dirt away from the end and see there's a third part. Each one of these pieces is thicker on the ends and thinner in the middle. And that's when I realize what I've been touching …

These are bones! They look like the bones of a finger! A huge finger!

I quickly draw back my hand. Bao comes closer. "What is it?" he asks as he brings his torch close to mine. The heat from both torches feels like it's starting to burn my skin, so I pull mine away a little bit until my hand cools down.

"I'm not sure, but I think it's a finger … a big finger."

"What! Like someone was buried here? Yuck!" he says, and I see a shiver make its way through his body. I start to giggle.

"Are you laughing at me?" he asks, starting to calm down. He lets a little laugh escape.

"You're just so big. I didn't think you'd be afraid of some bones in a wall."

"Those are some big fingers that belong to something, and I was so close to accidentally touching it when I dug my way through here. Just the thought gives me the heebie-jeebies."

I'm laughing hysterically now and holding my stomach with my other hand as I try to balance the torch and not put it out. I've never heard anyone use those words to describe how they felt. I can barely catch my breath as I struggle to ask, "It gives you the what?"

"The heebie-jeebies," he says, now laughing with me. "I suppose that is a funny way to say something, isn't it?"

I try to regain my composure so that we can finish looking

at the bones in the wall, and just as I catch my breath, I lean back and look above us. My mouth falls open. Bao follows my gaze, and I can see him starting to tremble out of the corner of my eye.

"Wha … what is that?" he stammers as he lifts his torch toward it. Since he's so much taller than me, he can get his light a lot closer than I ever could hope to.

"I'm not sure," I say, but in my heart I know exactly what it is. I just don't know how it got here.

Bao moves his torch back and forth and lights up the ceiling, bringing to life the glimmer of the bones that show another part to the owner of the finger we found earlier.

Bao draws in a deep breath and says, "It's a wing."

Forty-Four

"I think it's an angel," I say, not knowing what else to say. How much does Bao know? Does he know about me?

"I think you're right. But how would an angel get down here, and how would it get buried? I didn't think angels could die."

He's right. I don't think angels can die either. So what is it? The full wingspan of the skeleton in the ceiling must be huge. The one wing we can see is at least six or eight feet wide. Miriam would've had wings too, but I never saw them. How did she hide them if they're this big?

I look back up at Bao, and he's still standing there looking at the bones in the ceiling. He moves his torch from one tip of the wing to the place where it should've met up with the spine or the shoulders, but there's nothing there. I don't know how this creature got buried in here like this.

"You didn't see this when you were digging the tunnel?" I ask. He seems lost in thought as he looks at the bones that glitter in the light.

"Bao? Hello?" I nudge him with my elbow.

"Wha … oh, no, I didn't," he says. He turns and looks at me. His eyes are glowing the same way the specks in the bone glowed when we brought the torch by them. I wonder what's going on.

"Bao, are you okay?"

"I … I don't know … I think I need to sit down," he says as he stumbles a little and then leans against the wall next to the finger.

"Oh!" I exclaim as I reach out and grab his torch, watching his legs crumple underneath him. He slides down the dirt wall, hitting the floor with a flump. His legs flop out, and his hands lay palm-up on the dirt floor. What's going on with him?

He finally takes in a big breath and says, "I feel so drained … like my breath was sucked out of me. But I couldn't pull my eyes away. It was so beautiful …" He turns from me and starts to look back up at the bones, and when his eyes make contact with them, I look at the bones and see that they are glowing just like Bao's eyes. Whatever this creature is, it's draining Bao's strength. But for what?

I nudge him again and try to get him to stop looking at them, but he just falls over onto his side, never breaking his gaze with the bones. I can barely hear him breathing now. If I don't interrupt this, he may not survive it!

I lean against his massive arm and try pushing him, but he's so big that I can barely move him. I stand up and use my foot to push on his leg, and it moves a little, but he doesn't flinch or seem to know that I'm doing it. His head is now lying nearly lifeless on the dirt floor, and the dirt around him is starting to move toward him. I look up at the skeleton in the ceiling, and the dirt that was surrounding it is moving away, uncovering it. That creature is taking Bao's life for its own and swapping places with him! If I don't stop it, Bao will be the one locked away in this underground cavern, and that creature will be standing in front of me.

I look back to Bao, and the once giant of a man is starting to dwindle right before my eyes. The glow from the bones is now so bright that the tunnel is lit up, and I can see without the help of the torches, which is good because if I'm going to do anything, I have to set these down. I'm afraid that if I do that, the fire will go out. As I watch Bao still locked in the grip of the creature's enticing glow, I don't have much choice. I walk over to the other side of him and lay them down as gently as I can. One of them does snuff itself out, but the other one seems to stay lit for now. I turn to Bao and push my hands against his back as I try shaking him again, but nothing works. I have to break his gaze somehow. I run around his legs and trip over one of his feet that are lying lifeless on the floor, landing on my hands and knees. I land face-to-face with Bao.

Suddenly I see the glow in his eyes start to dim, and his breathing becomes more normal. I stay there with my face in his, blocking his view of the creature, and finally his eyes return to their normal color. Just when I think that he's going to be okay, he closes his eyes, and all of his muscles seem to completely relax. He passed out!

I brush away the dirt that has started to cover him and grab his face with both of my hands. I start gently shaking his face back and forth.

"Bao! Bao! Come on, big guy! You can't leave me now. I don't know how to get out of your tunnel. I need your help. Come on …"

And that's when I hear it.

Something rustles above me.

I look up and see that the bones to the wing are no longer just bones. They're covered in feathers, and the creature is starting to move. I then look toward where the finger bones were in the wall, and that's covered in flesh and starting to move too. I need to get him out of here! I need to get us both out of here! If that creature could drain him this much with just its bones, what will it do once it breaks free?

"Bao!" I whisper. I don't know if the creature has ears or not, but judging from its finger, I'm guessing it does, and I don't want it to know that we're still here. I push on his shoulders with all that I have and nudge him back and forth. Finally he starts to come to and opens his eyes.

"What happened?" he asks. He sounds like he's been woken up from a deep sleep, and as he slowly blinks, he starts to prop himself up on one of his elbows.

"We have to get out of here! Those bones … they aren't just bones, Bao. That creature is draining you of your life and taking it as its own. It's not bones anymore," I say as I point toward the ceiling.

I remember what Miriam said back in the library about how I can shield those around me like sunglasses. Maybe if I touch him when he looks up at the creature, it won't be able to feed off of him. I grab his hand and say, "Okay, I'm going to move a little bit so you can see what's up there, but don't look too long. I don't know if I can get you back."

I move out of his line of sight and watch his eyes as they move up the wall to the ceiling. There's a faint glimmer in his eyes but nothing like what it was before. I *can* shield him! When I see the horror flicker across his face, he breaks the hold I have on his hand and sits upright against the wall. His eyes never leave the creature, but now his eyes are fully lit up.

I grab both of his hands in mine. "Come back to me, big guy. Come on now."

It takes a few seconds, but the glow dims, and he starts to regain some sense of clarity.

"Wha … how … how can you do that?" he stammers. "When you touch me, I can feel the draw lose its grip on me, but when you aren't touching me, I have no control. I can't even force myself to look away."

"I don't know," I say. I don't know how much to explain it without giving away all of who I am. "What I do know is we need to move."

Just as I say that, the wing that was locked in the ceiling above us breaks free of its dirt prison and swoops down. The tips brush the top of my head, and as my hair lifts from my head, an electric current runs through me. It runs across my skin and centers on the feather that is trying to break free from my skin, driving a spike of pain down through my spine. It hurts so much that I fall to the ground and writhe in agony.

Bao somehow finds a bit of strength left inside and crawls to where I have fallen.

"Patrina! What's wrong? What happened?"

I hear the panic in his voice and then hear the wind swoosh as the wing makes another pass in the air, this time knocking Bao back onto his side. I look at him to see if he felt the same jolt by the wing, but he doesn't seem to have the same outcome that I did. As he gets back up, he shifts so that he's on his hands and knees and crawls across the floor to me. The pain has subsided in my spine now, and I'm able to move again.

"We have to get out of here," I whisper. "Now."

He and I brace ourselves against each other and use our joined strength to get to our feet. We stumble down the dirt cavern a little ways, just so that we're out of reach of the wing. I look back at the finger in the wall, and it's now a hand. The creature is digging itself out.

"Come on," I say to him. "There's no going back. We need to get out."

"I'm so sorry, Patrina. I had no idea ..."

"Don't worry, Bao. I know you didn't know this was in here." I turn to face the tunnel in front of us as I mumble under my breath, "You wouldn't have made it out alive if you did."

Forty-Five

We stagger our way down the tunnel to the first bend, and once we make our way around the corner, we both lean up against the wall and take a few deep breaths. It's dark in this part of the tunnel, and I realize something. I left the torches back by the creature.

"Oh no," I murmur.

"What's wrong? Is there another creature?" Bao asks as his eyes start darting around.

"No, but I left the torches over there," I say, pointing back toward the creature.

We look back to the wing that is flapping from the ceiling and then look at each other. There's no way we can go back there. Not now.

I remember the flashlight I have in my pocket, but before I can pull it out, Bao clicks on a flashlight, and I'm glad that he has one. I don't want to use up the battery in mine. I don't know what else lies ahead of me on this journey to Arcadia, and I will need all the resources I can keep.

He flashes the light on the wing, and I'm amazed as it sparkles like diamonds. The reflection from it dances on the wall like little fairies. Will my wings do that? Will my wings be that big? Where am I going to put them? Will I be able to fly?

If Miriam could fly, then why didn't she just fly out of here? Oh yeah … my uncle owned her. It always seems to come back to that. That still doesn't answer why I never saw her wings. Did he do something to them?

"Patrina? Are you okay?" Bao is looking at me with worry etched in his face.

"Yeah, I was just thinking." I turn to face the dark tunnel away from the creature and start walking. Bao is close to my side.

"So, if that wasn't one of the oddities that you found down here, what exactly did you find?"

He chuckles, and the light from his flashlight bounces on the floor.

"No, that is definitely not one of the things I found down here. We're actually coming up to one of the oddities, as you called it. Just right up here," he says as he points into the darkness ahead. The tunnel takes another twist and then opens up to a small room.

"Were you going to live down here?" I ask.

"Wha … oh, no. I started finding more and more little trinkets in this section, and the more I found, the more I dug until it was this big. I guess it does look like a room, doesn't it?"

"A little," I say as he shines the light across the wall and suddenly something glitters.

"There it is!" He walks over to the spot that we just saw light up. I hope it wasn't like the last thing we saw that lit up. That didn't turn out so great, and it's still working itself out of its dirt tomb behind us. We really don't have time to look at the stuff he found in here, but this has gotten my curiosity.

"See? There it is! I was in the process of trying to dig it out, but it really doesn't want to budge," he says, pointing to it like a little kid who's excited about a new treasure he just found.

I walk up to it and look. This thing does sparkle in the light and is very familiar. The piece that is sticking out looks like an end of a feather, like what someone would use back in the old days for writing. A quill? Is that what they called it? If it was a feather from that creature, that would explain the twinkling in the light. I'm about to tell Bao that it's just a feather and we should keep moving when I reach to touch it with my finger to prove it to myself before I say it aloud.

Just as my finger grazes the tip, it vibrates and makes the sound a tuning fork makes when you hit it against something. That clang is unmistakable. I remember it from when Miriam was teaching me about sound.

"What did you do?" Bao cries in agony. I look at him, and he has one of his hands on his ear. I'm sure both hands would be on both of his ears if he were not holding the flashlight.

"I just touched it. It looked like a feather ... but a feather wouldn't make that kind of sound."

I reach up and touch it again, and it makes the same noise, but this time I can see that it vibrates too. What is that?

"Can I have the flashlight?" I ask. Bao readily hands it over to me and places both hands on his ears.

The sound doesn't seem to bother me like it does him for some reason. As I'm about to touch it again, I look back to Bao, and he sees what I'm going to do and pushes his hands over his ears even harder. I get the flashlight really close to the end of the piece that's sticking out and grab it with my hand. The whole thing lights up and starts shaking! I shine the light up the wall above it and see that it's making a crack in the dirt. I pull as hard as I can, and it releases itself from the ground's grip, and I fly backwards, landing on the floor next to Bao's feet. I drop the thing that was stuck in the wall when I fall, and I start using the light to sweep back and forth across the floor in search of it.

I see rocks, roots from a tree here and there, and then I see it. It *is* a feather! How could a feather cause that much of a raucous? I look up to Bao, who is standing next to me, and he lowers his hands from his ears.

"How could a feather do all that?" he asks.

"I'm not sure."

I look back to it and stretch out my arm to pick it up, but when I do, the feather starts to slide across the floor toward me. I snatch back my hand, scared at what we just found.

"Did you do that?" Bao takes a step backward, away from me.

"No! That wasn't me!"

It's okay, child, The Guide says. *Do not be afraid.*

I wish The Guide would give me more information, but if he says it's okay, then it must be okay. Or maybe just okay for me? Bao doesn't seem to be able to handle even the sound of it. I don't know what would happen if he touched it.

I stretch out my arm toward it once more, and it starts sliding again, but this time I don't pull back. It skitters across the dirt, over a small rock, and dives into the palm of my hand. As I wrap my fingers around it, it starts to glow. I feel it heating up the brighter it gets, and then I feel it starting to change shape. I look to see where Bao is, and he has backed himself up all the way to the farthest wall behind me. I see a look of fear on his face.

The feather starts to make the noise it made when I first touched it, getting louder and louder until it explodes in a ball of light. I can't help but shield my eyes, and when the light has died back down again, that's when I see it.

I'm holding a sword.

Forty-Six

"Wha … how …" Bao rambles from behind me.

I turn my hand over and look at this new long sword in my hand. I grab the flashlight that I must've dropped next to me when it exploded and shine the light onto the golden hilt. The part that covers my hand is covered in feathers made out of gold, and when I shine the light down the blade, I can see words of another language etched in it. The blade isn't what I would think a normal sword blade would look like. It's black, like that stone in one of my books. I think it was called obsidian. It's one of the hardest substances around if I remember right. Why would it be attached to gold? Gold is pretty soft.

The hilt reflects the owner's heart, The Guide says. *The only thing better than gold, dear one, is diamond.*

How would someone have a diamond hilt? I ask in my mind.

That someone would have gone through many tests and tribulations and still come out with a pure heart. It's never been done, little one. There's usually something along the way that derails even the most kindhearted of them all.

"Patrina? Are you okay? Does it hurt your hand?"

I look up and see Bao standing next to me. I'm sure this hasn't been easy on him.

"Yes, yes, I'm fine. No, it doesn't hurt. See?" I flip my hand over and back again to show him that my hand still works even though I now have a sword in it.

"How did it go from a feather to a sword? Who are you?"

"I'm not sure ... of either of those. I hope to find out though." I smile up at him and set the sword down onto the floor. Immediately it becomes a feather again.

"Whoa," we both say.

"A feather is easier to get in my pack and travel with, but when I touch it, it seems to become a sword," I mumble.

"What happens if you just touch the feathery part? You know, the other end of it?"

"I don't know. It can't hurt to try though, right?"

I reach down and grab the tip of the feather, and it starts to glow, but it doesn't heat up or transform. I quickly slip my pack off of my shoulder, unzip it with my other hand, and place the feather inside. I don't know what I'll need a sword for, but at least I have one. I zip my pack back up and flip it over my shoulder.

As we stand there, we hear a rustling from the creature down the tunnel. I want to look to see how far it's gotten out of its tomb, but I know we should just keep going, so I motion to Bao that we should move on and hand him the flashlight. He takes it from my hand, careful not to touch my skin. I look up at him, puzzled.

"I don't know who or what you are, and I'd much rather not touch you and find myself blowing up into something else."

"Fair enough. Let's just keep going."

He shines the light up ahead, and we start walking. As we go, I see where he's made little chairs out of dirt along the way. I suppose it's probably easier to rest in a chair than just on the ground. He doesn't say much else to me and doesn't point out any of the strange trinkets he came across, although I'm not sure I would either if the one I did point out randomly exploded into a sword.

The farther we go, the less we hear the creature rustling until we can no longer hear anything coming from that direction. When it gets free, is it going to follow us? Or will it go the other way, under the house?

Before I have time to ponder that thought any longer, we come to the place where Bao dug upward. He made a ladder out of roots he found in his tunneling and strung them together with something. Maybe twine. I'm actually surprised he made it up this ladder because it doesn't look very strong.

"This is it," he says as he shines the light up to the piece of wood above us. "I tried to conceal that I made my way through. I just put a board there. If anyone tried to walk on it, they would fall straight in though."

"So are you going up with me? You can't very well go back that way. The creature will get you, and if it doesn't, my uncle surely will."

"What would I do once I got up there? I'm much larger than you. I would only slow you down. Where are you going anyway?"

I haven't thought about that part. He really can't go into Arcadia.

"I want to see where my mother came from … but it's pretty far away. You could always go with me for a while, and when you're ready to stay somewhere, well … then I guess I'll just go on ahead without you."

He stands there and thinks about it for a moment. I see him weighing his options in his head.

"I guess I don't have much of an option. I don't want to live out the rest of my life a slave to your uncle, and making it past that creature," he rolls his eyes and sighs, "I don't think I could get past that! We barely made it out, and that was only its wing!"

"Well all right then! Give me a boost, and let's get up top!"

He clicks the flashlight off, and I can see light peeking

around the piece of wood. He puts the flashlight back into his pocket and puts his hands around my waist. His hands are so big that if they were any bigger they would encircle my entire waist! He lifts me up to the third rung of the root ladder without even a struggle. As I make my way up, it hits me. How am I going to get that piece of wood out of the way?

I look back down to him at the bottom of the ladder. "Aren't you coming up?"

"Yeah, but two of us are too much for that rickety thing. You get up there, and I'll follow."

"How do I move the wood?" I know that I could move the wood by myself because it's an element, but I can't do it in front of him without making him wonder what I am even more.

"Oh! That's easy! Just push on one of the corners, and it'll pop it kittywampus and come right out."

"It'll do what?" I ask, starting to giggle. Bao has some of the strangest words for things.

"Um, it'll make it so that it's not lined up in the hole." He's starting to giggle now. "I guess that is a weird word, isn't it?"

"Yes, very weird!" I say, laughing. I turn back to the ladder, and as I finally reach the wooden door above me, I push on one of the corners. Sure enough, the rest of it pops out, and I'm able to pull it out of the hole. I hand it down to Bao, who is still at the bottom, and look back up to the blue sky above. I know it hasn't really been that long, but it feels like I've been in the tunnels forever.

I climb up farther so my head is able to peek out of the top of the hole. We are definitely in the maze. I listen for a moment, just to see if I can hear my uncle, but I don't hear anything. I wonder if he's still in the house. If he is and we can figure out how to get out of this maze, we may just be able to escape!

I put my hands on the top of the hole and feel the plush green grass underneath my fingers. It's cool and refreshing. If

I weren't on the run from my crazy uncle, I would love to just lie down in this and rest for a while. I've heard about people lying on the ground and pretending to see shapes in the clouds. That's something I would like to do. Someday, but right now I really need to get out of here.

I climb up out of the hole, and when I get my feet out, I swing around and look back in. I see Bao standing down there looking up at me.

"Is it all clear?" he hollers from below.

"It looks good to me!"

He climbs up nearly five of the rungs and then just stops. He looks behind him and after a moment looks back up at me with sheer terror in his eyes.

"Run!" he yells as he starts climbing as fast as he can. He makes it up four more rungs before I see what has caused such fear.

The creature has dug itself out and is standing at the base of the root ladder.

Forty-Seven

"Hurry!" I yell as I motion with my hand for him to grab it. He climbs, but just as he's almost to the top, his eyes get really big, and he starts falling. I look past Bao and see the eyes of the creature glowing in the dim light from the hole. The creature has grabbed his leg and is pulling him down!

As the creature comes more into the light, I can see that it looks like what I would think an angel would look like. It has skin that glimmers in the light and hair the color of the sun, but it's so tall. If it could reach Bao's leg when he was almost to the top, it must be almost nine or ten feet tall ... like that creature that was looking in my doorway. Was that one of these too?

Bao falls to the floor below with such a thud that I can feel the earth shake under me. The creature is struggling to get him to do something, but I can't figure out what it is, and I have no one that I can call to for help. What do I do? If I try to use one of my gifts against the creature, Bao will find out, but if I don't, he'll die.

Bao and the creature wrestle and tumble below, and then the creature suddenly gets its hands on Bao's face, and as it digs its long talon nails into his cheeks, Bao screams. The creature turns Bao's face toward itself, and even though Bao struggles against its grip, he can't seem to fight anymore, and

I watch as they lock eyes. There's such a glow that forms between them that it's hard to look at, and that's when I realize that the creature is drinking in his life. I watch as Bao starts to shrivel and the creature gets bigger, stronger. How do I even make it stop? I only know how to do a few things. Locks, doors, leaves … but not this, not a creature.

And then I remember something. Before, when I was really happy, I made an earthquake. I wonder if I could do that now. If I can, then maybe I can knock the creature off balance long enough for Bao to get away. I place my hands on the ground and close my eyes. I just let my emotions run, and soon I can feel a small tremble. That's not going to be enough. I have to move more.

I think about everything that was taken away from me: my parents, a life with them, Miriam, and now possibly Bao. I dig my fingers into the dirt under the plush grass as the thought of all that I've lost makes my heart hurt, and I feel my emotions drain out of me into the earth. The ground starts to pitch and roll under me, and I hear it growling as it moves out of place, time and again. I open my eyes, and the creature has broken eye contact with Bao and is now staring at me. I can't let it get out.

I dig my fingers in further, nearly up to my second knuckle, and I have to hang on as the ground convulses under me. I look to see the ground around them starting to tumble and fall. The creature loses its balance, and one of its hands lets go of Bao, but the other hand is still attached, and Bao is looking at me, pleading with his eyes.

I shove my hands into the ground, up to my wrist, and groan as everything in me is poured into the ground below. A huge boulder falls and launches the creature backwards, hitting its head against a rock, releasing its grip on Bao as he slumps lifeless to the floor. The ground is out of control and taking over, sapping all of my strength from me, and as it shakes one final time, I see through blurred eyes as the ceiling above them collapses, and the ground caves in from around me, covering them in a cloud of debris, blocking my view. And then everything goes black.

I can't feel my hands … or my arms. It's as though my body has become separated from my mind. I open my eyes and look around, but all I see is white … pale white. And then I feel the wind rushing past me. It echoes in my ears and pulls the back of my hair up. Where am I? My back is starting to get hot, very hot. It feels like it's on fire! Why isn't the wind putting it out? I look at my legs and my arms as they are floating in front of me and see that I'm encased in a fireball. I think I'm falling … but to where and from where?

I wiggle to turn myself over to see where I'm headed. My face is ablaze with the flames that are surrounding me, but I can just barely see through the flickers … what is that? It looks like a forest … like the one behind Uncle Vlad's house! Why am I falling to earth there?

Why am I falling to earth?

I start to roll and tumble. The whole world is out of focus now as I get closer and closer. The fire around me is so intense; it feels like my skin is boiling, and I can't right myself in the air to make the spinning stop.

I see the top of a giant tree as I near it and realize that I'm going to land right on it.

That's going to hurt.

I arch my back and brace for impact …

"Patrina! Patrina! Wake up!"

I open my eyes, but I can't see. Everything is so hazy, like something is covering my eyes. This is much softer than landing on a tree. It feels like someone holding me up, and my head is leaning against something. There's a steady thumping noise … a heartbeat.

I raise my arm to my face and rub my eyes, trying to grind out the grit that seems to be covering me. Once I get that off, I squint open my eyes, and I see him.

"Bao! You're alive! But how? How did you get out?" I try to sit up, only to fall back against his chest. It was his heartbeat that I was hearing!

"You should rest a while longer, princess." His voice sounds funny, almost breathless.

I look up at him, and he doesn't even look like the man I knew. His cheeks are caved in, and his eyes look so big, bigger than normal. I lean back so that I can really look at him.

"You look so different …"

"What? How? I feel the same … well … maybe a little weaker." He holds out his arm and looks at the back of it, turning it over, flexing it.

"The creature … angel … I don't know—it was draining you right before my very eyes. I was watching as you were locked in its grip and shriveling."

He looks down at himself and says, "I guess I did lose a little weight, huh?" He chuckles to himself, and I finally sit up all the way. The ground around us is a pile of rubble with pieces of sod strewn in between clumps of dirt and rock. I look around and don't see any way that he could've gotten out … and I don't see the creature.

"How did you make it out? It's all … such a disaster."

I scoot a little and turn so that I can look at him. He looks around at the mess I've created and says, "That creature lost its grip on me, and I woke up on the floor. The earthquake had everything tumbling around me, and I saw the ladder dangling. I was able to get most of the way up when the dirt caved in around me. I could see the top of your head before I was buried. The dirt was loose enough though, so I was able to dig my way out. But that doesn't answer my question ..."

"What question?"

"I saw you ... you were glowing. What were you doing?"

I didn't think he saw me. I didn't even see him coming up the ladder. I must've been hazy long before I realized it. I can't lie to him ... but I don't know how much he should know.

"How much do you know about Miriam?" I ask. Maybe, if he knows about her, it's not going to be a far stretch to know about me.

"I know that your uncle had something on her, but I don't know much. She was nice. Why? What does that have to do with you and why *you* were glowing?" He leans away from me and has a puzzled look on his face.

What do I say? He doesn't even know about Miriam. He probably doesn't know about my uncle and that he glows too. Where's The Guide now? Why isn't he telling me what I can tell Bao?

I decide that sometimes I just have to take chances on people and say, "I don't know how much of this is going to make sense. You know that creature down there?" I point to the remains of the hole.

"Yeah ..."

"I don't think that was an angel ... well, not a full angel. I think it's a nephilim."

"A what?"

"A nephilim. Part-angel, part-human. It's kind of hard to explain. Miriam told me about them. Some of them look like that ... and some of them look like ... me," I say as I look up at him and wring my hands together in my lap. I've never had to tell anyone this before, and as I impatiently wait for his response, I watch as he starts to process what I've just said to him. And then he starts to crawl backwards away from me, his eyes watching me the entire time, and I can hear his breathing start to go faster.

"Bao, please, I won't hurt you. I'm not like that creature. Please," I reach out my hand to him, "please don't run.

"But … but that creature … it drained me. It locked me in its mind with its eyes, and I couldn't get out. I couldn't get away from it. And you … you're like it?"

"No," I say, crawling across the rubble to him. "Not really. I mean, yes but no. Ugh, even I'm confused! Miriam told me that a long time ago there were the first nephilim, giants, and some of them died, but some didn't, and I think that creature down there is one of the first ones. Then there were more. These angels revolted and came down here to make new ones, better ones … stronger ones. These new ones look like normal people but can do things. Different ones can do different things, and the ones that come after them get the gifts of the ones before them. Miriam told me I'm the tenth virtue. I'm the tenth genesis of virtues."

He starts to calm down as he processes all that I've just spewed out at him.

"What does that mean? The tenth virtue?"

"It means I'm the strongest there has ever been. That's why my uncle wants to keep me locked up."

The look of it all coming together floats across Bao's face. "That's why …"

"That's why, what?"

"That's why he got so mad when you figured out how to get out of your tower! That's why he started being here more often. He used to be at his office a lot more."

"Yes," I agree. "And that's why he's hunting me now. But I can't stay here, Bao! I have to get out! He only wants to use me for all the wrong reasons. He just wants to be more powerful, and I need to get to Arcadia before my feather …" I stop midsentence as I realize that I've said too much.

"What feather? Arcadia? What are you talking about?" His face is scrunched up in confusion as he looks at me.

"Nephilim have wings too. I don't know how or where they go when we just look like humans; I don't really understand it all. But I have to get to Arcadia so that I can know my true purpose, not doing the bidding of my—"

"Patrina!"

Forty-Eight

Bao and I freeze and look at each other. Bao scrambles to his feet and then looks at me again for a moment before sticking his hand out for me to grab.

"He found us," Bao whispers. "I don't know how he knew we were in here, but he does!"

I quickly glance around us, but all I see are the green hedge walls of the maze. I can't see my uncle, but I clearly heard him. And if I can hear him, it won't be long before he finds us here.

"Sssshhh! If we stay quiet, maybe he'll go around us and look in the other parts of the maze," I whisper to Bao.

"Your uncle can find anything if he wants it bad enough."

He's right, unfortunately.

"Then we need to move, quietly," I say, pointing toward where I think we should be headed.

"Patrina! I know you're out here! I know you're out here too, Bao!"

Bao crouches low beside the maze wall as though my uncle's words will hit him as he screams them at us.

"How? How does he know you're with me?" I ask, crouching next to Bao.

"I'm not sure ... I don't know how he knows the stuff he

knows. He just does. I understood some of it because of the cameras, but there are times that he just knows things, and there's no explanation."

I nod and motion for us to move. As we turn and start walking, I hear every step that Bao makes. I turn to him and put my finger to my lips in hopes that he understands he needs to walk quieter. He nods and tries to tiptoe, but it seems to just make it worse. His noisy feet are about to be the least of our problems though. Just as we start to turn the corner of the maze, the hedge wall shifts and slides, blocking us in and making us have to go a different way. If we started in the middle, would the maze try to keep us in the middle? Or would it prevent us from getting to the house and be our way out?

I look to Bao, and we both nod as we decide to follow the maze and see if it takes us away from my uncle. We make another turn, and it shifts again. I hear my uncle yelling for us. It sounds like he's farther away from us. Maybe this is working!

And then I hear a boom.

Bao and I freeze in place as we hear the walls slide again, but this time it's so loud. I turn around toward the noise and see the wall that was behind us shift and slide. Suddenly I'm looking down a wide path, cleared by my uncle, and he's standing about twenty feet away from us.

"How did he do that?" Bao mumbles, but I don't say anything. There's no time to explain my uncle's powers.

"I knew I'd find you," my uncle says as he saunters his way across the open maze.

"Why can't you just let me go? Why must you keep me a prisoner here? I'm not yours to keep!" I yell as I start backing up. I bump into the wall behind me and stop. Why isn't that wall moving?

"Girl, you know why. You know you are the one investment that's going to make me the most powerful man in the world."

"I'm not an investment! I'm a human being!"

"No, you're not. Does Bao know what you are?" He waves his hand in Bao's direction. "Does he really know what he's got for a traveling companion?"

"Yes, he does! Well kind of … but that's not important!" I start making my way toward Bao, who is standing there, dumbfounded, watching as my uncle and I banter back and forth. When I'm finally standing next to Bao, I reach up and grab his hand. He squeezes mine, letting me know that he's on my side, even after all that he's gone through and knows.

"Vlad, you don't own us anymore. We're leaving here and never coming back," Bao says as he straightens his back and puffs his chest out.

"That's what Miriam said too. She's not saying much anymore now," he says as laughs the most horrific sound I've ever heard.

The tears start streaming down my face, and though I try to fight it, I can't control them.

"What did you do to her? You're such an awful man! My mother was right in not wanting to leave my father for you!" I scream. My heart is hurting now more than ever before.

My uncle stops laughing and starts walking toward us, closing the gap, causing me to feel as though he's suffocating me. "You will never leave here, girl. Never!"

Bao starts backing up, nudging me, and whispers, "Patrina, what's happening? What's going on? Why is his neck like that?"

I see it too.

I've seen that mark before, but it only looked like that in the reflection pond. It's glowing bright red now! It seems to be tied with his anger, and the angrier he gets, the redder it glows.

Bao pulls me toward him and starts to push me behind him to hide me from this maniac of an uncle who's relentlessly coming at us. The more he pushes me, the more the leaves of the hedge wall start to grab me. First my arms, then my shoulders, and soon I'm halfway engulfed in the hedge behind us.

"You're not going to ruin her life like you did mine, Vlad. I won't let you." Bao keeps pushing me behind him, and now I can barely see around his arm, but I can hear my uncle's footsteps coming straight for him.

"What are you going to do? You're nothing! I'm the one who saved you from yourself. I'm the one who gave you a job and a place to stay. And now you're going to betray me? You don't know what you're up against!"

"I know enough, and you'll have to go through me first!" And with that, Bao pushes me the rest of the way into the hedge wall and starts barreling toward my uncle. The leaves of the maze keep pulling me in, and just as I see Bao and Vlad hit each other, the leaves block my view and pull me through to the other side of the maze.

"Run, Patrina!" Bao yells from the other side. "Run and never look back!"

I hear the sounds of fists hitting flesh and bone and the cries of agony from Bao as my uncle relentlessly takes out his anger on this man who just saved me from my jailer.

"Run!" Bao yells once more, as if knowing that I am stalling just beyond the wall.

I decide to do as he says and turn to face where I think the back woods are, where the lake is that Miriam told me about. Just as I do, it's almost as if the hedge maze knows who I am and opens a straight path to the woods.

You must run, little one.

Where were you before? Where were you when I really needed you? I'm so angry at The Guide that I don't run. I just stand still with my hands clenched into tiny balls of fury.

Special one, sometimes I have to let you figure things out on your own. But right now, you need to run!

I guess now isn't the time to put up a fight. I start to run.

The wind is whipping through my hair, and I hear the clashing between my uncle and Bao reach a crescendo. I see the line of trees up ahead of me. These must be the trees that I could see from the garden on the roof. But isn't this where that nine-foot-tall creature I saw peering at me through my doorway came from?

I stop midstride at the realization of that and start scanning the trees, trying to see if I can see anything standing in the woods. But what if it's not standing? What if it's crouching? Or perched in the trees? I'm starting to panic at the thought of going into this forest without knowing what I might be coming up against when a huge thunder clap shatters the air behind me.

Forty-Nine

I whip around to see the remnants of a giant cloud that resembles the nuclear bombs I read about in one of my books. The ground is moving but not like it was when I caused the earthquake. This time it looks like a big tidal wave coming right at me.

I turn around and start running as fast as I can right into the woods. I have no other way to go. I either run into the creepy woods with who knows what waiting behind the trees, or I get pummeled by the wave of dirt coming at me with a crazed uncle behind it.

I dodge under and weave between the branches that reach out from the colossal timbers towering above me. I barely make it into the forest before I hear the dirt come crashing up against the trees at the front line. I find one of the bigger trees and hide behind it. I can't outrun this wave, but I can brace myself behind something.

I look up to see just how big the tree is that I'm behind, and it's a monstrosity of a tree. I recognize the leaves on it as belonging to the same family as a black oak, but the acorns give it away. This is a red oak! It's exciting to see the things in real life that I've learned about in books, but just as I'm about to forget what made me seek refuge here, the first spattering of soil from the wave hits the tree.

I turn my face toward the bark and try to shield my eyes with my hands. As I press myself against the tree as tightly as I can, the tree shakes as the wave hits it with its full force. The dirt starts to engulf my shoes as it piles around the red oak, and I feel as though I may not make it out of this mess.

Help me, I cry silently in my heart.

Just then, a door in the tree slides open in front of me. I'm so surprised by it that I almost fall in, but I catch myself by grabbing the edge of the doorway. It's pitch-black inside! I sweep my hand just within the opening, trying to see if I can feel anything on the other side, but my hand disappears into the black void in front of me. I remember I had a dream like this! Except in my dream, I never actually made it through the door. I woke up and was standing by my closet. I remember feeling afraid to go inside, kind of like now, except right now I have a tidal wave of earth coming my way.

I cling to the edge of the opening and pull my foot from under a pile of dirt. I can feel granules of dirt and muck that have made their way inside my shoe, so I shake it a little, but only a small amount comes off. I gingerly stick my toes just past the opening into the blackness, and just like my hand, the tip of my foot disappears. The wave has picked up even more in its move across the field, and the pile surrounding the tree has started to creep up to my knees. I have no choice but to go inside.

I place my foot down where the bottom of the ground should be, but it just keeps going down. Had I not been holding on to the tree, I would've surely fallen inside. I keep stretching downward until I feel something hard underneath the sole of my shoe. Are these stairs?

As I steady myself, I bring my other foot inside, still clinging to the side of the doorway, and I can no longer see the lower half of my body. I can still feel it though, so I know it's there. Just as my other foot hits, the tidal wave of dirt has started to take on a life of its own. Instead of the tree blocking most of it, it's starting to assemble and climb on top of itself, piling up just outside the open doorway. I feel the door trying to slide shut, and it knocks one of my hands off the edge. If I let go and completely go inside, I won't be able to see anything, but if I don't, the dirt that my uncle must've sent will bury me alive.

Before I can think about it much more, the tree tries to slide the door shut again. The motion of it surprises me, knocking my other hand off of the edge. I lose my balance for a moment and reach to steady myself by placing my hands out on either side of me. They both hit something hard and rough. It feels like the inside of the tree has been carved out by something … or someone. Just as I regain my balance, the door slides shut behind me, blocking out the creeping dirt and, unfortunately, any light.

I stand there, motionless, hoping that I am actually standing on a step, but to where? I don't dare let go of the wall because I don't know what's in front of me, and I don't want to fall into the dark abyss.

Suddenly a red glow comes from inside the tree all around me. I wonder if my eyes are adjusting to the darkness, but when I look to where one of my hands is pressed on the rough wall, I start to see the outline around my hand. The tree itself is lighting up. How can it do this?

This tree grew up out of the ashes of a very intense fire, little one. A long time ago, long before your uncle made his claim on this piece of land, there was once a beautiful forest with almost every tree imaginable. It was a masterpiece of nature. When the Fallen came to earth, this is where they landed on that fateful day. You had a dream of falling, didn't you?

Yeah, I did. Wait … was that what I was reliving?

There are many things your dreams will teach you, but yes, that was what you were reliving.

289

But who was I reliving? Couldn't I only relive someone from my line?

Oh but you were, Patrina. You were reliving the first virtue.

Adena? I ask in my mind. *I read her entry in my diary.*

No, dear one. You were reliving Engelbert. He was the first virtue. The very first the Monarch created.

But I thought I was part of Adena's line? I'm a little confused.

You are, child. Adena is part of Engelbert's line, The Guide continues.

Then how did Adena get here? Didn't they fall? I would think that I would've relived her falling, not him.

Adena and several others were kidnapped by The Six. Engelbert was one of The Six, but he didn't have her with him. Bronx, who was the leader of their group, had smuggled them out with him when they fell. He had them in his pack.

Uh … what? Wait. How can someone smuggle that many angels in a pack out of Arcadia?

Angels aren't always in the form you think they are, dear one. They're true form is a little ball of light. In that form, they easily fit into a pack.

My mind is swimming at just how complex my life has become recently. It wasn't that long ago that I was just in my room, waiting for Miriam to teach me something new, randomly getting another book or trinket from an uncle who was never around, and eating the delicacies of Bao from the kitchen. Now I'm running for my life, trying to protect a feather that's growing out of my shoulder, while standing on what I hope is a stair to somewhere in the middle of a tree, surrounded by dirt possessed by a maniacal uncle who is trying to capture me, all while learning that my heritage stemmed from kidnapped angels. Somebody could write a book about me!

"All right, Guide, now what?" I ask aloud, hearing my voice reverberate inside the tree. It sounds a lot bigger on the inside than it looked on the outside.

You can make it brighter in here, The Guide says.

"How?"

You're the reason it's already starting to glow. You can make it glow brighter. You just have to let it.

"Like the diary?"

Yes, like the diary.

I take a deep breath in, releasing the tension in my shoulders, and as I breathe out, the walls glow brighter and brighter until they look as though someone turned on a whole room full of lights. I see something in front of me, but I can't tell what it is. It just looks like the inside of the tree that I'm in. How peculiar! When I spoke, it sounded as though my voice carried for a long ways. I look down at my feet and see that I am standing on the top stair to a very long staircase that goes down far below the tree. The echo of my voice must've come from down there. I squint, trying to see farther, but all I can see is stair after stair. It looks as if the staircase was carved right out of the main center root of this giant red oak tree. I turn around, looking for the door that led me here. What was I thinking?

Life's adventures go forward, little one, not backwards. In order to get to where you need to be, you must move forward.

I sigh, leaning against the wall, knowing that The Guide is right. Going back, even if I could get out of the door and past the dirt that was trying to bury me, would only land me back in the clutches of my uncle.

Sometimes going back just seems easier, I say in my head.

Life isn't supposed to be easy, dear one. It's supposed to help you learn and grow so that you can go on.

On to what? What could there possibly be?

There's a lot more after this realm, dear Patrina. This is only your beginning.

Fifty

I look down the winding staircase below and start my descent. There's a ridge cut out in the side of the trunk that acts as a handrail, making it easier to steady myself, as the stairs aren't all the same. Some are lumpier than others and my foot rocks on those parts when it hits. Some are shorter, making my toes hang off the edge uncomfortably, and some of the steps are a lot farther away, making me wonder if there's even another step for me to stand on.

I climb down for what must be hours, but when I look back up to where I came in, I see that the tediousness of the climb just made it seem like I've been going for a lot longer than I have, because I can still see the top where I came in. This is going to take a very long time, and the events of the day have really taken a toll on me. I'm so tired. It's almost as though something in this tree is dragging me down and causing me to be so sleepy I'm suddenly wishing I could lie down in my nice, soft bed and listen to Miriam tell me a story of my parents.

Miriam.

I don't even know what happened. Did she make it out? And what about Bao? He sacrificed his chance at freedom and fought my uncle long enough for me to get away. What happened to him? Did he make it out?

I lower myself down onto a step that's a little bigger than the rest and sit for a moment before sliding my pack off of my shoulder. I've been carrying it for so long on that side that it feels like I should have a dent in my shoulder where the strap was hanging, but when I reach up and rub my hand across the spot, it just feels normal.

I wish I packed a pillow.

I pull my pack up onto my lap and unzip the main zipper. I barely remember what I put in there when I was in such a rush to get out. I find my jacket and contemplate putting it on but then decide to roll it up to use as a pillow instead. Once it's rolled, I lay it on the stair off to the side of me and continue digging for the blanket I packed. My fingers graze the diary, and it vibrates under my touch. I ignore it and pull out the blanket, laying that on my lap, and then zip my pack back up. I slide my pack to the step below the one I'm on and then lay down and place my head on my makeshift pillow. It's not very comfortable, and there are some lumps in the step that are poking me in my side, but I pull my blanket up and wrap myself in a cocoon, slowly feeling it reflect my heat and relax my muscles. I'm so tired that I quickly drift off.

I finally reach the bottom step. My legs ache from the descent. I look back up to where I came from, but the staircase disappears into a mist and then dissipates into nothing.

Strange.

I turn around and look to see where the stairs have brought me, and I'm amazed at what I see. It's a crystal blue lake, perfectly round, surrounded by more trees like the one I just stepped out from behind. I wonder if all of these trees have stairways inside.

I walk up toward the water, and my feet skim across the

ground, barely feeling the pebbles beneath them on the beach that surrounds the lake. Is this the lake that Miriam talked about?

Just as I get to the edge, I see a splash off to the far left near the edge. The water is so clear that I can see most of the bottom of the lake, but something is in it causing such a ripple, and I can't make out what it is. Suddenly it disappears, and the water calms once again.

I decide to walk around the edge to the place where I saw the splash. As I make my way around, I see the massive trees bend toward me and then away, but there's no wind. It's as if they're dancing to a tune only they hear.

I finally reach the spot in the water where I saw all of the disruption, but I don't see anything there. Whatever it was seems to have disappeared. I sit down on a giant boulder near the edge and look at the reflection of the trees in the water, and that's when I see it out of the corner of my eye. Or should I say her?

I see someone small with long, curly brown hair duck behind one of the monstrous trees surrounding the lake. I get up from my seat and walk over to where I think she is, but when I get there, I don't see her. I only see more trees.

What am I supposed to do here?

Just as I turn around to walk back over to where I was sitting before, I see a pair of eyes open up behind the tree. What is that?

The tree starts to move and dance, making the ground shift underneath me.

🌿

I awaken to the feeling of falling. Down one step, two steps, then three, and then I tumble down four more. I grab the side of the wall, catching a root that's sticking out, and stop my fast track down the stairs. What happened? I think I was dreaming of that lake Miriam told me about, and then the tree shook me awake, making me fall, but when I look, I see that my pack is still up where I was laying. I climb back up and retrieve my pack, blanket, and jacket, shoving them back inside. I sling my pack back on and start my journey downward once again.

I look back up to where I came from but don't see anyone behind me. What could've caused the tree to shake like that? Did my uncle find the tree I'm hiding in? Did he make the tree give off something that made me sleepy?

I decide to go faster and start skipping down the steps. The farther from the top I get, the more awake I feel. After a few minutes, I relax, and my mind drifts as I start reliving the dream I had, wishing I had Miriam to talk to about it.

You may not have her, but you have me, The Guide reminds me.

"What was that dream about then? You know what I dreamt, right?"

Yes, little one … who do you think sends you these dreams?

"Wait, do you send me all of my dreams?"

Mostly. Sometimes your human part dreams random dreams, but mostly the visions I send to you are things you need to know. Whether they are from the past or from what you will soon endure.

"What was the lake dream?"

What do you think? he asks, making me wish, once again, that he would just tell me what he means.

"I think that's where I'm going. Am I right?"

I guess we will find out, won't we?

Ugh.

I trod on, plodding down, step by step. The staircase starts to swirl around on itself tighter and tighter until it feels as though each step is more next to the other one than below it. After a few minutes of walking like that, I have to stop. My head is spinning. The staircase around me is spinning. Everything is spinning.

I close my eyes and sit down on the step that I'm on and put my head in my hands, resting my arms on my knees as I try to keep from passing out. I feel a chill on my skin, and when I raise my head to look at my arms, there are goose bumps all over them. I slip my pack off and get my jacket out, but just as I'm about to slide my arm into the sleeve, I feel it.

A breeze … a very cool breeze.

I lift my eyes to where it's coming from, and I see something amazing.

There's a giant ball of light about twenty feet ahead of me … what is that?

Fifty-One

I stand up, and my pack falls onto the next step. When I look down, I realize that I stopped three steps from the bottom. I didn't know I was that close! I would've just pushed on! I step down while putting on my jacket, finally feeling like my head has stopped spinning, and grab my pack. Once I swing it up onto my shoulder, I get a good look at the light up ahead of me.

It touches the ground and is taller than me. I stand still for a moment, watching it. It doesn't move. I take a step forward, but nothing happens. I take another step, and then the light pulses loudly and flashes. It scares me, and I freeze in place.

Did I do something to make it do that?

Suddenly my pack starts vibrating. At first only a little and then more and more until it's shaking off of my shoulder. What is going on?

I let it drop, hitting the ground, and when I open it, the diary is glowing and shaking violently. Why is it doing this?

I reach in and quickly grab it before it slides under the blanket that's in there. Once it's in my hand, the shaking lessens to an intense vibration and then to a pulsing that matches my heartbeat. I watch as the light starts pulsing in rhythm with the diary, all of it is syncing with the beat of my heart.

Slowly, with every beat, the center of the light opens up. At first it's just a small dot, and then it's bigger, about the size of a fist. Finally it's the size of me.

This is the next step of your journey, dear one. There will be many steps along the way that are similar to this one, but there will always be a key. This time it's the diary. It won't always be that way though. Once you make it through, there will be new challenges, new friends, and new enemies. Do not for even a little bit think that your uncle cannot find you once you pass through. He is not of this world, my little one. He will hunt you until he no longer has a reason to hunt.

"But … what do I do?" I ask.

What do you think you should do?

I pause for a moment and then say in my heart, *I think I'm supposed to go through that opening … but I can't see what I'm walking into.*

If you knew what was going to be on the other side, you wouldn't need to take a leap of faith, would you? Sometimes you just have to go and let me guide you through the adventures ahead.

I know he's right.

I lift my pack so that it's not dragging on the ground, sling it onto my back, and hold the diary out in front of me with one hand. The light is still matching my pulse, even though it's racing. I slowly walk toward the strange light that has formed a giant circle in the air. I try to look into the circle, but there are so many squiggly lines that I can't see through it. If I squint my eyes, I can just make out that it looks like green grass or something on the other side.

I stretch out my other hand out so that I can put my fingers through the circle, anxious about what I might feel in there. My fingers disappear, like they did when I put them into this tree, but it doesn't hurt. In fact, it feels warmer where they are on the other side of this opening. What is this opening anyway?

I guess there's only one thing to do—just walk through.

Standing in front of it, somehow I know that once I go through, I may not be able to come back. What if Miriam is okay? And Bao? What if my father is still alive somewhere? Maybe my uncle has him imprisoned somewhere like he did me. If I go through, I won't be able to help them.

But if I don't, I might end up just like them.

I take in a big breath and hold it as I step through, stretching my arm out in front of me with my diary in my hand. If the diary is the key, I don't want to lose it if the circle closes on me. I hold my pack onto my shoulder with my other hand as I fully step into the lighted circle, now blinded by the brightness that is surrounding me.

Before I can see anything, something grabs my hand that's holding the diary, and even though I try to keep it tightly in my grip, it slips and falls. I don't hear it land, so I hurry, trying to fight my way through the light so I can find it before I'm snatched as well. I finally make it through, and as my eyes adjust, I'm stunned to see that I've walked right into my dream.

M. C. Meinema is an executive administrative assistant by day and a wife, mother, and author by night. She spent ten years working with local teenagers and was then encouraged by them to go on to pursue her dream of writing a novel. She and her husband have one child and live in Michigan.

Printed in the United States
By Bookmasters